Children's Bible-story books are a dime a dozen. But how about adult Bible-story books? Few and far between? No longer! Linda Rios Brook tells Bible stories like I've never heard before—and I have four graduate degrees in religion! *The Deliverer* is an intriguing and fascinating insider's view of the stories of Moses and Joshua. Trust me; this is top-drawer literature. It may be fiction, but Linda's sparkling imagination probably comes closer to the real facts than you or I have ever imagined. You'll love this book!

—C. Peter Wagner
Chancellor, Wagner Leadership Institute

THE DELIVERER

LINDA RIOS BROOK

REALMS
A STRANG COMPANY

The Deliverer by Linda Rios Brook
Published by Realms
A Strang Company
600 Rinehart Road
Lake Mary, Florida 32746
www.strangbookgroup.com

Design Director: Bill Johnson
Cover design by Justin Evans

Library of Congress Cataloging-in-Publication Data:

Brook, Linda Rios.
  The deliverer / Linda Rios Brook. -- 1st ed.
    p. cm.
  ISBN 978-1-59979-476-1
  1.   Bible.   O.T.--History   of   Biblical   events--Fiction.   2.
Demonology--Fiction. I. Title.
  PS3602.R64273D45 2009
  813'.6--dc22
                                                    2008055613

First Edition

09 10 11 12 13 — 987654321
Printed in the United States of America

CHAPTER 1

S AVE ME, SAMANTHA. I didn't mean to do it."

The disembodied spirit called out to her, begging her for help. She blinked hard and peered into what seemed like an endless sea of putrid fog.

The eerie voice cried out again.

This time she had to find him. If this was a prank, it had to stop. If it wasn't, well, she was less sure what she would do if it turned out to be real.

"Stay where you are," she cried. "Don't run away again." Her voice shook with fear.

"You know I'm innocent, Samantha. I don't deserve to be in hell. Hurry! You must help me while there's still time."

Her heart pounded so hard it seemed to catch in her throat and she couldn't breathe. Fear welled up within her. But fear of what or whom?

It didn't matter; she must pursue the desperate cries for help.

The ghostly voice cried out in anguish again as she groped her way through the gloomy maze that she already knew led to nowhere. She'd been this far before. It was always the same: a mournful voice pleading for her help, and each time the voice faded before she could reach its source. This time she wouldn't stop until she found the one calling out to her.

The foul-smelling fog thickened and concealed the path beneath her feet, and like the times before, she knew she was descending lower and lower with each erratic step forward. How far did she dare to go? She opened her mouth to call out, but her own voice failed her. An invisible hand tightened around her throat, holding her words captive.

This isn't real. I won't be stopped by something that isn't real. I must keep going.

"Where are you?" she screamed, surprised with the force of the words as they broke free.

Stumbling on through a darkness that grew denser with every step, a cold, slithering tentacle tried to wrap itself around her feet. She screamed again, kicked it away, and ran faster.

"Who...who are you?" Her breathing was becoming more labored. "How can I help you if I can't see you?" Her voice was raspy, and her throat hurt. The thickening haze was hot, and a nauseating odor assaulted her nasal passages. She paused and gagged.

"Pray for me, Samantha." The voice drifted farther away.

Gasping for clean air but finding none, she wiped her mouth on her sleeve and pushed onward toward the black hole that swallowed every glimmer of light. How much deeper could she go? What if she couldn't find her way back? She swallowed her terror and pressed downward into the darkness. He must not get away again.

"Wait!" Her throat was tightening, and her cries faded into hoarse whispers. "I'll pray for you. I'll find a way." Desperation percolated through her body as she lunged forward, her arms grabbing for someone who wasn't there.

"Stop running," she pleaded, her words barely audible. "How can I pray for you? I don't know your name."

The slithering tentacle returned and tripped her. She gasped and fell to her hands and knees on a rippled surface that had once been a river of molten lava. It had cooled and hardened but was still active below the thin crust. The steam continued to rise from beneath, and it burned her hands as she struggled to stand.

It was becoming impossible to see. Disoriented from the fall and fearful of careening into an abyss, she spun in circles, unsure of which way to go. A night bird flew near her head, pulling out strands of hair and mocking her as it sped away.

"Run away, Samantha. Run away while you still can."

"Stop it! Leave me alone!" She tried to cover her hair with her blistered hands.

"Pray for me, Samantha. Pray before it's too late." The voice faded even more.

"Wait! I don't know your name." Her desperation gave way to panic as if she were about to fail a critical mission. "Why won't you tell me your name?"

"Pray for yourself, Samantha."

"Please, don't go."

"Good-bye, Samantha."

She dropped to her knees, wailed in defeat, and sobbed.

A terrified scream.

A ringing telephone.

Samantha wasn't sure whether her own cry or the ringing BlackBerry had startled her awake, but she bolted upright, escaping the nightmare that had plagued her for weeks.

The cell phone rang again.

Still groggy, she blinked hard, sat up straight, and glanced about the room, trying to remember where she was. She rubbed her eyes and blinked again. Of course she was in her office at the University of Jerusalem. Alone.

The phone was still ringing amid the stacks of paper on her desk.

"Don't hang up." Her hands trembled as she groped for it, knocking over a cup of forgotten tea from the day before. "Just don't hang up."

Still disoriented, she fumbled with the BlackBerry as she pushed a strand of hair away from her ear with one hand.

"Yes, hello," she managed.

"Dr. Yale?" The unsteady voice on the phone was unmistakable.

Samantha Yale slumped down behind her antique desk, ignoring the spilled tea dripping onto the floor. Carefully, she cupped the telephone with both hands, afraid she might drop it and lose the connection she had been anxiously awaiting. She breathed in deeply and measured her words lest she startle her nervous caller.

"Yes, this is Samantha Yale."

"Dr. Yale, it's..."

"Yes, Wonk, I know who you are. Where are you?"

Silence.

It had been six months since the mysterious Wonk Eman, the nervous little man with no address, no telephone number, and no e-mail, had visited her and delivered the ancient scrolls to her office. His silence told her she was moving too fast. She took a deep breath, slumped back in her chair, and tried again.

"All right. You don't have to tell me where you are. Are you safe?"

"Why do you ask that?"

Before she could answer, he blurted out, "Am I in danger? I'll call back."

"Stop it, Wonk." She took another deep breath and lowered her voice. "You're in no danger."

"Then why did you ask me if I was safe?"

"No reason." She rose from her desk and walked over to the window where the Dome of the Rock could be seen in the distance against the blue Jerusalem skyline. Maybe a shift in position would make her sound less tense. "It's just that when we last talked, you were concerned about safety. Remember? You were worried someone else might try to contact me about the scrolls."

"Has anyone contacted you?"

"No, no one at all." She heard him slowly exhale.

"Have you told anyone else?"

"No one, just as you directed me."

She restrained herself from asking questions too soon. Slowly she began a silent count from one to ten. If he didn't speak again in ten seconds, she would prompt him. She only got to five.

"I have more scrolls."

"Good. When will you bring them to me?"

Another of his interminable pauses. She ran her fingers through her rumpled hair and tried to control her exasperation at how long it took him to say anything. Her ring caught the edge of the newly formed scab just above her right ear. A drop of blood smeared on her fingertip. *Now what have I done?* She turned to the wall mirror to examine the injury but gave up when she couldn't make her eyes shift far enough to see it. *OK, that's long enough.*

"Wonk?" she said, attempting to prod him back into the conversation.

"Yes. How long will it take you to translate them?" Impatience, anxiety, or both had crept into his voice.

"You know that's almost impossible to say. It's a difficult task to translate cuneiform."

"But you're an expert."

"Even for an expert, it requires a thought-for-thought translation, as opposed to a word-for-word technique. Besides, you haven't told me how many more scrolls you have."

He ignored the bait.

"Tomorrow, then," he said.

"Will you bring them yourself?"

A thud told her he had dropped the phone. She could hear him scrambling to retrieve it.

"Hello?" His fumbling sent piercing beeps into her ear. "Sorry. No, no, I...very risky...not wise at all." His voice had become shriller as he floundered to answer her question.

"That's OK." *Take a breath.* "Don't worry." *Pause; let him calm down.* "How will they be delivered?"

"By messenger; same as before. Good-bye, Dr. Yale."

"Wait—" She stopped him before he could hang up. Did she dare go any further? He was so high-strung he might flee at the slightest provocation. Maybe she should wait until she had the scrolls safely in her possession. Too late. She had to say something.

"Can I ask you something else?"

"What is it, Dr. Yale?"

"When we last talked..." She hesitated. *Do I really want to go down this road?*

"Dr. Yale?"

"Yes, sorry. When you were in my office and we talked about the Torah and other relics of antiquity, you brought up Noah's ark. Do you remember the conversation?"

"Yes."

"You were concerned about someone who might have survived Noah's flood—besides Noah's family."

"Og," he whispered.

"Yes, that's it. Og, the Nephilim king." She waited for his reaction.

There was none. She ran her fingers through her hair again. Afraid he might hang up, she preempted her ten-second rule and pressed in.

"What did you mean?"

"Why do you want to know?"

"No reason except it seemed important to you. Suppose such a thing had actually happened. Why would the idea distress you so?"

Silence.

I shouldn't have said "distress."

"Then he has contacted you." His voice *was* distressed. "You said no one..."

"What? No, of course not. Don't be ridiculous."

Seeing her reflection in the mirror on the wall, she began a silent exchange with herself.

You're having a conversation with a deeply disturbed man about someone who's been dead for five thousand years—if he ever existed at all. No wonder you can't sleep. Wonk doesn't seem capable of playing mind games, but what else can he be doing?

"I was only curious to know what you meant," she continued gently. "It's hard to understand why you would care about something that might have happened so long ago."

Silence.

One second, two seconds, three...

"He must not get the scrolls, Dr. Yale. You must promise me that will not happen. You have no idea the consequences if..."

"No, it's OK. I'm sure I can keep them safe." She glanced at her reflection again to see if she looked sincere.

"Tomorrow, Dr. Yale. Wait for them. Remember your promise." The dial tone signaled the end of the conversation.

Samantha clicked the END button on her phone, sighed with relief that the conversation was over, and sat down on the window seat as she lingered at her personal portal of the world.

"Sign here, Dr. Yale." The burly man in the brown delivery uniform handed her the electronic notebook to register her signature as the authorized recipient of a carefully packed crate. She scrawled her name in silence, not wanting to engage him in any conversation that might delay his leaving. The man was barely out the door before she found a sturdy letter opener in the desk drawer and began prying open the container. At last the lid slid off, and Styrofoam peanuts went flying as her hands carefully reached inside the box. Just as she had done with the first scrolls, she gently removed each of the twelve and laid them out in what she guessed would be a somewhat chronological order on her conference table. Her only hope was that Wonk, or whoever packed them, had some appreciation for sequence.

Selecting the first scroll, she carried it to her desk and gently unrolled it. To an untrained eye it would have looked exactly like any one of the others she had already examined and locked away. Only an expert would recognize the difference in the markings of the ancient written language of the Phoenicians, cuneiform, which predated hieroglyphics by who knew how many centuries.

"I wish I knew what this material is," Samantha said, talking to herself as she fingered the scroll kept her from rushing through the delicate process.

With magnifying glass in hand, she peered intently at the first line.

"Are you in there?" She spoke aloud as if the scroll was listening. "A fallen angel with no name; what do you want to tell me? How can I help you if I don't know your name?"

CHAPTER 2

S AMANTHA GLANCED AT the clock to make note of the time. Reaching for her pen, she took a slow, deep breath and began the meticulous translation of each symbol.

"Talk to me," she whispered to the scroll.

"Come with me, Samantha," the voice inside her head answered. "This is how it was."

If he had remembered the first thing about God, Satan could have expected this to happen eventually. God would not leave the children of Abraham in slavery forever. Granted, after four hundred thirty years of silence, a casual observer might wonder if God had finally cut His losses with the Hebrews and gone on to other things, but a person who really knew God would never indulge such a thought. A person who truly knew God, as Satan most certainly had at one point, would never come to such a conclusion no matter how bad the situation looked or how long it might take to fix it.

God promised the Hebrews that He would send a deliverer. It was certain to happen one day, and then one day it did. As soon as I knew the expected one was on the earth, I flew directly to Satan's lair to let him know. Satan ran right over the top of me as he raced to the edge of the second heaven and began yelling at God.

"Go away, God. Go far away. Nobody remembers You here. Give them up. Find another hobby. Cut Your losses. You are not wanted. Your creation has turned against You. They worship *me*. I will kill them before I see them turn back to You. I will die before I allow them to escape."

Those were his exact words as he stood on the rim and berated God. Then it got worse.

"You think You can save them?" Satan bellowed. "Go ahead. Try to snatch them out of my hands. But it will cost You, God. Oh, it will cost You more than You are willing to pay."

Satan rolled in laughter at his threat against the Almighty, as if he had caught God in some terrible joke only they knew. His countenance changed again, and with yellow, hideous eyes, he roared and then bleated as if he were some tortured animal. Next, he began frothing from his mouth and spinning on the floor like a captured tornado. He was completely mad; there was no other way to describe it. At last he collapsed in a heap; it was finally over.

It took awhile, but Satan eventually pulled himself together and made his way back to his den. The demons stepped aside, avoiding eye contact with him and pretending not to have noticed the public meltdown of their ruler. I tried to slip out quietly without being seen by His Horribleness. I hoped I could avoid the badgering I knew Satan would assail against me because of this turn of events. I had nothing to do with the arrival of the deliverer, and the last thing I wanted was to be the depository for his anger at God. So, of course, that's the very first thing that happened.

"Come with me," Satan ordered.

I braced for a tongue-lashing and followed him into his dark abode. He sat down on his granite throne, and I knelt down before him. For what seemed a long time, he said nothing at all. His silence was almost harder to bear than his tantrums. I didn't dare look up at him. I thought about the news I'd delivered and wondered whether there might have been some other way to have done it, a way that would not have triggered the rage Satan had unleashed against God. I couldn't think of any. It was what it was. The deliverer was now on the earth. I didn't cause it, but I had to tell it. That was my job, to watch and report. Finally he spoke.

"Does he have a name?"

"Yes, sir. His name is Moses."

"How many soldiers has he got?"

I didn't answer because I had no idea why he was asking me about soldiers. I dared not ask for clarity because doing so might imply that his question was vague, and Satan's interrogation skills were not subject to criticism. I continued to kneel before him, trying to figure out what he meant. When he rightly discerned I didn't have a clue what he was talking about, he grabbed me by the wing and stood me upright before him.

"The deliverer, idiot," he said as he thumped me on the head. "How many men does Moses have in his army?" He let go of my wing and then turned away, which gave me a moment to think.

"Army?" What can he mean? I'm sure I didn't I say anything about an army. I could feel Satan losing patience with my

inability to follow this line of questioning, so I answered the best I could.

"If you mean an army in the conventional sense, sir, he doesn't have an army per se."

Satan turned back and looked at me as if I had spoken some incredulous thing.

"No army?"

"No, sir."

"No soldiers at all? Don't lie to me."

"No, sir, I would never dare lie."

"How does he expect to come against the Egyptians without a militia? Does he think he can simply saunter into Pharaoh's court and walk out with the slaves without a fight?"

I felt faint when I realized that in giving my report, I'd left out an important detail.

"Oh, I see what you're asking, terrible one. My fault entirely; of course you'd expect the deliverer of the Hebrews to be a man, a mighty warrior. Why would you assume anything else?"

I might have gone on groveling all afternoon had Satan not leaned into my face and snarled, "I didn't assume anything. You said the deliverer had come. Are you tracking with me on this?"

I nodded but didn't make a sound.

"Then he must be a man. God has obligated Himself to work through humans."

"Yes, sir. I mean no, of course not. But I can see how you might think that. I should have been clearer. Of course he's a man—just not quite yet. But one day soon. You know how fast they grow." I continued to prattle on when Satan grabbed me by the tail and jerked me to attention.

"Are you anywhere close to making a point? If he's not a man, what is he?"

"Well, right now, to be completely accurate, he's a baby, sir. A little one about this long." I held my claws about two feet apart to show him. "Not very big at all. Like I said, he will grow into a man, but..." Satan cut me off with another jerk on my tail.

"You dared waste my time over a Hebrew baby? Not even a grown man?" He thumped me on the head again. "What makes you think he's the deliverer? Who told you?"

"It was like this, sir..."

Satan cut me off and began mocking me by clapping his claws together as if suddenly figuring it all out.

"Let me guess. God must have taken you into His confidence."

I was about to tell him about the baby's eyes but knew it would be a waste of time.

"I'm quite sure of my facts, my lord. There's no doubt about who he is. He's the only male baby to have survived the Egyptians' sword. He floated right down the Nile in that wicker basket, slick as you please, no leaks, no alligators, no capsizing, right under the noses of the Egyptian soldiers and right into Pharaoh's backyard. An escape like that has the fingerprints of God all over it."

Satan had a puzzled look on his face as if I had said something baffling.

"What did you say? What do you mean he went right into Pharaoh's backyard?"

"That's just how it was, sir. Pharaoh's daughter and all her girlfriends were down there splashing around in the river when this baby in a basket came floating by. You know how women are, sir. They can't resist a baby, no matter what kind of baby it is. Pharaoh's daughter laid claim to him immediately. Gave him a name right away. Instant motherhood."

"She will kill him when she figures out he's a Hebrew."

"No, I'm quite sure she plans to keep him. She's already found a nanny for him. Interesting how that happened. She sent someone to find a woman to nurse him, and wouldn't you know, the friend came back with the baby's very own mother in tow. What are the odds of that? Of course, the girls didn't know I was watching. I saw the whole thing."

By now some of the other demons had decided it was safe to come in to see what was going on. They'd heard most of my explanation. Bezel spoke first.

"Now that we know where he is, we can kill him. End of problem."

"Oh, really? You'll kill him? Just like that, will you?" Satan's sarcasm dripped with hostility as he mocked Bezel's solution. "Then why didn't you kill him when you had him? You let him get away. Wasn't I clear enough? Watch the Hebrew babies and make sure the Egyptians kill the boys. Why do I have to do everything myself?"

Satan threw his arms up in disgust while Bezel kept his head down and his mouth shut, but, oh, I knew what he wished he had the nerve to say. Satan barely took a breath before continuing his tirade.

"Your dereliction in duty has allowed things to become much more complicated. If Pharaoh's daughter has him, we won't find any Egyptian soldier brave enough to touch him."

We hadn't been dismissed, so we stood in place, avoiding eye contact and waiting to see if Satan had any plans as to what he would do with this turn of events. None of us had any ideas of our own, or if we had, we weren't about to say so. Ideas were not allowed in Satan's realm unless they were his. Finally he spoke again.

"Leave him alone." He turned to me as if daring me to say the wrong word. "You did say Pharaoh's daughter has him; you did get that part right?"

I nodded.

"Then he'll grow up in Pharaoh's court. They won't keep the nursemaid for very long. After that, they'll be careful not to let him associate with the Hebrews. They won't tell him who he is, of course. He will be raised as an Egyptian with all the wealth and religion of Egypt." Then Satan started chuckling. (Hard to imagine that, isn't it?)

"The Egyptians will do our work for us. Whatever or whoever he is now won't matter; the environment of Egypt will change him. I'm not convinced he's who you think he is, but we take no chances." He glared right at me again. "After all, why would God save him from death only to send him into

Pharaoh's court to be raised among the people who are in our camp? It's not like God to make a mistake like that. You're probably wrong about who he is."

I knew I wasn't wrong, but I also knew enough not to challenge Satan's flawed reasoning.

"Nevertheless," Satan whirled back to Bezel. "Watch him, but don't touch him. In fact, make sure he gets every indulgence in Egypt. See to it the girl spoils him. Baby him, pamper him, overprotect—keep him away from the influence of men. Make sure he's a mama's boy. If he *is* the deliverer, we can circumvent his destiny. When God calls him, he won't go. He won't leave the posh comforts of Egypt. Don't let him make any friends among the Hebrews. Visit Pharaoh's daughter in her dreams. Tell her if she lets the boy spend any time with them, the Hebrews will try to steal him away from her. Plant fear and distrust in her mind.

"And you." Satan turned back to me. "Get back out there on guard duty. If he makes any moves toward God, let me know instantly."

I went back to my perch and began my watch. Mostly I watched nothing happen for what seemed like forever. I stood guard for years, and after a while, it seemed as if Satan might have been right. Moses grew up as a brother to Ramses, Pharaoh's true son. And...oh my...yes, those boys were spoiled rotten. God never intervened as far as I could tell, and Moses never indicated any particular affinity for the Hebrews. Maybe I'd been wrong about him after all; still, I couldn't forget what I'd seen in that baby's eyes.

Then one day, something quite unexpected happened. Moses was walking along the edge of the mud pits where the Hebrews were making bricks for the new pyramid. Nearby an Egyptian soldier began savagely beating one of the Hebrew slaves for no good reason I could see. Nothing new in that; it happened all the time. But all at once, Moses was in the fight.

He caught the soldier completely off guard and killed him. Looking around to see if anyone had seen what happened (no one had except me, of course), he dragged the soldier's body behind the pits and buried it in the sand. When I say that no one saw, I mean no one of any importance. None of the Egyptians were around to see it, but wouldn't you know, the Hebrews who were working in that same pit saw the whole thing. But so what? They weren't going to tattle to anyone about a dead Egyptian; one less for them to worry about. For whatever reason Moses had done what he did, he appeared to be home free. And that is exactly what I reported to Satan.

"He knows," Satan murmured as he paced restlessly in front of his throne.

"Knows what, sir?"

"Moses knows who he is."

He seemed quite certain, which was always the case with him, so I should've known to say nothing and nod in agreement whether or not I thought he might be right. But I didn't.

"Oh, I don't think so, sir," I quipped, forgetting for a moment that no one quipped a contradiction Satan's way. I tried to explain what I meant.

"He can't know, sir. He's had no contact with the Hebrews. No close encounters of any kind—nada, zilch. Further, God hasn't yet made a move toward him. I wouldn't have missed something like that. Maybe Moses didn't like the attitude of that particular soldier. Who knows what may have motivated him to kill the Egyptian? Whatever it was, I'm quite sure it could have had nothing to do with any empathy toward the slaves."

Satan ignored my explanation. "Did anyone see him do it?"

"No one who counts. Some of the slaves saw it happen, but they're not going to tell anyone, and even if they did, who would believe them? And if someone did believe them, who would care?"

It was as if I hadn't said a thing. Satan turned from me and summoned Bezel, who was hovering outside the den listening to every word. He took Bezel by the arm and instructed him as they walked toward the door.

"Go out there and watch Moses. When he goes near the pits again, stir the Hebrews up. Cause a disturbance and see what he does."

Bezel followed me back to my perch and crowded in beside me. Together we watched the pits for several days without leaving. I tried to make small talk, but he wasn't much of a conversationalist. He seemed content to simply sit there and stare at the slaves. He was much bigger than me, and when he stretched his wings out, he knocked me right off the end. Where did he think I was supposed to sit? I was already bunched up in a knot because of his size. He never once apologized. I hoped something would happen so Bezel would go home. Finally it did.

Moses was once again walking along the rim of the pits. Bezel jumped off the perch and took off for the earth so suddenly that it flipped me right off, like what happens when a child jumps off the low end of a seesaw while someone else is on the high end. I straightened myself out and watched him hover over two of the slaves in the pit. I couldn't hear what he said, but suddenly, there they were slugging each other. Moses ran down to the edge and separated them and asked them why they were fighting. One of them began berating Moses.

"Who made you our judge when you're nothing but a murderer?"

Moses turned pale. He looked around to see if anyone had heard, and someone had. One of the Egyptian guards heard every word. At first, the guard did nothing, but then I saw Bezel whispering in his ear.

"Report it to Pharaoh; there's a reward in it for you."

The guard took off for the palace, and I followed right behind him, but Bezel got there first and seated himself on the cushion right next to Pharaoh's throne.

Pharaoh listened to the guard's report with one ear and listened to Bezel interpret it with his other ear. A fight among slaves would have been a nonevent if it hadn't been for Bezel. He told Pharaoh how Moses had found out about his heritage and was trying to start a rebellion among the slaves.

"Not only that, but look how ungrateful he is for all you've done for him, treating him like your own son."

Pharaoh was immediately offended. Offense works every time.

"Seize him," Pharaoh ordered. The palace guards took off after Moses. Bezel followed the guards, and I followed Bezel. They quickened their pace when they spotted Moses not far from the city gate. While they were still at a distance, a strange wind coming from nowhere and going nowhere begin to swirl around Moses's head.

This was trouble. I hadn't seen Him for hundreds of years, but I recognized the whirling wind that was a dead giveaway when Ruah Ha Kadosh arrived on the scene. Bad, very bad for any demon when He showed up. Seeing no convenient place to hide, I remained completely still, hoping Ruah Ha Kadosh would focus on Bezel and not notice me. His voice was unmistakable to anyone who had ever encountered Him, which Moses had not. Moses had no idea the third person of the Trinity was speaking into his mind. When he heard the words, "Flee to the desert," he was off like a flash, not giving a second thought as to who had spoken to him. He ran so fast I was sure one of the guardian angels of the earth must have been zipping him along, but I quickly realized how unnecessary such a thing would have been. Ruah Ha Kadosh had breathed on him; Moses could have outrun a team of horses on that one breath. Immediately, I flew back to Satan's den to tell him what had happened and how Moses was on the run.

I was fast but not fast enough to beat Bezel back to the lair. He sat near Satan, gloating and taking credit for running Moses out of town.

"Whether or not he was the deliverer," Bezel bragged, "he will be nothing but a bad memory in a few days."

Satan chortled, and much as I hated to agree with Bezel about anything, it looked like he was right. Moses would die in the desert, no doubt about it. The wasteland was ruthless and Moses had grown up a city boy. Out there alone with no servants to take care of him, he wouldn't stand a chance against the desert.

Even if he were able to find someone in the wilderness who might take him in, all desert people worshiped one of Satan's demon gods. They wouldn't let Moses hang around their camp unless he joined in with their worship. They'd be too afraid he'd offend one of their easily angered deities. To survive, he would have to go along to get along, if you know what I mean. Once he joined in exaltation of one of Satan's surrogates, he would have done the one thing from whence there were no do-overs with God: worship of a false deity...or real demon, same thing. Moses was toast. We didn't think about him again for forty years.

CHAPTER 3

ONE DAY, WHO knows why, Satan began to fidget. He jumped at the slightest noise and then glared at anyone he thought might have noticed. He paced back and forth near the rim of the second heaven, stopped at the edge, leaned over, sniffed the air, and paced again. We didn't know *who* he was, but he was definitely not himself, which was an improvement since himself was pretty hard to take most of the time. While the other demons pretended not to be watching Satan fidget, I used the distraction to slip away by myself to my perch.

I'd been there only a moment when I felt the air temperature change. Satan came and sat down on the other end of my perch. I tried not to hyperventilate. He'd never done such a thing before, and it made me so nervous I wasn't sure I could breathe at all.

"What's the matter with you?" he asked noticing my heaving wings.

"Nothing, sir. I wasn't expecting you, that's all."

"I sit wherever I want."

"Of course, to be sure." I tried to breathe normally.

He sat there for quite a while not saying anything, just staring at the earth, particularly the Hebrew slaves. I wondered if I should say something to try to sound empathetic, although I wasn't and didn't feel anything except stress. What does one say to an out-of-sorts ruler of iniquity? I tried out several salutations in my head.

"How is it going, sir? Can I get you anything? Can I fetch you a slave for dinner?" No, that wasn't right. I tried again.

"Oh, it's you, sir. I was just sitting here, holding my post and admiring the way you've messed up the earth again." Maybe not.

Before I could think of anything safe and clever to say, he spoke to me. Well, not *to* me exactly. It was more like *at* me, if you can picture it. He never turned his eyes toward me, just kept staring at the earth, but there was no doubt as to whether or not he was talking to me; he was. If for no other reason, it was because I was the only one there. When he spoke, I knew to listen and obey immediately, whatever he said.

"Find him."

"Right away, sir."

I was so anxious to get away from him that I jumped up, stretched my wings, and flapped off toward the earth as if I understood my assignment perfectly, when in fact, I did not. Not only did I not understand it, but also I didn't know what it was. I looked back to see if Satan was still sitting on my perch. Yep, still there. I thought about turning back to get a few more details on my mission but then changed my mind.

Best not to look tentative. I'm sure I can figure this out. I wonder who I should be looking for?

In my zeal to get away, I hadn't asked enough questions. I'd foolishly taken off unsure of where I was going or whom I was supposed to find. Now, it may seem obvious to you, a reader with the benefit of history, what "find him" meant, but try to remember that at the time, I lived under the rule and whim of a crazy person where nothing could be assumed. Besides all that, no one had said the name "Moses" in forty years. Truth be told, I'd all but forgotten about him.

I guessed I was to go to the earth because I couldn't recall he'd ever sent me anywhere else. I flew in that direction, but when it came time to veer right, I got worried I might be wrong.

Maybe whoever he wants me to find isn't even on the earth. What if he meant for me to find another demon who was somewhere else in the second heaven? I could end up looking silly. No way around it; I had to go back for clarification.

I was halfway back to ask Satan exactly who it was he wanted me to find, but I changed my mind in mid flap. I knew he wouldn't be civil about it. More than likely he would get mad and tell me to figure it out. So I banked left and resumed my original flight plan.

But since I don't know who I'm looking for, how will I know if I find him? What did Satan tell me to do with him if I do find whoever it is? I convinced myself I really *had* to go back and get better instructions, so I made a U-turn and headed toward my perch where Satan waited.

When I saw his face, I changed my mind again. *No, better not. He's in no mood for questions.*

I made another wide turn, realizing I had now flown in a complete circle. A crowd of demons had gathered near Satan and were making bets as to which way I would go next. Of course, that made me all the more nervous, so I just kept flying in a circle, trying to decide what to do.

Eventually, Satan ceased to be entertained by my predicament and dispatched one of the other demons who caught me by the tail as I flew past and then dragged me back to His Awfulness. The next thing I knew, it was Satan who was holding me by the tail, seething into my upside down face.

"I'm sorry. I didn't know who I was to find," I whimpered.

"Why do I let you live?" he snarled at me.

I know a rhetorical question when I hear one, so I didn't answer, but, oh, how I would have liked to tell him what I thought about the way he ran things. Just once I wished I could stand up to him. I wished anybody would, but nobody dared. He slammed me to the floor and continued berating me, belittling every single thing I'd ever done as if I'd never once gotten anything right. I wanted to remind him how over the centuries of human history I had an exceptional track record for being right. Not that he would have cared anyway.

"Find Moses, you idiot," he steamed. "Who else did your pitiful mind think I meant? He's living in the desert with the Midianites."

"Oh, I really doubt that, sir," my mouth uttered before my brain engaged. "Not that you could be wrong, you understand, but it's quite unlikely Moses would still be alive after forty years or we would have surely heard something from him by now. And as for living with the Midianites? Highly doubtful, if you please, sir. They don't like Egyptians, and they don't like Hebrews, so there you go. Whoever Moses thought he was or claimed to be, it wouldn't matter. No one of either race could have lasted long with the Midianites."

It was Tammuz who hissed at me and said, "If you had been doing your job, imbecile, you would know Moses is married to Zipporah, the daughter of a Midianite priest."

How could I have missed such a thing? Tammuz interacted on a regular basis with the territorial principalities over Midian, and if something strange was going on in their territory, they would be sure to know. One of those demons must have come across Moses somewhere in the desert lands and reported it to Tammuz. I needed to think of something fast.

"But what of it?" I blurted out as if Tammuz's news flash were no news at all. "If Moses married the daughter of a Midianite priest, there must have been a religious ceremony of some kind."

"And so?" Satan asked.

"And so it could not have been kosher, so to speak. Moses would be in violation of the no-god-but-Yahweh rule or at least complicit in the goings-on."

They all looked at me as if I hadn't finished a sentence, so I knew they hadn't put the obvious two and two together.

"If Moses had ritual with another god," I spoke slowly so they'd understand, "it means he abdicated, flunked the test, jumped the fence, whatever you want to call it. He's forfeited his opportunity to be the deliverer."

It was as if I hadn't said a word.

Once Satan made up his mind about something, he wouldn't change it regardless of evidence to the contrary or even if it was in his own interest to do so. Why? you ask. Well, let me just tell you it wasn't because he was always right or even usually right. The extraordinarily stupid idea of rebelling against God to start with and getting all of us tossed out of paradise into the ghetto of the second heaven ought to be proof enough of that.

No, the reason Satan never changed his mind was because God never changed His. Never mind the simple fact that God was always right, always thinking ahead, always moving the earth forward through time (though toward what I do not know), while Satan was rarely right. He spent most of his time wasting everyone else's and overreacting to the last thing that happened. This whole manhunt was a case in point. But nothing would do except for me to launch out on a pointless search for Moses.

"And if I find him?"

Satan glared, and I tried again. "*When* I find him"—*that was better*—"then what?" Which was a very good question seeing as how I couldn't do anything *with* him or *to* him. I was a watcher, end of function.

"Watch him," Tammuz growled.

"Watch him do what? Count goats?" I muttered under my breath. I'd stalled as long as I could, so I set my course and started winging it toward the desert.

You might wonder how I could have been so sure of myself when I said Moses was no longer a threat to Satan because he'd flunked the test for being the deliverer. The truth is I took a chance and lied to Satan; I thought just the opposite of what I said. Oh, I know I took a big risk because I'm not a convincing liar and Satan would devour me if he caught me lying to him, but I was highly motivated.

The truth is I disparaged the idea to Satan that Moses was still in the running to be the deliverer because I desperately did *not* want to go to the desert to look for him. Nobody did. The desert was the training ground for hell. There's no other way to describe it. The worst of our kind inhabited the hot, arid sands of the wasteland. The desert devils weren't anything like the fat and happy—at least by comparison—demons in Egypt who indulged on the spoils of the land.

No, not at all. The desert rulers were deprived of any of the booty of the earth. Although they were ravenous to gratify their demonic nature on human flesh, like all the rest of the demons, they were assigned, or sentenced, to an empty place with few humans to hunt. Their prey was limited to unsavory life forms that lived under rocks or deep in the scorching sand. If I was discovered soloing it in their territory, there would be a food fight, and I would be the food they were fighting over. Never mind that I was on a mission from Satan. No one would have bothered to ask why I was in the neighborhood.

So try to imagine my relief when I flew deep into the wilderness only to find no one at home. The spiritual realm was silent. It wasn't just a case of no demonic chatter going on; it was deadly silent. It was empty. The territorial rulers were out of town, gone, completely gone. There were no telltale signs of demonic activity or presence. How could I be sure? Sometimes you know what *is* by what is *not*.

What *was not* was the unmistakable odor that emanates from demons. Most humans still haven't learned how to interpret smell. When demons are anywhere about, the air smells bad because they smell bad. The worse they are, the worse they smell. One time in Egypt during a demonic orgy, the odor got so bad I almost threw up. When I couldn't stand it anymore, I took off for one of the gardens by the Nile and plopped myself right down in a patch of pansies. I breathed in the fragrance of flowers until I was tipsy. I didn't even bother to exhale.

Unless you have personally wallowed in a flower bed, you might not know that the perfume from flowers is an intoxicant. When the others found me, I was rocking back and forth on my tail with a snootful of pansy petals, reminiscing about the good old days before we were thrown out of heaven. Satan was in a dither because I'd left my post. He had me locked in the dungeon until the effects of the pansies wore off and then assigned me to the morning-after crew for the cleanup of the orgy. I'll spare you the details.

The only smell in the desert now was, you might say, the desert—rocks, sand, clean air, nothing else. Where were the demons? They had no place to go. Even if there had been a place to go, they would never have dared leave a whole section of ground unoccupied. There would be no excuses with Satan on that one. He was positively paranoid about unoccupied ground. If the principalities were gone, and they most definitely were, what could have happened to cause them to leave? It could only be one thing: something scarier than them. But what?

I settled down on the side of a sand dune and tried to figure out what to do next. When I heard the bleating of goats, I crawled up to the top of the dune and peered over to the other side. I didn't have to see his face to know that the man with the goats was Moses. After all those years, I still recognized his voice.

Demons brag about how they can read the human mind, an undocumented claim at best. But whether *they* can or can't, *I* can't, so I was grateful when Moses began to talk to his goats. That was the only way for me to know what was on his mind. There he stood, an old man by then, leaning on his staff and carrying on a one-sided conversation with a nanny goat. It wasn't as odd as you might think. After all, most of you humans talk to animals now and then. It doesn't seem to bother you at all that the animals never talk back.

It wasn't like that in the beginning, you know. When God first created the animals, they could speak. They chatted with Adam and Eve all the livelong day. How do you think Adam got them to line up and parade by so he could name them? He simply told them what to do. He actually made up a little song for them to sing as they marched along. Let me see if I can remember how it went. Hum along with me.

> Single file, elephant style, we went to the animal fair.
> There were lions and tigers there.
> The monkey made fun of the skunk, who sat on the
> elephant's trunk.
> The elephant sneezed and fell to his knees and that
> was the end of the monk, the monk, the monk.

Something like that anyway. The animals all laughed at Adam's silly song.

Not convinced about the talking animals? Have you ever wondered about why neither Adam nor Eve panicked and ran away after encountering a talking snake in Eden? They weren't the least bit surprised the serpent could talk, because in the beginning, all animals in the garden could talk. At least they could until the Fall. That knockout punch God delivered to the serpent was so powerful that the ripple effects spilled over into the whole animal kingdom, and every species lost its ability to speak the human language. I've always wondered if God really meant to do that. Anyway, now you know why all people in all cultures talk to animals, even stuffed animals. It's in that genetic code thing God put into humans. Until now, you probably never thought about how odd it really is to see a grown person talking to a dog.

Moses seemed to be looking at something over the rim of the next sand dune when he turned and asked the lead goat, "What is that?"

The goat didn't seem to know, so Moses said, "Let's go over and see this strange sight." I stayed low to the ground and followed after the last nanny, who kept turning her head and sniffing in my direction.

Moses had never seen anything like it, but I had. Well, not exactly like it. I'd never actually seen a bush burning brightly yet unconsumed by the fire, but I had witnessed enough of the creative antics of Adonai to know one when I saw it. No wonder the demons had vacated the territory. God Himself had shown up once more on the earth.

The burning spectacle was so beautiful. I was captivated myself, so I could just imagine what was going on in the mind of Moses. When the voice called out of the bush and said,

"Moses, Moses," he jumped backward with such force that half the flock panicked and headed for cover over the next hill.

The voice continued, "Do not come any closer." Judging by his trembling, I could see that going any closer was about the last thing Moses intended to do.

"Take off your sandals, for the place where you are standing is holy ground."

Moses obeyed, and the voice spoke to him again.

"I am the God of your fathers, Abraham, Isaac, and Jacob."

"I knew it," I jumped up and yelled out before I caught hold of myself. Moses didn't hear me, but the goats did, and they all began bleating like a tripped burglar alarm. If the angel of the Lord saw me, He ignored me, but just in case, I dove back to the ground and hid along with the frightened goats. Moses didn't know what was going on, so he fell to the ground also and buried his face in the sand. Whether he believed it really was God or not, it was something strange, and he was too scared to find out what.

From His long experience with His humans, God knew the goats would die of old age before Moses got it together enough to ask a few obvious questions, such as, "If You're really God, why are You pretending to be a bush?" For most people, a burning bush that wasn't burnt up would be a real conversation starter, but not for Moses, who was much more comfortable talking to goats than to humans.

Knowing He would have to make the first move, God began telling Moses what was on His mind, just as if Moses had a perfect grasp on the idea that God Almighty had dropped by.

"I have seen the misery of My people in Egypt. I have heard them crying out because of their slave drivers, and I am concerned about their suffering. So I have come down to rescue them from the hand of the Egyptians and to bring them up out of that land into a good and spacious land flowing with milk and honey."

Moses still had his head in the sand, but he pulled back slightly and opened one eye when he heard this. He didn't speak, but I knew what he was thinking.

Is this something I'm supposed to care about? I tried to help them once, and look what it got me.

"So now, go," the voice continued. "I am sending you to Pharaoh to bring My people the Israelites out of Egypt."

"You have got to be kidding, God," Moses said. No, wait. Moses didn't say that; I said that.

Moses actually said, "Who am I that I should go to Pharaoh and bring the Israelites out of Egypt?"

But it meant the same thing. As far as Moses was concerned, this was not an idea that could work at all. His window of opportunity to be a hero had long since closed, and he no longer had the desire or the will to try to open a new one.

God tried to reassure him. "I will be with you. This will be the sign to you that it is I who have sent you: when you have brought the people out of Egypt, you will worship Me on this mountain."

When I heard that, I couldn't help but feel a little bit sorry about the fate that awaited the desert demons who had abandoned their posts. They'd given it up without a fight, and now

God had it staked out as an altar to Himself. Satan would have a fit when he learned about it. Not that I would have acted differently in their circumstances. Spiritual warfare against the heavenly host is one thing, but if any one of the Trinity enters the fray, *see ya'; wouldn't want to be ya'.*

At first, Moses was tracking with me; it was all over his face that he had no appreciation for why this was a good idea. Slowly rising to his feet, he stared at the ground, shifted from one foot to another, and finally spoke to God.

"Mighty God, You know I am a murderer. My execution awaits me if I go back to Egypt."

"Those who wanted your life are now dead," God responded.

"But suppose I go to the Israelites and say to them, 'The God of your fathers has sent me to you,' and they ask me, 'What is His name?' then what shall I tell them?"

Good question; very good question, Moses.

I knew God by many names: Yahweh, Elohim, Hashem, El Shaddai, and others. His creation called His name by what it saw Him do. I wondered which of these names God would assign to Himself for the task He was proposing.

God said to Moses, "I am who I am. This is what you are to say to the Israelites: 'I AM has sent me to you.'"

Moses was still standing, but I wasn't. I was slammed to the ground by the force of God's words. I tried to get up, but I couldn't. The weight of "I AM" sat on top of me.

"Say to the Israelites, 'The God of your fathers—Abraham, Isaac, and Jacob—has sent me to you.' This is My name forever, the name by which I am to be remembered from generation to generation."

It went on like that for seven days. God would lay out the plan for Moses, and Moses would explain to God why His plan could not possibly work. Finally, God told Moses to go to the elders of Israel and tell them the cavalry was coming and Moses was leading them. Together they were to go to Pharaoh and announce the exodus of the Jews. With my face still smashed into the sand all that time and goats sniffing around my protruding backside, I found myself wondering how God thought this was going to happen.

"Surely God doesn't think Moses can just drop in unannounced on the ruler of Egypt and get past the front door. How would Moses, a goatherd, a nobody, get in front of Pharaoh?" I puzzled it for a moment.

"Of course he can," I mumbled into the sand. I tried unsuccessfully to levitate myself up out of the dirt as I answered my own question. "The old pharaoh is dead. Ramses is on the throne. He and Moses were once brothers. Of course he'll get in."

God told Moses exactly what would happen. Ramses would resist. There would be signs and wonders. Plagues would be unleashed, but at the end of the day, Moses and the Israelites would leave Egypt with the plunder. Moses found his tongue and began to negotiate with God.

"What if they don't believe me or listen to me and say, 'God did not appear to you'?"

Now God had been talking to Moses for about a week, saying the same thing over and over. When God didn't strike him dead right there on the spot for lack of belief or at least terminal thickheadedness, I couldn't stand it. It was probably a good thing for me that I was stuck in the sand, because if I could have gotten up, I would have risked my life to get in front of God just to ask Him a few questions of my own.

"God," I would have said, "just what is Your definition of *fair*? How do the humans get away with it? Why do You allow them to question You? They express serious doubts about You, and not only do You let them live, but You also answer their doubt. Take just a moment here and think about my case. I never doubted You in the least. I had one fleeting moment of uncertainty, a simple question for clarity's sake when the rebellion started. Do You think I would have followed that maniac in his self-destruction if I had been allowed just one minute to think things over? Why do You allow the humans to do what You would not allow the angels to do—question You? How is that fair?"

Not even a little put out by Moses's doubt, God said to him, "What is that in your hand?"

"A staff."

"Throw it on the ground."

Moses threw it on the ground, and it became a snake, and he ran from it, which is just what I would have done if I could have stood up.

Then God said, "Reach out your hand and take it by the tail."

So Moses reached out and took hold of the snake, and it turned back into a staff in his hand.

"This is so that they may believe that the God of their fathers has indeed appeared to you."

I thought I couldn't bear to hear another word as God went on and on as to how He was going to address Moses's every concern. When I thought Moses had gone as far as he dared, he went further.

"O Lord, I have never been eloquent. I am slow of speech, and sometimes I stutter when I'm nervous."

With my head still in the sand, I couldn't see it, but I could feel the bush flame hotter. I could tell God was just about done negotiating.

"Who gave man his mouth? Who makes him deaf or mute? Who gives him sight or makes him blind? Is it not I? Now go; I will help you speak and will teach you what to say."

If Moses had any brains, he'd get going while the getting's good. He may have been treading on holy ground, but it sounded to me like he was close to treading on God's last nerve.

When Moses spoke again, I was convinced he was addled. It must have been those years of talking to goats. Talking goats, talking bush, probably not all that different in his mind. That must have been it. Otherwise, he never would have dared say what he did.

"O Lord, please send someone else to do it."

The sand where I was planted got hotter and hotter as God's wrath burned against Moses. This had to be it. I couldn't see how God could indulge him any further. But He did. When I heard God agree to allow Aaron, Moses's brother, to accompany him and speak for him, I quit trying to get up and hoped

I would die right there in the sand. I was exhausted and frustrated at the way God let these humans get by with things that would never have been allowed in the angelic realm. The last thing I remember was the crumpling of my wing as a goat laid down on it.

The ground was cold, the night was dark, and everyone was gone when I came around and realized the weight of "I AM" had lifted from my back. Shaking my wings back into shape, I looked around and, seeing no one, wondered if Moses was still alive after challenging God the way he had. Dead or alive, he was nowhere to be seen; even the goats were gone. Finding a flat sandstone, I sat down and tried to think about what had happened.

After a while, I figured it out. The desert had not killed Moses, but it had humbled him. So much so that he was likely the humblest man on all the earth. His questioning God was not because he doubted God but because he doubted himself. Moses couldn't get over his sense of unworthiness, so he begged God to use someone like Aaron, a person he thought to be holier than himself and more worthy of being chosen by God. At least Aaron was not guilty of ever having killed someone like Moses had done. Moses believed he had failed God years ago and was now of no use to Him at all. And God, of course, could not resist that kind of humility.

If I had ever doubted, there was now no possibility Moses might fail.

As I flapped my way back to the second heaven, I thought about the contrast between the arrogance of Satan and the humility of Moses. Satan's unrestrained pride caused one-third of the angels to fall to their doom. Moses's complete lack of self would redeem a nation. I wanted to rub the irony in Satan's face when I returned to his lair, but I would never have had the nerve to do such a thing. I couldn't help but think about the Hebrews and their unrelenting belief for more than four centuries that someday, some way, a deliverer was coming for them. Even as hundreds of them died every day in the mud pits, the rest of them continued their song of hope.

"My deliverer is coming. My deliverer is standing by."

I wondered how they knew.

CHAPTER 4

I s THAT THE best you can come up with?" Satan's sarcasm
was intended to minimize the importance of my report
lest for one minute I might take pride in bringing him
useful information. "Am I supposed to believe God came up
with a ridiculous plan like this?"

I told him word for word the conversation I'd heard between
God and Moses in the desert, but he wouldn't believe I hadn't
left something out of the story. It sounded too simple. That's
another of the countless ways in which Satan is different from
God. God makes things simple, especially when it comes to
humans. Satan, on the other hand, makes things as convoluted
as possible.

"Let me see if I have this right. Moses will just mosey into
Ramses' throne room with a stick in his hand, and Ramses will
hand over the slaves. Is that what you expect to happen?"

"Something like that, sir. Of course there's going to be hail,
frogs, flies, blood in the river, all that at first, but at the end of
it all, Moses will leave with the slaves."

"Are you suggesting I don't have the power to stop the exodus
of the Hebrews?" Satan was beginning to sizzle. Trick question. *What should I say?* My mind worked double time trying
to come up with an answer with the least physical consequences
for me.

"No, of course not, Your Terribleness. With the humans,
you've always got a shot because of that misconceived idea of

free will God programmed into them. Moses has to obey every step of the way by an act of his will. It hasn't been hard for him so far. But he's been out of town for a long time, and when he comes back and sees the grandeur of Egypt and its gods (us, of course), he might realize the absurdity of the whole idea and go home. He might begin to doubt whether the burning bush really happened; maybe it was just a mirage. That sort of thing happens in the desert a lot, you know. We could help with that. Speak confusion into his dreams; suggest to his friends that he got into a hallucinogenic weed or something. It could work."

Satan ignored my suggestions and turned to Bezel and the other chief demons.

"Station your guards in Ramses' court. Be ready when Moses arrives."

"We've had a platoon on the wall for forty years, master," Bezel answered. "Do you really think we need more guards?"

Satan didn't have to answer. All he had to do was cast those awful eyes toward the demon who thought he could question Satan's decision.

"Right away, sir," Bezel said meekly as he backed away.

Off they went in blind obedience whether they had a game plan or not. As they were leaving, I decided it would be a good time to slip out the side door and get back to my perch. Satan stepped on my tail as I crept out.

"Did I dismiss you?" he scowled. "Let me know the moment Moses steps into the city. Don't let him get past you. You will rue the day if he does. Now get back to your post."

That was exactly what I was trying to do.

I supposed God must have spoken to Aaron when I wasn't paying attention. That would explain why he was headed out to the desert to meet Moses. In any event, the two of them met with the elders, handled the protocol of leaving, and before he had a chance to rethink the whole idea, Moses, his son, and Zipporah were on their way to the city.

I couldn't wait to see the look on Moses's face when he stepped over the crest of the sand dune and beheld Egypt in all of its glory, something he hadn't seen in forty years. I left my perch and flew down to where he was standing, careful not to make any noise or do anything to let him know he wasn't alone. I wanted to see what the Temple of Karnak looked like from his perspective.

I closed my eyes tightly and tried to imagine I was a human. I do that from time to time because even after all these centuries, I'm still amazed how the human race has survived against Satan's demons. I've often wondered if God secretly regretted having made mankind of such inferior materials. He handicapped the entire race right from the beginning. Think about it. The whole mortality issue for humans is a terrible motivator when He needs them to go to war. Man knows he is finite. No matter how he lives or how he dies, at the end of it all, his death will be the same as the worst or best who ever lived. By contrast, even if a demon loses a battle with a human, he doesn't die. God should have fixed this inequity centuries ago.

Humans, on the other hand, not only die, but also many of you are *willing* to die on the basis of your perceived relationship with God. Why? You die and then what? You can't be sure what, if anything, awaits you after death. Why jeopardize the life you at least have some control over now by taking impossible orders from a God who you can't be sure exists at all. And if He does exist, He's been known to disappear for hundreds of years at a time with no explanation at all as to where He's been.

And while we're talking about it, the whole idea of the natural combating the supernatural, man against the demonic realm, is preposterous. Whose idea was that? I have a hard time imagining God came up with it on His own.

Look at the facts. Demons don't bleed. Let's start right there. You humans function as a result of your blood. Poke a hole in your feeble flesh, let the blood run out, and there you go—dead human. Demons cannot be physically hurt by man, and that's just the plain fact of the matter. Humans can swing at us all the livelong day, but you cannot actually touch us. The only warfare weapon you have against us it to entreat God to dispatch the warring heavenly angels against us on your behalf. Fortunately for us, most of you never figure it out. Demons have extraordinary strength and are cunning and invisible. You humans are weak by comparison, not all that bright in my observation, and clearly visible. What kind of contest is that? Unless God has some idea of a better line of defense for you somewhere down the road, you cannot possibly win. Tell the truth—at least some of you from time to time must have thought that God set you up for failure. Certainly Satan has tried telling you that for years.

I stood beside Moses, scrunched my eyes shut, and pretended I had no supernatural powers, could not fly, and was made of flesh and blood. Then I opened my eyes and beheld Karnak, the city of the pharaohs. I have to tell you it was impressive.

Although it was built entirely by humans, the temples, the architecture, the sheer grandeur of it all almost overwhelmed me, and I had the perspective of paradise to compare it with.

Then I looked at Moses. Five feet eight inches tall—five-nine tops—one hundred sixty pounds more or less, weathered skin of a shepherd, and long gray beard and hair of one who has fought the desert all his life. Not all that impressive. Certainly he didn't look like a man in search of a midlife career change. I wondered if he felt as small as he looked.

He stood there a long time staring at the city. At a minimum he must have been reevaluating the whole idea. I wondered if he was thinking how this would be a good time to turn back before anybody realized he was back in town. God had appeared in the earth realm as a burning bush and declared him to be the deliverer of Israel. So, what of it? No one else saw it, and no one else would ever have to know, save those few elders he talked with, and who really cared what they thought about anything?

Moses continued staring at Karnak, and I continued staring at Moses. I couldn't figure it out. Why would Moses at eighty years old, a person who had escaped death and slavery and had ended up in a desert oasis with a pretty good life, care anything at all about what happened to the humans who remained in bondage in Egypt? I don't get that about you people. Why do you humans care about the sufferings of other humans? More than that, what motivates you to try to do something about it?

Here's how I would have handled the whole situation. If I'd been Moses and God showed up to tell me how the sufferings of the slaves were of concern to Him, I would have suggested to God—very respectfully, you understand—that He go get them Himself or at least send a SWAT team of angels to do it. I would have pointed out the logistical nightmare of what He was proposing. Here's what I would've said:

"So, sovereign Lord, let me see if I heard You right. You want me to lead two million Hebrews into the desert to have a party and worship You, and Pharaoh is going to go right along with the whole idea. I can see how You are about worship and all that, but say, did You have some sort of follow-up plans for after the prayer meeting? Or were You thinking all the AWOL slaves and I would just wing it after that? Where did You say this Promised Land is, and how many demonized tribes are already living there? Of course, You're probably planning to have them surrender to us when we get to the border, right?

"That's only fair if Your idea is to send me into the middle of them with just the slaves, who, I might point out, make a lousy conquering army. Why don't we just sleep on this tonight and see how we feel about it tomorrow?"

Yes, that's what I would have said. I looked to see if Moses might be thinking the same thing, but he was gone.

He was halfway to the city gate by the time I caught up with him again. I thought about going back to Satan's lair right then to let him know where we were in the process, but then I had a reality check. When Moses got to the gate, how was he going to get in? I know what I said about him being raised as Ramses' brother, but that was a long time ago. These guards wouldn't remember him; they were too young. They wouldn't know or care who he was. They were highly unlikely to let a wandering goatherd enter the gates without any prior authorization. Maybe it wasn't worth getting Satan riled up just yet. I decided to follow Moses and see what would happen.

When we got to the gate, it was just as I thought. The Egyptian guards were posted on top of the wall over the massive doors. Beside each one of them was one of Satan's henchmen to make sure the guards did not let Moses through in case he ever showed up again. As Bezel tried to remind Satan, the demons had been stationed there since Moses fled forty years earlier just in case he ever tried to come back. Moses banged on the gate with the staff the Lord had given him. I must say it did make quite a loud noise for a piece of wood. I thought I'd better wave a wing at the demons on the wall to let them know I was with Moses in case they were planning some sort of attack. They had a habit of overlooking me, and I didn't want to end up as barbecue if there was a fight. I took a step forward to get in a better position, but when I looked back up to the place on the wall where they had been, they were gone. The human guards were still there, but every last one of the demonic horde was gone. Now, that was odd.

I stayed behind Moses, simultaneously wondering where our side went and not believing it when the gates began to open. You know how you get that funny feeling down your scales—or in your case, down your spine—when you realize you're not alone? I was getting that feeling when all at once I heard a snort and felt hot breath right down the back of my neck. I turned around and was face-to-nostril with the biggest white horse I'd ever seen. In fact, there were six of them. I had to step back to see how grand they really were. When I did, I saw on their backs the elite guard of the heavenly host.

No wonder the demon guards had fled. Moses couldn't see them and had no idea the angels were even there, much less that they had arrived to ensure he got into the city. He looked first at his staff and then at the opening gates in pure amazement, having no idea that the cavalry of heaven stood round about him. The great stallion stomped his glistening hoof and snorted at me. Time to go.

I tried to flee, but I'm not at my best under stress. Those snorting horses made me so nervous I couldn't get my hooves and wings going in the same direction. I hopped around trying to get liftoff, but my tail acted like a sack of rocks. The lead horse was now bearing down on top of me with those flaring nostrils right in my contorted face. I just knew he was going to step on me.

I decided to play dead. I whimpered and rolled up in a ball under his massive chest. I figured out right away this was not a great idea, but as I said, I'm not good under pressure. The horse sniffed at me and then tossed his head, turned, kicked with those powerful legs, and sent me flying into the vast expanse. When I stopped spinning, I began flapping for all I was worth as I beat a quick path back to the second heaven.

But I wasn't as fast as the demon guards who had already made it back to Satan's court. He was furious when he learned they had left their posts. They stood cowering before him as he blasted them for abandoning their assignment. I tried not to show it, but I enjoyed seeing someone besides me on the receiving end of his thrashing. He glanced my way, seeming surprised to see me.

"Why are you here?"

"I live here, Your Majesty." Never try to be flip with Satan. I ducked whatever it was he threw at me and went on. "What

I mean is that I'm back to report. Moses got into the city." I was going to tell him about the horses and the elite guard, but he cut me off.

"How many of you imbeciles do I need to tell me Moses got into the city? I got it, all right? And here you all are comfy at home while Moses wanders around Egypt completely unopposed." His eyes seared each of us. I knew not to say anything right then, but one of the others did not.

"What did you expect us to do when the heavenly host showed up?" he blurted out. "You were certainly no match for them when we were in heaven. Don't blame us for getting out before they saw us and turned the wrath of you-know-who on us again."

Oh, my. Bad, bad answer. No one was ever allowed to remind Satan of how Michael had thrown us out of heaven after the rebellion.

Over the centuries, I'd seen Satan throw just about every kind of fit you might imagine. I'd seen rage that melted demons' wings and violence against his own kind that in any other created species would be unimaginable. But I had never seen Satan do what he did that day to the demon who dared to say what all of us were thinking. I dare not say what happened, but suffice it to know our former comrade was no more.

"Any other comments?" he snarled to the rest of us as he wiped away the demon ooze that dribbled out of his mouth. Disgusting, I know, but it gives you a hint. Of course, not a word was spoken. No one even thought out loud. Everyone fled for his post. I was glad to be going back to my perch to resume my duties of watching the Hebrews when Satan stopped me in my attempted exit.

"Does Moses have any weapons to use against Ramses?"

"Not to speak of, sir. He has his shepherd's staff, but that's about it. Nothing to worry about, although it does have one pretty impressive add-on feature." I was remembering what I had seen in the desert. "He can turn his staff into a snake. I saw him do it back there at the bush."

For a moment, Satan didn't seem to know what to do with this information. God hadn't been all that favorably disposed toward using snakes for anything since that episode in the garden. Satan summoned one of the demon princes who specialized in magic and told him to position himself with the court magicians.

"Whatever Moses does with his staff, make sure they can duplicate it," he hissed to the prince, who did not speak but just nodded and whisked away toward Ramses' palace.

"You." Satan was speaking to me again. "Dog his steps. Watch every move. If he hears from God, I want to know about it. Do not allow Moses to leave Egypt with the Hebrews."

I took to flight in search of Moses without asking any questions, but I kept thinking about that last statement. Surely Satan was not suggesting that I might be able to keep Moses from doing anything, much less liberating the slaves. Since we were not allowed to ask follow-up questions, it was a constant battle to guess what Satan meant by what he said.

CHAPTER 5

AT FIRST THEY just stared at one another as if each had seen a ghost. Moses, weathered and leathered, a man who had battled the desert and survived, seemed out of place but oddly at ease in the opulence surrounding him. Aaron stood by his side, uncomfortable and unsure of where he was supposed to look, so he stared at the floor. Ramses sat on his throne in splendor, dressed in his royal robes, with a look of confusion and disbelief all over his face. Moses had no trouble getting in to see the pharaoh because as soon as Ramses heard that someone claiming to be his long-lost brother had arrived, he canceled the business at hand and had Moses ushered into the throne room.

Ramses spoke first. "You've returned from the grave, my brother. Have you come back to us to take your place in the royal service?"

"No, Ramses," Moses said. "We both know I have no claim to the royal lineage. I am the son of Hebrew slaves."

"Nonsense," Ramses replied. "We played together as children. We were as brothers. You're welcome here, and you will be safe. After all, those who wanted your life are now dead." He rose from his throne and walked around Moses as if seeing him from every side might reveal some hidden thing.

Ramses must be psychic, I thought to myself. *That is exactly what God said to Moses in the desert. Why else would Ramses think to say it?*

Moses turned around to face his brother. "Pharaoh knows that I am a Hebrew, a brother of the slaves you hold in bondage. Their cries have gone up to the God of heaven, who has sent me for them."

I swear the temperature in the room dropped ten degrees as Ramses' eyes iced over at the words of Moses. If you ask me, God skipped an important step in the "get ready" phase when He failed to insist that Moses brush up on his diplomatic skills before encountering the ruler of Egypt. Moses had spent too many years talking to goats. God should have provided him with a life coach for a couple of weeks. Someone to help him learn the social graces he'd long forgotten, such as how monarchs like a little polite chitchat to break the ice before jumping right down to the nonnegotiables. At least a few opening words like this, maybe:

"Hi, how are you doing, brother? What's new with the family? The castle looks great; I like what you've done with the place. Sorry I haven't written. By the way, I just dropped by to walk out with your entire labor force. Nice seeing you."

No, Moses didn't give Ramses a chance to warm up to the idea at all. No sugarcoating whatsoever. All eyes were on Pharaoh. Maybe Ramses thought Moses's comments were so ridiculous they didn't merit a response. After an uncomfortable silence, it was Moses who blinked and spoke again.

"This is what the God of Israel says: 'Let My people go so that they may hold a festival to Me for three days in the desert.'" The snickering in the court came from the palace guards who couldn't contain their giggles at the absurdity of what Moses had said.

Pharaoh laughed as well. "My brother hasn't lost his sense of humor. You were always the prankster."

Moses remained silent.

Ramses stopped smiling and sat down on his throne. "Who is this God that I should obey Him and let the slaves go?"

"He is the God of Israel and the Creator of all that is."

Moses had summed it up nicely, I thought—briefly but nicely.

"Is he greater than the gods of Egypt?" Ramses shot back.

"He is."

Again I was concerned Moses wasn't investing nearly enough words into this conversation. Ramses opened the door to dialogue, but Moses was not walking through it.

"So your God cares about the Hebrews, does He? They've been the slaves of Egypt for four hundred years. Where's He been all this time if He is so concerned?"

"Let them go, Ramses."

"Here's what I think of your God." With that, Ramses turned to the foreman of the slaves.

"Give them no more straw to make bricks. Obviously they have too much time on their hands. Now let them gather the straw themselves, and let the daily quota remain the same."

Moses didn't flinch, but Aaron looked like he might run. They should have anticipated that Pharaoh would resist the idea of a total shutdown in the brick-making business. Aaron swallowed hard but didn't say a word as he waited to see what Moses would do with this unfortunate turn of events.

"Pharaoh, for your own sake, let them go."

Ramses bristled in indignation. He rose from his throne and stormed out of the room without saying another word. Moses and Aaron were summarily dismissed and booted out the same door they'd come in. It didn't take very long for the word about the straw to get to the slave masters, who themselves were Hebrews. In one grumbling group they petitioned a meeting with Ramses and got it.

"It can't be done," they said, groveling before him. "The people can't gather straw and produce the same number of bricks. We'll fall behind. The building projects will suffer. Why has Pharaoh done this to his subjects?"

"If your people have enough time to ask for three days off to party in the desert to worship your God, then they have too much time."

The foreman looked stunned. "Did we ask my lord for any such thing? It would never cross our minds to think about a long weekend. Who brought such a request to Pharaoh's ears?"

"Moses."

Well, you can guess what happened. The slave masters went back to the brick pits and told the people what Ramses had said. When Moses and Aaron showed up a little while later, the whole Hebrew population had turned on them. The brothers were flabbergasted. God had never given the slightest warning this might happen. From their ashen look, it was clear they hadn't expected things to go quite this way. Neither said very much in the face of the verbal assaults being hurled at them by the throng, but once they got out of earshot, Moses began to cry out to God.

"O Lord, I tried to tell You I wouldn't be very good at this. I've made things worse for the very people You are trying to help."

"Tell the Israelites I will bring them out from under the yoke of the Egyptians. I will free them from being slaves, and I will bring them to the land I swore to give Abraham, Isaac, and Jacob. I will give it to them as the inheritance I promised."

Aaron was in a quaking heap on the ground in the presence of the Lord, but Moses just kept talking to the Creator of the universe as if they were old chums.

"O God, here's my idea how we can turn this around. Would You mind doing the burning bush thing one more time? I told the Hebrews about it, of course, but I could see in their eyes that they didn't believe me. But if You could just fire that bush up again right there in the middle of town where the Egyptians and the Hebrews can both see it, I'm pretty sure we can be out of here by morning."

God didn't think much of his idea, so Moses and Aaron went to the Hebrews and told them what the Lord God had said. Moses was right. They didn't believe one word of it.

Satan squealed with delight when I gave him this news. He walked over to the edge of the second heaven and looked off into the distance.

"Where are they now? Hightailing it back to the desert for sure. Who does God think He's messing with by sending two country bumpkins into my territory?" Satan swung his fist in an uppercut for effect.

The other demons were congratulating themselves on running Moses and Aaron out of town, but I just stood there saying nothing at all and looking at the floor. I just knew Satan was going to comment on my silence.

"You don't see anything here to cheer about, moron? The deliverer and his sidekick are on their way back to the sticks. It's over."

I chose my words carefully. "Did anybody actually see them leave the city gates, sir?"

Satan looked at the demons, and they looked at one another. When the heads started shaking in response, Satan dispatched one of the lower-ranking devils to scour the city streets for them. They weren't hard to find, and it was only minutes before the scout was back, reporting what I knew all along. Moses and Aaron had gone nowhere but to bed.

I spent the rest of the night perched on the ledge above the door of the house where Moses and Aaron slept.

"Dog their steps," Satan had hissed at me as he sent me out on the graveyard shift.

The next morning, God appeared to them again. "You are to say everything I command you. Tell Pharaoh to let the Israelites go. Aaron can help you."

Well, I can just tell you that Aaron's face fell like a rock when he heard that bit of news. He knew he was to stand behind whatever Moses said, but his idea was to stand about forty feet behind and under a rock if one was available. Aaron had zero plans to get in the line of fire between Moses and Ramses, much less to actually enter into the conversation.

"I will harden Pharaoh's heart, and though I multiply My miraculous signs and wonders in Egypt, he won't listen to you."

Moses didn't say a word, but I knew what he was thinking because I was thinking it myself. *What are You saying, God? Number one, Ramses' heart doesn't need to be any harder, and number two, he's not listening to me now.*

"Then I'll lay My hand on Egypt, and with mighty acts of judgment, the Egyptians will know that I am God when I stretch out My hand and bring the Israelites out of it by divisions."

Here's what I've learned about God over the eons: if you don't listen carefully to every word He speaks, you can miss something big. And that's just what happened to Moses. He missed two remarkable things. God said He was going to bring the Israelites out by divisions. Out of divisions come *soldiers*, not *slaves*. Slaves come out in a mob. I didn't know what He meant by His word choice, but I knew it meant something.

I was more than merely interested in the other thing God said. He was going to play this thing out for a while so the Egyptians would know He was God. Why? Whatever for? What good would it do? As far back as I could remember, at least since Abraham, God had never before cared one way or the other about anybody but the Hebrews. Why would He suddenly be interested in what the Egyptians knew about Him?

Unless...

I couldn't bear to think about it, but I knew I must. Why would God care what the Egyptians knew about Him unless

He intended to save some of them? Impossible. Completely out of order and not fair. The Egyptians were sold out to Satan, way beyond redemption of any kind. The idea that God might be thinking of saving the Egyptians took hold of my mind, and I completely forgot about Moses and Aaron. All I could think about was how I wanted to have a little chat with God.

"God," I cried out. Sometimes I've complained to God with great bravado, secure in the knowledge that He did not hear me. This time I wished He would hear me, although I knew I was just shaking my wing at empty space. "I'm right, aren't I? You're trying to find a loophole to save some of the Egyptians, aren't You? How could You even think about it? How could You give those who don't know You and don't care about You time to repent when You wouldn't spare me five minutes? That's all I needed to recover my sanity that awful day when the war in heaven happened. Five minutes more and I could have reached Michael's side to tell him I'd changed my mind. Five minutes more and I would never have followed that lunatic Lucifer."

In total despair at the mere thought of God counting the evil Egyptians worthier of salvation than me, I flew hard into the nearest wall and tried to kill myself. Of course, it didn't work and only made my head throb. By the time I pulled myself together, God was still talking to Moses and Aaron.

"When Pharaoh says to you, 'Perform a miracle,' then say to Aaron, 'Take your staff and throw it down before Pharaoh,' and it will become a snake."

You should have seen Aaron snap to attention at that comment. The first thing he did was throw the staff on the ground to see if it was working. Nothing. Next, he started pulling on Moses's tunic with one hand while continuing to thump his staff on the ground with the other. He tried to point out to Moses that the staff was just a common tree branch with no supernatural qualities. Moses ignored him and continued listening to God while Aaron feverishly practiced behind his back, trying to make something happen—*thump, thump*. No snake.

The next day I followed them into Pharaoh's throne room to see what would happen. Moses strode with calm confidence and walked directly to the place where Ramses was seated. Aaron followed a few steps behind, continuing to thump his staff on the floor as he went along to see if it wriggled at all. Nothing. He stopped thumping and came alongside Moses, not looking at all well.

Right on cue, Pharaoh demanded proof that the God of Moses was real. "Perform a miracle," he chided.

Everyone in the room snickered. Moses turned to Aaron and told him to do what God had said. With trembling hands and closed eyes, Aaron threw his staff to the ground and prepared to run. It was the cumulative gasp from the eunuch slaves that caused him to open his eyes and jump back in disbelief at the writhing snake on the palace floor.

With nary a raised eyebrow, Pharaoh summoned wise men, sorcerers, and the Egyptian magicians to do the very same thing by their secret arts. Each one threw down his staff, and each staff became a snake. But to everyone's amazement, Aaron's staff swallowed up their staffs. No one in the room was more surprised by this than Aaron. When Moses reached down and picked the serpent up by the tail and it turned back into a staff, there was a chorus of sighs of relief from every corner of the room. Ramses, however, pretended to be unimpressed. He ordered Moses and Aaron to leave.

I was about to fly back to Satan's lair to give him an update when it occurred to me that Moses and Aaron wouldn't go home without reporting to God. I knew I'd better follow them lest I miss something. When they got to the city's edge, they called out to God. I listened with both ears to what God told them to do next.

"Go to Pharaoh in the morning as he goes out to the water. Wait on the bank of the Nile to meet him. Take the staff that was changed into a snake, and say to him, 'The God of the Hebrews has sent me to say to you, "Let My people go so that they may worship Me in the desert."' With the staff that is in your hand, strike the water of the Nile and it will be changed into blood. The fish in the Nile will die, the river will stink, and no one will be able to drink its water.

"And you, Aaron, take your staff and stretch out your hand over the waters of Egypt, the streams, canals, ponds and all the reservoirs, and they will turn to blood. Blood will be everywhere in Egypt."

Moses seemed to be taking it in fairly well, but Aaron was getting that woozy look again.

As I flew back to the second heaven to report to Satan, I wondered how he was going to take this news that God had upped the stakes in the battle for the Hebrews. He was enabling mere humans to operate in the supernatural realm. I knew Satan would demand to know if this was legal. I wasn't sure.

He took the news much better than I thought he would.

"So what? God's losing His touch if that's the best He can come up with. I can do the same thing."

He summoned two of his demons who were specialists in black magic and sent them to the quarters of the court magicians. The next day, Satan summoned all the demons to come and stand on the edge of the second heaven to watch the show. He was very smug about how this would turn out.

There they were, Moses and Aaron, standing before a full house of spectators on the banks of the Nile. They did just as God had commanded. Aaron, with newfound confidence after the snake episode, raised his staff in the presence of Pharaoh and his officials and struck the water of the Nile, and all the water was changed into blood. The fish in the Nile died, and the river smelled so bad that the Egyptians couldn't drink its water. Blood was everywhere in Egypt.

"Well, *all right*," Aaron whispered to Moses as he nodded his head proudly at this new supernatural power he had obtained.

But his satisfaction didn't last long. The Egyptian magicians did the same things with jars of water by their secret arts. Now, right there is where Moses should have thrown down the yellow flag and yelled, "Foul." Who did the magicians think they would fool with that old parlor trick? What unbiased observer would equate changing the waters of a river into blood with changing a couple of gallons in a primed jar? Obviously, the magicians tossed a little dye into the pots with all their gyrations and hocus pocus. *Unbiased observer* is the key phrase here, which there were none of in the audience that day. I have to tell you, I was sorely disappointed with the cognitive abilities of Moses and Aaron in their failure to identify the trickery.

Pharaoh watched with a smug look on his face as if this were a perfectly legitimate contest. It appeared that his heart became harder just as God had said. He wouldn't listen to Moses and Aaron, and instead, he turned and went into his palace.

The demons laughed out loud at the puzzled expressions of Moses and Aaron. God failed to mention that part about how the magicians would appear to be able to turn water to blood as well. The crowd found better things to do and left, but Moses and Aaron stood there for a long time looking at the Nile and wondering what had gone wrong.

It was seven days before anything else happened.

CHAPTER 6

AFTER BEING PUBLICLY humiliated by Pharaoh's magicians, Moses and Aaron didn't venture out much during the next week, preferring to avoid the chiding of the Hebrews and Egyptians alike. Some of the demons thought it might soon be all over and Moses would head back to the goats. I couldn't be sure what Moses would do, but I was certain what God would do. He would up the ante again.

Just as I predicted, He summoned Moses and Aaron and said, "Go to Pharaoh and say to him, 'God says, "Let My people go so that they may worship Me. If you refuse to let them go, I will plague your whole country with frogs. The Nile will teem with frogs. They'll come up into your palace and your bedroom and onto your bed. They'll come into the houses of your officials, on your people, and into your ovens and kneading troughs. The frogs will jump up on you and your people and all your officials."'"

Moses swallowed hard but didn't say a word to indicate the doubt he must have had about God's new plan. Aaron was bursting to ask the obvious question but didn't. I decided to help them along by projecting my thoughts Moses's way. Other demons were always sending thoughts into human minds and seeing immediate results; I'd never given it a try but thought now might be a good time. I stared intently into his eyes and thought hard.

Are the court magicians going to be able to do the same thing and make you look foolish again?

No response. I couldn't tell if Moses received my thought transfer or not. Since he didn't repeat my question, I presumed he must not have heard me, otherwise he would have seen the wisdom in asking God whether the court magicians were going to make him look silly by making their own frogs. I myself didn't know the answer. The ability of Satan's minions to create amphibians had never come up before, although I personally doubted they could do it. I was still stumped over how they managed the snake trick. I wondered if I should dash back to the lair and ask about our ability to do frogs, but then I realized there wasn't enough time. We were about to find out anyway because Moses and Aaron, without protesting at all, turned and walked right back to Pharaoh's court.

Pharaoh was busy with the scribes when the two entered.

"So you're back, my brother," Pharaoh waved the scribes away. "What new entertainment did you bring me today?" The court laughed.

Moses motioned for Pharaoh to follow him as he and Aaron walked across the room and stepped out on a balcony over-looking the city. No one else heard it when God whispered to Moses.

"Tell Aaron, 'Stretch out your hand with your staff over the streams and canals and ponds, and make frogs come up on the land of Egypt.'"

Moses obeyed, and so did Aaron. The frogs came up out of everywhere and covered the land. But, wouldn't you know, the magicians did the very same thing by their secret arts.

The frog-making question was settled, and it was a mess. There were frogs all over the place. They hopped out of soup kettles and salad bowls and bounced across lunch tables all over Egypt. They popped out from under the long togas of women who went screaming hysterically into the street, demanding that someone do something. Even in Ramses' throne room, the soldiers and slaves couldn't contain the frogs. Moses and Aaron walked out of the chaos without much notice from anyone because every free hand in the room was slapping at frogs. The court magicians had also tried to slink out when Pharaoh ordered the guards to stop them. The guards grabbed them by their collars and deposited them right back in front of Ramses.

"Now get rid of them," Ramses seethed just as a really big jumper landed right on top of his bald head.

The nervous magicians waved their arms and spoke in Egyptian and then in gibberish, but nothing happened. If anything, there were more frogs than ever. The more the magicians cursed the frogs, the more there were, and the more aggressive they became. The one on Ramses' head would not budge, even with all the slaves swatting at him. All at once, I knew what was happening.

I couldn't help but be impressed all over again by the cleverness of God. He allowed the magicians to call the frogs in (which must have surprised them if the truth be known), but they couldn't get rid of them. God set a hook, and the magicians swallowed it, worm and all. Ramses rose to his feet in anger, dumping a dozen or so frogs out of the folds of his robe as he moved toward the magicians and slapped the main wizard to the side.

"Where are they?" he roared.

Obviously, he meant Moses and Aaron, who were outside on the front porch, trying to decide what to do next. The guards didn't have to be told to bring them back inside. Ramses stared at them, shook his head, then sat down on his throne and waved a hand of resignation at Moses.

"Tell God to take the frogs away from me and my people, and I will let your people go to offer sacrifices to Him."

Moses was stunned. So was I. This wasn't like Ramses to give up without a fight. Satan would be furious when he found out Moses and Aaron were about to leave town with the slaves in tow without any resistance at all.

Moses composed himself. "I leave to you the honor of setting the time for me to pray for you and your officials and your people, that you and your houses may be rid of the frogs, except for those that remain in the Nile."

"Tomorrow," Pharaoh waved his hand again, signaling their dismissal.

"It will be as you say so that you may know there is no one like our God. The frogs will leave; they will remain only in the Nile."

Moses and Aaron walked out in silence, having no idea what had just happened.

The next day, just as he promised, Moses cried out to God about the frogs. God did what Moses asked, and the frogs died in the houses, the courtyards, and in the fields. They were piled into heaps, and, I tell you, the land reeked of them.

In fact, it was so bad, the smell drifted all the way to the second heaven, where even Satan held his nose at the stench. He heard the whole thing and had already dispatched one of the demons to stand beside Ramses while the frog killing was going on. When it looked like most of the frogs were gone, the demon spoke into Ramses' ear.

"You can't let them go. They've made a fool of you. The brick pits will be shut down if the Hebrews leave. Your own people will turn on you. They're laughing at you right now for letting Moses pray in the presence of the great gods of Egypt. What were you thinking?"

Pharaoh listened to the demon, and when he saw that all the frogs were dead, he reneged on his promise to Moses and Aaron.

Now, this should have been the moment when Moses and Aaron stomped off in a huff after being lied to by Ramses. But they didn't. They stood quietly as if waiting for something else to happen. Satan turned to me and jerked me up by one of my ears.

"What are they doing? Why don't they leave? Did God give them any further orders?"

"No, no, not at all. I was there the whole time. He didn't say anything else."

I was frantically trying to remember if I'd left them alone at any time when God could have spoken to them and I missed something important. No, I was there the whole time. Well, except for the brief fit when I tried to commit suicide by flying into the wall. I might have blanked out there for a moment, but, no, I was sure that wasn't it.

I found myself airborne again as Satan tossed me off the ledge of the second heaven with orders to get on the ground by Moses to find out what was about to happen. I arrived just in time to hear God speak. No one could hear Him except Moses, and me, of course.

"Tell Aaron, 'Stretch out your staff, and strike the dust of the ground,' and throughout the land of Egypt the dust will become gnats."

"Gnats?" Moses asked.

"Gnats?" I echoed. Neither of us saw the wisdom in gnats. They were common in Egypt as it was. I couldn't see Pharaoh being one bit impressed by gnats, and I knew Moses couldn't see it either, but he didn't question God.

Moses did as God said, and when Aaron stretched out his hand with the staff and struck the dust of the ground, a torrent of gnats came upon men and animals. All the dust throughout the land of Egypt became gnats. Did I ever miscall that one! You can't imagine the catastrophe it was. Millions, make that billions, of flying, biting, miniscule gnats all over everything, everywhere, including me.

Pharaoh bellowed for the court magicians to come and clean up the mess. Any idiot would have known Pharaoh meant for them to get rid of the gnats, but at first they thought they were supposed to create more, which they couldn't do. It was easy to see how a person might be confused. It didn't matter anyway; they couldn't create more, and they couldn't get rid of the ones that were there. Men, women, cats, and dogs were swarmed over by Aaron's gnats.

Miserable as it was walking around in a cloud of gnats, I found myself momentarily forgetting about them as I pondered what was going on. The magicians could not make gnats. Why not? How was it the magicians could produce frogs but not gnats? Basic biology proves that a leaping, croaking, multidimensional amphibian just has to be harder to conjure up than a gnat. Therefore, it could only mean one thing, which should have been obvious to me all along. The magicians never really *produced* any frogs either. For all the things we demons can destroy, we cannot create a single thing. God Himself had summoned the frogs when the magicians called for them. It was all part of His plan to make Pharaoh show his hand.

If you think the frogs might have been annoying, you should have been there for the gnats. Arms waving, everyone running for cover, the animals going crazy...there was no escape. Ramses himself grabbed the lead magician by the throat and ordered him to get rid of the gnats. The magician struggled to get free and gasped for breath.

"We can't do it. This is the finger of God."

Pharaoh threw him to the ground and set off in search of Moses and Aaron.

I flew back to Satan's lair in time to hear him giving instructions to the demon he was dispatching to Ramses.

"Do not let Ramses give in to Moses. Kill him first."

Then he turned to me. "What will God do next? What have you heard?"

"I, uh, haven't actually heard anything."

Satan threw a fireball at me. I ducked but knew there would be more and worse if I couldn't come up with something.

"I can guess if you like, Your Horribleness. I've gotten pretty good at guessing what God will do next."

I ducked the next fireball but remained ready to run at any moment.

"Then guess," he snarled through his fangs.

"He will release another plague. No doubt about it. He will throw something new into the equation. It will be something to make Pharaoh look weak in the eyes of the people."

"What would that be?"

"No idea, sir."

"What good are you?" He threw another fireball at me as I dove for the floor. I didn't have to be told to return to the earth to see what would happen next. I arrived just in time to hear God speaking to Moses.

"Get up early in the morning, and confront Pharaoh as he goes to the water. Say to him, 'This is what the Lord says: "Let My people go so that they may worship Me. If you do not let them go, I will send swarms of flies on you and your officials, on your people and into your houses. The houses of the Egyptians will be full of flies.

""But on that day, I will deal differently with the land of Goshen, where My people live; no swarms of flies will be there, so that you will know that I, the Lord, am in this land. I will make a distinction between My people and your people. This miraculous sign will occur tomorrow.""""

If I had been Ramses, the gnats would have been the finisher for me. Let the people go with Moses. I would've given in while it was still an option. Make them promise to come back right after the weekend, but call for a time-out. I guess Ramses' head must have hardened right along with his heart, because once again, he defied God.

So, God did it. Dense swarms of flies poured into Pharaoh's palace and into the houses of his officials. Throughout Egypt, whatever the gnats missed before was completely ruined by the flies.

This time, it looked as if God's plan was beginning to work. As soon as the word got out that there were no flies in Goshen where the Hebrews lived, mobs of people began to gather outside of Pharaoh's court. The guards could barely keep them in line. The magicians, fearing a coup, pleaded with Ramses.

"The crowd is out of control. They're going to overrun the palace unless you do something."

"You do something," Ramses roared back, pushing the chief magician aside and storming to the window to see for himself.

"Ramses, you must listen. It's been fun, but the jig is up. Our hat tricks aren't going to help."

"What am I supposed to do?"

"Cry uncle. Here's my hankie; wave it at them—just do something."

Fearing the riots were at the boiling point and about to break out, Pharaoh summoned Moses and Aaron.

"Go! Sacrifice to your God, but stay here in this land."

I thought Moses might take that deal, but he didn't.

"No, that won't work. The sacrifices we offer our God would be detestable to the Egyptians. If we offer sacrifices in the city, they'll stone us. We must take a three-day journey into the desert to offer sacrifices to our God, as He commands us."

Pharaoh sighed and slumped back on his throne. One of his advisers leaned over and whispered in his ear.

"He's right. They cannot worship their God here."

"Why not?" Pharaoh whispered back.

"What if their God proves superior to the gods of Egypt? Then what are you going to do?"

The look on Ramses' face showed he hadn't thought about what might happen in a one-on-one between the gods of Egypt and the God of Moses.

"All right. I'll let you go offer sacrifices to your God in the desert, but you must not go very far, and you must come back in three days like you said."

Then Ramses ordered everybody out of the room except for Moses and Aaron. When the guards were gone, he turned to Moses and said, "Now pray for me."

Moses never flinched, but I was dumbfounded at Pharaoh's request. Not that I wouldn't have done the exact same thing, in case there were to be a showdown between the gods. Either he was getting over himself, or he was hedging his bets.

"As soon as I leave you, I will pray, and tomorrow the flies will leave. Only be sure that you do not act deceitfully again by not letting the people go to offer sacrifices to God."

Moses's naïveté was more than I could stand. Even though he couldn't see me, I waltzed right over and got in his face.

"Are you serious, Moses? How many times are you going through this before you catch a clue? Get over the sentimentality that this man was once your brother, if that's what your problem is. You just agreed to pray for Pharaoh, who not only worships the gods of Egypt, but he also thinks he is one. He doesn't honor our God—I mean, your God—and you know it. Don't even think about asking God to cut him some slack. Do you think God could ever overlook the fact that Ramses sacrifices the Israelites to the gods of Egypt on a regular basis? If you want to go out on a limb and ask God to bend the rules for somebody, let me tell you my story."

I dropped my wings in remorse and resignation to my fate as I watched Moses walk away. He left Pharaoh and prayed to God, and God did what Moses asked. The flies left.

Then, once again, Pharaoh hardened his heart and would not let the people go.

What a surprise.

CHAPTER 7

THINGS ON THE earth were quiet for the next few days, so I returned to my perch, continued my watch, and tried to guess what would happen next. I found myself wondering about Ramses.

"By now, he's got to know he's up against something stronger than he is. Why doesn't he give it up? The consequences can only get worse the longer he holds out. What is he thinking?"

"Not only that," I paced back and forth on my perch. "What's up with God? Why does He keep sending Moses with 'Tell Pharaoh this, and tell Pharaoh that'?" I couldn't recall God ever before engaging His enemies in conversation. This messaging back and forth to Pharaoh through Moses looked like a negotiation for the release of the Hebrews, which made no sense because God doesn't negotiate with anyone who isn't a Hebrew and about to be sent out on some impossible scheme. Abraham came to mind.

Satan instigated mandatory daily debriefings from all of his hordes for as long as Moses and Aaron were in town. When I heard the report from the demon assigned to Pharaoh's side, at least I got the answer to my first question about why Ramses didn't simply give up the slaves.

"Does Ramses know what this is all about yet?" Satan asked.

"No, sir," the demon answered. "I don't give him time to think about it. I keep telling him that it's all about him and

Moses, nothing more. I remind him how Moses would have been the prince of Egypt, not him, if it hadn't been for that murder years ago that drove Moses into hiding. I tell him that it's obvious to everyone that Moses is back to take over. He thinks it's a power struggle between two brothers with a little magic thrown in."

Soon it was my turn before the evil inquisitor.

"Now you tell me what God will do next."

I thought he was serious until I realized that the rest of the demonic corps was snickering. They were waiting for me to become flustered and say something silly as I usually did when I was nervous, and I was always nervous when Satan spoke to me. I gave what I thought was a good answer.

"He will send Pharaoh another message."

"*Ooooh*, so scary," the horde began chiding me. "Big whoopee, a message to Pharaoh; we better worry now."

They continued to make fun of me as if I were the village idiot whose sole purpose was to provide comic relief for their staff meeting. They kept on for a while until one of them realized that Satan wasn't laughing. One by one, the snickering subsided as they saw the steely look in Satan's eyes as he glared at me.

"Why did you say that?"

"Because that's what He's been doing. He sends Pharaoh a message warning him about what He'll do if Pharaoh doesn't let the Hebrews go, and then He does what He said. That's all I meant."

I desperately hoped Satan wouldn't pursue this line of questioning. I just wanted to slink back to my perch, but Satan stared me down, reading my eyes and knowing there was something more.

"It may be all you *said*, but it isn't all you *meant*, is it, imbecile?" The snickering started up again. In a rare burst of public vexation, I turned on the demonic crowd and railed at them.

"Does nothing about this look a little strange to any of you? Have you learned nothing at all about God? How many times has God ever negotiated with His enemies? Let me count them for you: none. Something big is happening under our collective noses, I tell you, and we have no idea what it is. And do you want to know why we can't figure it out? It's because He never does anything the same way twice. Do you seriously think you can outguess God? You've forgotten everything you ever knew of Him. You don't remember how He thinks, so you can't possibly know what the fight is about. You're pathetic. We're all pathetic."

It was Satan himself who held them back from attacking me. Maybe he intended to personally destroy me.

"So God will send a message to Pharaoh, and then He will do what He threatens, and therein is supposed to be some cosmic mystery that you alone have figured out. Is that it?" Satan's eyes narrowed as he glared at me.

I looked about the room at the seething demons and whispered my response for fear of triggering some celestial crisis if I actually said out loud what I now knew was true. I lowered my voice.

"It isn't just about the Hebrews anymore."

"Of course it is. It's always about the Hebrews." Satan slammed his claws down on a nearby rock and then turned toward me, daring me to tell him something about God he didn't already know.

"We've made a wrong assumption. It isn't just the Hebrews God cares about. He cares about the Egyptians as well." I ducked down in case this revelation triggered a demonic fit.

Instead, the whole lot of them broke out in body-shaking laughter. Again, Satan was the only one who didn't laugh.

"For a moment I thought you were serious," he said, dismissing me with a swipe of his claw.

"No, think about it, sir. What does He say when He sends a message to Pharaoh? He says something like this: 'Tell Pharaoh this, that, or the other *so that he will know that I am God.*' Why would God care whether or not Pharaoh knows He alone is God? Why would He care what Pharaoh or the Egyptians think about Him unless by realizing that He is God, they might repent and He would save them?"

"Impossible," Satan roared and then stormed across the lair, knocking the other demons aside as he paced back and forth. "It's only the Hebrews. It's always been about the Hebrews. He doesn't care about the rest of humanity."

I ventured a bit further. "Technically speaking, sir, it's about a people who will believe Him and obey Him. It just happens that Abraham's descendents are the only ones who have done this—so far. It isn't in the rule book that He only wants the Hebrews. It has just turned out that way. Clearly, He's trying to get the attention of the Egyptians. Nothing else makes sense. He's trying to give them a way out. And isn't that His nature?"

"No, it's not His nature," Satan bellowed at me. "He can't suddenly meddle in our strongholds just because He's had a change of heart about the rest of mankind. Their sin is too deep. Their sin demands restitution; I'm entitled to that. Even if they repent, which we will not allow, they have to be paid for by blood, innocent blood of which there is none in all the earth. Those are the rules."

Suddenly Satan stopped pacing and whirled around, facing the throng as if he had just realized some magnificent truth.

"In fact, why didn't I think of this before? He can't save the Hebrews without a blood payment. Just because they're slaves doesn't mean they're innocent." He turned to the demon who kept his records. "Check that out. I know I'm right. No blood, no restitution. Game over."

I didn't know how to answer because I'd never understood Satan's fixation with the blood issue to start with. None of us knew what he meant when he went off on a blood tangent. I nodded my head like the rest and agreed that he was probably right. By now all of the other demons were nodding and chattering about how Satan was always right and how he had it over God. I took the opportunity to crawl out of the room and sneak back to my perch.

He's not right, I thought to myself. *I don't know what it is, but God has a plan.*

I wondered if Moses knew what it was.

CHAPTER 8

I WAS BEGINNING TO think it would never end. How many ecological catastrophes could God come up with? He just kept going and going. Next, there was the plague that came upon all the livestock. With one exception, of course: none of the animals belonging to the Hebrews got sick. Pharaoh buckled a bit at the knees when this happened because nothing disrupts the economy and sends merchants into a panic like cattle, sheep, and goats dying all over the place. I thought Ramses might give it up on that one, but he didn't.

Next were the boils. Ugly, oozing sores broke out on every single man, woman, and child in Egypt, except the Hebrews. By now, all the magicians and advisers were begging Pharaoh to make a deal with Moses.

It was then God summoned Moses and Aaron and gave them a verbatim message to take to Pharaoh. When I heard it, I knew that God was getting closer to making His point.

"Get up early in the morning, confront Pharaoh, and tell him I said, 'Let My people go so that they may worship Me, or this time I will send the full force of My plagues against you so you will know that there is no one like Me in all the earth. By now, I could have stretched out My hand and struck you and your people with a plague that would have wiped you off the earth. But I have raised you up for this very purpose, that I might show you My power and that My name might be proclaimed in all the earth.'"

"I knew it! I knew it!"

I shouted as I jumped straight up in the air and missed my perch altogether, coming back down with a thud and landing on my bottom side. I got myself together and headed back to Satan's lair to tell him how I'd been right all along. God wanted Ramses to repent so the Egyptians could be saved. They would declare that God alone is God, and it would spread over the entire world. I stopped short of take-off when I realized I had no proof of anything and still had no answer for that blood-for-sin detail. I thought it better to restrain my excitement and watch and see what would happen next.

It was a good thing I waited. Otherwise I would have missed hearing the very proof I was looking for. God continued His message to Pharaoh: "'Therefore, at this time tomorrow I will send the worst hailstorm that has ever fallen on Egypt, from the day it was founded till now. Bring your livestock and everything you have in the field to a place of shelter because the hail will fall on every man and animal that has not been brought in and is still out in the field, and they will die.'"

There it was, shattering every assumption Satan held. God moved sovereignly, asked permission from no one, and offered the guilty-as-sin Egyptians a way out of judgment. God promised to save the animals belonging to the Egyptians, just like the animals belonging to the Hebrews, if only they would take one step toward Him by believing His word and hiding their livestock. Not one word about letting the Hebrews go so they could worship was in the deal.

When Moses delivered the word to Pharaoh, he did it in a loud voice so all the people in the neighborhood could hear what God was offering them. Those officials of Pharaoh who feared God couldn't move fast enough to bring their slaves and their livestock inside. Others, in misguided loyalty to Pharaoh, ignored Moses and left their slaves and livestock in the field.

Satan did not take this news well at all.

"You're making it up. I should cut your tongue out." Satan threatened me as he dragged me by the tail to the edge of the second heaven to watch for himself what was about to happen on the earth.

When Moses stretched out his staff toward the sky, God sent thunder and hail, and lightning flashed down to the ground. It was the worst storm Egypt had ever seen. Throughout the nation hail struck everything in the fields—both men and animals. It beat down everything growing in the fields and stripped every tree. The only animals that remained alive belonged to the Egyptians who had obeyed God. The only place it did not hail was the land of Goshen, where the Hebrews were.

"NGYAAAAAGH!" Satan shrieked as he jumped up and down on my tail as if I'd caused this to happen. He only stopped because he wanted to hear what Pharaoh was about to say to Moses and Aaron.

"This time I have sinned. Your God is right, and I and my people are wrong. Pray for us, for we have had enough thunder and hail. I will let you go; you don't have to stay any longer."

Moses left Pharaoh and went out of the city. He spread out his hands toward God; the thunder and hail stopped, and the rain no longer poured down on the land.

Satan whirled about and stomped right in the middle of my already sore bottom side, flattening me into the floor as he sped back to his lair of demons. He was back in a flash, dragging one of the demon princes by the collar, and then he flung him over the rim of the second heaven toward the earth.

"Get Ramses back in line," Satan yelled after the soaring demon. "Invalidate his repentance."

I didn't move a scale or a hoof. I lay there perfectly still, pretending to be unconscious, so I'm certain Satan was talking to himself and not to me when he spoke.

"No blood, no restitution. The repentance is meaningless without the shedding of blood," he assured himself as he slouched away back to his den.

I continued to lie there thinking about what Satan had said. *No blood, no restitution.* Even though I'd never figured out what it meant, I remembered exactly how and when Satan began his obsession with blood. It went all the way back to the garden when God should have killed Adam and Eve for their sin. Instead, He killed an innocent animal and made clothes for His errant humans. Satan had never been the same since that happened. It's like he knows some terrible secret he's too afraid to share.

Satan, scared? Seems unlikely, doesn't it? Especially when one remembers there's nothing in heaven or Earth scarier than him. Of course he fears God, and he knows about the judgment that will come to him—to all of us—at some point in time. He knows he is sentenced to Tartaroo like the rest of us who rebelled; there's no question about that. But he's sort of resigned himself to the inevitable because he knows that judgment day won't come until God either redeems the earth with His puny humans or cuts His losses and starts over with a better model. The day of sentencing could be pushed out to who knows how long—at least for as long as Satan holds the souls of humans.

As I peeled myself up from the floor, I thought more about it.

"The only thing in heaven or Earth that scares Satan, really scares him, is the idea of shedding innocent blood for sin. But why? Innocent people die all the time. What does he know that the rest of us don't?"

CHAPTER 9

AS FAR AS I was concerned, the locusts and the darkness were anticlimactic, if you know what I mean. I suppose the humans might not have seen it that way, but from my perch, it was just one big yawn after the frogs, gnats, boils, and hail. I figured it wouldn't be much longer before this whole misadventure to try to save the Hebrews, much less the Egyptians, would run out of gas. The Egyptians were not redeemable, and it didn't look like Pharaoh was ever going to let the Hebrews go. Not today, not tomorrow, not ever.

I wasn't surprised when God summoned Moses again, but I was baffled by what He said.

"Moses, I will bring one more plague on Pharaoh and on Egypt. After that, he will let you go from here. Tell the people that men and women alike are to ask their neighbors for articles of silver and gold."

"Like that's going to happen." I shrugged. "Why would the Egyptians give the slaves silver and gold?"

Then it hit me. The Egyptian people figured out that Moses had been right every time about what disaster was going to happen next. They had also seen how the Hebrews had escaped every plague that visited Egypt. So, by now the Egyptians were favorably disposed toward the slaves. More importantly, Moses himself was highly regarded in Egypt by almost everyone, including Pharaoh's officials.

After all, if it hadn't been for Moses warning the magistrates as well as the Hebrews about the hail, the Egyptians would have been eating hamburger for years from all the dead cows. The people had learned to pay attention to what Moses said, so when the Hebrews asked for silver and gold, they gave it to them. They probably thought of it as a commission, so to speak, or a down payment for future information. They weren't one bit reluctant to pay Moses for his timely advice. It seemed no one thought about the fact that slaves have no use for silver and gold. What could they do with it? The slaves weren't allowed to go anywhere but to the brick pits, and there were no boutiques or blue-light specials in that neighborhood.

This could only mean one thing: "The Israelites believe they're leaving town, and the Egyptians must think so as well," I reasoned. "They're packing up because they must know they're going somewhere."

I followed Moses as he walked straight into Ramses' throne room unannounced. He slipped right by the guards as if he'd been invisible. I slipped in right behind him because I was invisible. For several minutes, Moses stood quietly before his childhood brother and stared at him as if trying to find the words to make him listen. How could he make Pharaoh understand the irreversible consequences he was about to trigger if he resisted God one more time? Ramses stared back, and the longer he stared at Moses, the more it seemed that a cold fear rose up in his eyes, but he said not a word.

"This is what the Lord says." Moses paused, swallowed hard, and then went on. "Around midnight He will go throughout Egypt. Every firstborn son in Egypt will die, from the firstborn son of Pharaoh, who sits on the throne, to the firstborn son of the slave girl, who is at her hand mill, and all the firstborn of the cattle as well. There will be loud wailing throughout Egypt—worse than there has ever been or ever will be again.

"But among the Israelites not a dog will bark at any man or animal. Then you will know that the Lord makes a distinction between Egypt and Israel. All these officials of yours will come to me, bowing down before me and saying, 'Go. Leave quickly, and let all the people who follow you go with you!' After that I will leave."

Ramses didn't blink; he just kept staring at Moses. When Moses saw Ramses wasn't going to seize the last chance being offered him, he turned in frustration and left the room. I flew my fastest back to Satan's lair.

"Is that all He said?" Satan demanded. "You're certain?"

"I'm certain that's all Moses said."

"What about God? You're certain He said nothing more?" Although Satan grilled me as if he didn't believe me, he had a strange look in his eyes, as if he was hoping I would say, "Nothing more."

I've learned how to take a cue, so of course I answered, "No. Nothing more."

But he didn't stop there. He kept pressing as if I might be keeping something from him.

"Not even an *except for* or an *all but*—nothing like that; no qualifiers at all. You're sure?" His eyes narrowed as if probing into my mind to see if something else was there.

"No, sir. No ifs, ands, or buts. I'm certain of it."

I don't know quite how to describe what he's like when Satan thinks he's put something over on God. He danced a sort of jig and made a guttural noise in his throat that sounded something like the noise a cat makes when you try to give it a bath. He jigged all around, poking at me with his long claws as if I were supposed to giggle right along with him. I never really know how I'm supposed to respond to these antics, so I hopped around a little and tried to hum a little tune to go along with the jigging and to appear as thrilled about whatever it was as he seemed to be.

"You don't get it, do you, moron?" I didn't need to answer. The sum total of my not getting it was all over my face.

"Don't you see it? He didn't give them a way out. He's getting sloppy. He didn't exclude the Hebrews. He's bound by what He said. The firstborn of the Hebrews will die along with the Egyptians."

"Oh, I don't think so, sir." The words went right by the stop sign in my brain and out my mouth before I could rein them back in.

Satan stopped jigging not two inches from my face. I closed my eyes and tried to keep on humming like I wasn't worried. He didn't say a word. He didn't have to. He just breathed on me, daring me to tell him something he didn't want to know.

"It's like this, Your Evilness." I tried not to stutter, but I couldn't help it. "I mean, it's like, well, I don't really know what it's like, but..." I grasped for words, hoping to make a complete sentence as he bore down on me. "But I know what God is like. He will find a way to save them."

"Oh, so now you know what God is like, do you? Has *He* taken you into *His* counsel? Has *He* asked your opinion on anything at all?" He snarled and growled at me at the same time. "Or is there something you forgot to tell me? Some little detail you left out."

"No, no, sir." My voice was barely audible.

"If you're so sure He's got a plan, get out of my sight and find out what it is. You make me sick."

As soon as he turned his back, I slunk out and went in search of Moses.

I arrived just in time to hear Moses giving the people instructions to prepare a hasty supper. So hasty, in fact, they were not to use any yeast in making the bread. It was obvious they weren't going to have time to let it rise. Wherever they thought they were going, they expected to make a quick exit. I followed Moses into another room, where he gathered the men. I must tell you that I wasn't the least bit comfortable being in the middle of the Hebrews like that. I don't know what it was about them, but to be honest, I really wanted to run. But I didn't dare leave without hearing what Moses had to say.

Moses summoned all the elders of Israel.

"Go at once and select the animals for your families, and slaughter the Passover lamb. Take a bunch of hyssop, dip it into the blood in the basin, and put some of the blood on the top and on both sides of the door frame. Not one of you shall go out the door of his house until morning. When the Lord goes through the land to strike down the Egyptians, He will see the blood on the top and sides of the door frame and will pass over that doorway, and He will not permit the destroyer to enter your houses and strike you down."

When I heard the word *destroyer*, then I *really* wanted to run. I knew Satan would be livid when he heard that this new deal had blood in it, but how bad could it be? Lamb's blood would be the last thing he would care about once I told him the destroyer was about to be released into the earth realm. We knew all about him all right. He had only one job. He carried out the wrath of God. His authority transcended the realm of humans and demons alike. I flapped with all my might to get back to the den to report what I'd heard.

I tried as hard as I could to get in control of myself and stop trembling before delivering the news to Satan.

"The destroyer is coming," I blurted out, reaching as high as I could to remind him how big the destroyer was. "And there's going to be a lot of dead sheep everywhere..."

Satan stopped me short by slapping my face back and forth like a cartoon.

"Get a grip," he seethed at me. I settled down except for some minor whimpering.

"Are you telling me that the destroyer is being dispatched from the third heaven to kill sheep?"

"No, no. Well, I suppose he will kill some sheep, but only if it's the firstborn. But, no, hardly, I didn't mean that's his primary purpose. Oh, my, no..."

Satan slapped me again. "Spit it out."

"It's the Hebrews who are going to kill the sheep. Well, not all of the sheep, of course. Just some of them. The destroyer is being sent to kill the firstborn of every household, just like God said."

Satan cocked his head to one side and waved one of his claws in a circle.

"So, help me out here. God is going to kill people, and the Hebrews are going to kill sheep. This means what to me?"

"Don't you see?" I was exasperated that he couldn't see the obvious. "It's the escape clause in the whole last plague deal. They'll smear the blood of the lamb on the doorposts of their houses, and the destroyer will see it and pass right over."

I was about to point out the distinct possibility that the destroyer might not stop with the firstborn of Egypt but might step into our realm as well, but I didn't get the words out in time. The change in Satan's countenance silenced me. He stood completely still as all emotion drained from him. I wouldn't dare say so, but I'm sure he actually slumped, which he would never do in front of one of us.

"They're going to use the blood of a lamb? You're sure?"

"Well, I'm sure that's what Moses said, but who knows how well that idea will really work. It doesn't seem like much of a deterrent to the destroyer."

Satan didn't say another word. He didn't take a swipe at me as he usually did in circumstances like these. He didn't jump on my tail as he often did when I brought him bad news. He did nothing. The prince of darkness turned and quietly walked out of his lair.

Not knowing what else to do, I returned to my perch and tried to make the pieces of the puzzle mean something. It was hard to say whether Satan thought the destroyer in the earth realm was the big deal I thought it was. Why had he acted so strangely? All he seemed to care about was the part about the blood.

"What is it with the blood?" I asked myself for the millionth time. If I could just figure it out, maybe I could find a way to...never mind. I looked up toward the third heaven and called out to God.

"God, what is it? What is Satan afraid of? What does he know? Why doesn't he tell us? Why won't You tell me?"

God said nothing.

CHAPTER 10

AT MIDNIGHT, JUST as Moses said, the Lord struck down all the firstborn in Egypt, from the firstborn of Pharaoh to the firstborn of the prisoner, to the firstborn of all the livestock. Pharaoh, all his officials, and all the Egyptians awakened to the massacre as loud wailing broke out such as had never been heard in Egypt. Even to the demons it was chilling. There was not a house anywhere without someone dead in it—except for the houses of the Hebrews.

Pharaoh was beside himself with grief when he summoned Moses and Aaron. He slumped over the body of his dead son.

"Leave us alone. You and the Israelites go, worship the Lord as you have requested. Take your flocks and herds, but before you do also bless me."

Can you believe Ramses had the nerve to ask for a blessing after he single-handedly brought such devastation on his own people?

The Egyptians urged the Israelites to hurry and leave the country in fear that more death might be coming if they stayed. The Hebrews took their dough before the yeast was added and carried it on their shoulders in kneading troughs wrapped in cloths. Their animals were laden down with the gold and silver of Egypt, and off they went.

It was hard to tell how Satan felt about the exodus of the Hebrews. One moment he seemed depressed, then angry, and finally exasperated. He shifted his eyes to and fro over the ranks of the demons who returned from Egypt and now stood on the rim of the second heaven, awaiting further orders and staring at the parade of departing multitudes. I knew what he was doing. He was looking for someone to blame. For once, I was pretty sure it would not be me.

Finally, Satan walked behind Bezel and half whispered his instructions: "Get them back."

Bezel raised his great wings and leaned over the edge as if he were about to leap across the chasm that divided our realm from the earth. But just before he took to air, he stopped abruptly, turned back to Satan, and asked the obvious.

"How am I supposed to do that? We cannot touch Moses."

"Send Ramses after them."

"Have you seen Ramses lately? He's a sniveling wreck. Did you hear what he said to Moses? 'Pray for me.' He's so close to repentance. He's of no use to you anymore."

"Am I the only one who can think around here?" Satan roared. "*Close* doesn't cut it with God. Move in. Talk to him about his public humiliation. Turn his grief into revenge. Send the armies of Egypt after the Hebrews. If the slaves don't turn back, the armies will kill them all."

I followed Bezel as he flew straight to the bedroom where Ramses lay weeping over his dead son. Hearing loud voices from another room, he decided to check it out before speaking to Ramses. The voices belonged to the financial magistrates, who were dealing with the reality that the entire labor force of Egypt had just left town. Bezel contributed to their confusion by releasing visions of a crumbled economy into their minds. Then he flew back to Ramses' side and whispered into his dreams. Ramses saw himself publicly humiliated by Moses, removed from the throne, and Moses placed upon it. By the time the magistrates knocked on his door, he was primed. I tell you, that demon was good at his job.

It was as if Pharaoh and his finance men were waking from a shared nightmare.

"What have we done? We have let the Israelites go. Who's going to work?"

Who's going to work? Can you believe it? Never mind all the dead bodies—get that assembly line going!

Meanwhile, Moses was doing his best to get the masses of people organized and facing the same direction. Knowing God was sure to give Moses new orders, I hurried over to join him. Satan would have my head if I missed anything. When God told Moses which path to take out of Egypt, it should have been his first clue that in spite of what Moses had told Ramses, this was not going to be a weekend outing. Never having been out of town before, the ex-slaves were unaware they were about to travel the longest possible way when a much shorter route was available. Moses (who *had* been out of town before) tried to point out to God that this was the long way home.

"You must take the people this way. The Philistines are waiting for them. If the people are attacked, they will turn around and try to run back to Egypt. You won't be able to stop them. You can't let them leave Egypt along a straight path."

That's why for three days they simply wandered around in circles, having no idea they weren't really going anywhere. The reason no one noticed how many times they passed by the same rock was because their attention was fixed on the cloud by day and pillar of fire by night, which God had set in front of them to lead them on.

It wasn't till the third day when God revealed His strategy.

"Tell the Israelites to turn around and make camp at Pi Hahiroth, between Migdol and the sea. Camp on the shore of the sea opposite Baal Zephon."

"Are You sure, Lord?" Moses asked, not thinking about how utterly ridiculous the question was, although I might well have asked it myself because God couldn't have picked a more dangerous campsite. It was occupied territory.

Baal Zephon was one of Egypt's favorite gods and one of the few idols still standing after the calamity with the plagues that had toppled most of the others. I knew for sure the demon residing in the idol was still very much at home there. It was hard to see how thumbing one's nose at an entrenched principality was a good idea, considering the Israelites were skittish enough without more provocation. Why stir up a skirmish if you didn't have to? Moses couldn't see the logic either.

"Are You sure, Lord?" Moses asked the same ridiculous question again.

Thinking back to how it had been with Abraham and Noah when God told them to go somewhere they had never been, and never mind about taking along a map, I knew how God's marching orders usually didn't come with a lot of explanation. I wasn't expecting God to answer Moses at all, much less share His whole strategy, but that's just what He did.

"Pharaoh will think you're lost and confused. When he's told of your location and sees you are surrounded by the wilderness, he'll think you're vulnerable to an attack."

That was when Moses first realized that some of Pharaoh's spies had been following them the whole time. Right then I put one and one together and was sure Moses had to be doing the same math. Pharaoh was going to chase them, and God was the One who set it up that way. Moses must have figured it out, but being the man of few words he was, he said nothing.

The spies were about to hightail it back to Egypt to tell Ramses the slaves had been wandering aimlessly through the desert for three days and were now hopelessly lost, at least that's the way it looked to someone who hadn't heard God tell Moses to take the loop. From his nervous look, I was sure Moses had figured out the danger they were in. That's when God chimed in to confirm Moses's worst fear.

"Then I'll make Pharaoh's heart stubborn again, and he'll chase after you."

"Now, there's a good idea," Moses answered.

Moses didn't actually say it, but I knew he was thinking it. Or maybe it was me who was thinking it. Whichever one of us was thinking it, this would have been a dandy time for Moses to ask the Lord why He was planning such a thing. Knowing Moses wasn't much of a conversationalist and would likely never get around to holding up his end of the dialogue, God decided to tell him why without being asked.

"I'll use Pharaoh and his army to put My glory on display. Then the Egyptians will realize that I am God."

Moses shook his head in confusion, not understanding this line of thinking at all, but I did. It was just like I said when I tried to tell Satan it wasn't just about the Hebrews anymore. God wanted the Egyptians to be saved. Why else would He care whether they knew He was God or not? Satan would want to know all about this right away, so I began flapping my way back to the second heaven to give him the update.

He wasn't all that impressed with the news.

"So, let me see if I have this right," Satan began. "God caused all the hoopla with the plagues just to get Ramses to let the slaves go, who would then wander around lost in the wilderness for three days to provoke Pharaoh to chase after them again to take them back to Egypt, and somehow along the way the Egyptians figure out who God is. Is that what you're telling me?"

"Yes, yes, that's it. Just like I've been saying. It's more than the Hebrews."

I don't know why Satan never took my warnings seriously. In all the centuries I'd been assigned to watch and report what happened on the earth, I was rarely wrong when it came to predicting what God was going to do with you ill-conceived humans. Still, Satan always sent someone else to verify what I told him.

"Go find out what's really happening." He dispatched Bezel back to Pharaoh's court to check it out. I was dismissed, so I decided to follow the demon, if for no other reason than to satisfy myself that I was right. By the time we got to the throne room, the spies were already telling Ramses and the magistrates about the pitiful state of affairs with the runaway slaves.

"They've wandered in circles for three days, Your Majesty. They're lost. They don't even realize they've set up camp under the watchful eye of Baal Zephon. We can easily overtake them."

He listened, but Ramses didn't see the situation the same as the spies saw it.

"Why should we do that? Moses said they would be back in three days. They're not lost; they're just coming back to Egypt. That was always the plan."

The spies were not about to correct Pharaoh, so they stood silently, looking at the floor, each hoping the other would say something. When neither said a word, Bezel, who had been observing the whole thing, positioned himself beside the throne and whispered into Pharaoh's ear.

"Pay attention to the spies. You're getting sentimental. They know Moses has no intention of returning with the slaves. Why do you think they carried out all the gold and silver when they left? You're looking a little naïve here in front of your men."

Maybe he was addled from having to deal with the frogs, the gnats, the blood, the hail, and the deaths, but I do believe that was the first moment Pharaoh really figured out what had happened. Just as his magistrates had tried to tell him, the entire workforce had taken a hike. Of course, they weren't coming back. I watched the color drain from his face as he realized the situation he was now in. He jumped to his feet, startling the two soldiers who stepped back in fear when they saw the anger in Ramses' eyes.

"What have we done? The slaves are not coming back. There will be no one to do the work."

Can you believe he was just now figuring that out?

CHAPTER 11

"WE HAVE TO go get them," Ramses said in a state of panic and in full command of the obvious.

"Yes, yes." The soldiers were relieved it hadn't been necessary to point out Pharaoh's failure to grasp the situation. "It will be easy. They're trapped with their backs to the sea."

"Get my chariot," Ramses commanded. "Bring six hundred of the best charioteers. The slaves will not escape."

It was amazing how quickly the Egyptian soldiers mobilized. In less than an hour, six hundred war chariots were zooming toward Moses's camp with Pharaoh himself leading the charge.

Meanwhile, back at the campfire, only Moses knew that things were about to get ugly. The ex-slaves still hadn't figured out that they literally were between the devil and the deep blue sea. They went right on congratulating themselves over having escaped Egypt and the brick pits, as if any of them had a single thing to do with it. It wasn't until one of the women noticed the cloud of dust appearing over the horizon that they realized company was coming.

"What is it?"

"Can you see anything?"

Before anyone could venture an answer, the unmistakable rumble of chariot wheels thundered toward them.

"It's the Egyptians! They're after us." They cried out to each other and to God. God didn't say anything, so they quickly turned on Moses.

"Weren't the cemeteries large enough in Egypt so that you had to take us out here in the wilderness to die?"

"Why have you done this to us? Why did you take us out of Egypt?"

"Back in Egypt, didn't we tell you this would happen?"

"Didn't we tell you, 'Leave us alone here in Egypt—we're better off as slaves in Egypt than as corpses in the wilderness'?"

Of course, not one of them had ever said anything of the sort. They were all too happy to gather the booty and leave town.

Moses tried to calm them down. "Don't be afraid. Stand firm, and watch God do His work of salvation for you. Take a good look at the Egyptians today, for you're never going to see them again. God will fight the battle for you."

Moses sounded surer than he looked. He turned from the people and ran a few yards away, where he began calling out to God.

"God, please. It's time for You to do something."

"No, it's time for *you* to do something. Why cry out to Me? Tell the Israelites to get moving. Hold your staff high, and stretch your hand out over the sea. Split the sea! The Israelites will walk through the sea on dry ground."

Split the sea? Moses looked like he might faint.

"Meanwhile, I'll make sure the Egyptians keep up their stubborn chase. I'll use Pharaoh and his entire army, his chariots and horsemen, to put My glory on display so that the Egyptians will realize that I am God."

"The Egyptians don't need any encouragement," Moses muttered under his breath as he hurried to try to get the Israelites moving again. I could hear him, so I was pretty sure God could as well.

As much as God seemed to me to be enjoying what was going on, He must have taken one look at Moses's face and realized his last nerve was about to unravel. God ordered the angel who had been leading the camp of Israel to shift and get behind the people. Then the pillar of cloud that had been in front also shifted to the rear. The cloud was now between the camp of Egypt and the camp of Israel, enshrouding one camp in darkness and flooding the other with light. Pharaoh's army screeched to a halt when the horses reared up with fear and neighed at the site of the angel. Several chariots almost overturned from the panic of the strong steeds as they attempted to run away. Let me tell you, the soldiers weren't all that gung ho to try to get around that angel either. The army was at a standstill, and it stayed that way all through the night.

Meanwhile, Moses was leading the racing Hebrews toward the sea. When he got to the edge, he paused and looked around to see if God was anywhere about. Not seeing Him, Moses cried out again in that loud whisper.

"Now what, God?"

"Do what I told you. Stretch out your staff, and split the sea."

"Right, OK. I'm about to do that very thing." Moses had no conviction in his voice whatsoever.

He didn't dare look back at the people to see if they were watching. He knew they were. Every eye that wasn't fixed on the stalled Egyptian army was on Moses. He lifted his shaky arms and extended his staff out over the foreboding water before him.

Glancing toward heaven one more time, he muttered to himself, "I hope this works."

I was nervous just watching the whole thing.

Moses took a deep breath and stretched out his hand as far as he could reach over the sea, and right on cue, God, with a terrific east wind, made the waters split. It was magnificent. The sea stood up, forming two walls of water on either side of the dry land that now lay where mud had been before. I was so excited I wanted to clap, but I wisely restrained the impulse.

"Run! Run!" Moses shouted to the people. "Cross while you can."

Well, you can just imagine how the people were temporarily paralyzed with sheer terror, not knowing which was worse—the soldiers behind them or the towering sea walls in front of them. Moses couldn't get them going, but God could. He recalled the angel and released the army to race toward the hordes of people.

"Run! Run!" I shouted at the people, getting caught up in the drama before I realized what I was doing and stuffed my claw into my mouth.

And run they did. The Israelites hurried through the sea on a narrow path of dry ground with the walls of water to the right and to the left.

The Egyptians came after them in full pursuit, every horse and chariot and driver of Pharaoh racing into the middle of the sea. God looked down from the pillar of fire and cloud on the Egyptian army and threw them into a panic. The chariots were too many to stay on the slim trail of dry ground, so they were forced into the mud, which clogged the wheels of their chariots until every last one of them was stuck in the miry clay.

Then the Egyptians began yelling at each other: "Turn around! Retreat! Run from Israel! Their God is fighting on their side against us!"

The soldiers beat the horses with their whips, but the frightened animals could not dislodge the wheels from the thick mud. Some of them abandoned their chariots and tried to run back to the sea's edge, but they sunk to their knees in the mire. The glory that had been Egypt's military elite was hopelessly trapped between the lofty walls of water on either side.

Then God said to Moses, "Stretch out your hand over the sea, and the waters will come back over the chariots and the drivers."

Moses obeyed quickly and stretched his hand out over the sea, and immediately the waters crashed down upon the entire Egyptian army. Not one of them survived.

I was worn out from the stress. Since I knew he would be watching from the second heaven, I wondered if I had time to lie down for a while before heading back to give Satan my report.

When the Hebrews turned back and looked at the Egyptian dead, some of whom were already washing up on the shore of the sea, they realized the tremendous power that God brought against their enemy. The people were in reverent awe and pledged their everlasting trust in God and in Moses. There was no mistaking the relief on Moses's face. He was as exhausted as I was and sat down to rest, thinking the worst of it was over.

I could have told him it wasn't.

Chapter 12

THE DEMON HORDE stood on the rim and watched the sea return to normal as if nothing unusual had happened to it, much less that the fighting glory of Egypt now lay at the bottom. I wondered how Satan was going to respond to all of this.

At first, he didn't seem to be all that worked up about what had occurred. Then I remembered that Satan could not have cared any less about what happened to the Egyptians. They were of no further use to him. In fact, Egypt was of no further use to him. There was no leadership left to manipulate, and the people themselves were just a mess what with dealing with the dead firstborn and all that.

Deciding to cut his losses, Satan ordered the demon hordes to evacuate. I naturally assumed he would send them after the Hebrews into the desert. Everybody else thought that would happen as well. When he ordered the troops into Canaan instead, we looked at each other, wondering if we had heard correctly but not daring to ask. Finally, Bezel spoke up.

"We can still catch them."

"Forget it," Satan said. "We don't have to waste our time chasing them. They are slaves. They don't know how to take care of themselves. They can't function without someone driving them. There's six hundred thousand of them and one of Moses. Moses will have a heart attack from frustration before long. They'll wander around in the desert, and most of them will die there. If any of them make it across, we'll be waiting on the other side. Besides, the Nephilim are in Canaan. If some of the Hebrews do get through the desert, the freaks we created will be all too happy to have another chance at them."

The others congratulated Satan on being a brilliant strategist and then began forming battalions to move out. I assumed I would be going along and joined up with Bezel's brigade when Satan grabbed my tail.

"Where do you think you're going?"

"Obviously, I don't know, sir. Where would you like for me to go?"

"We have unfinished business."

I didn't like the look in his yellow eye, but I followed him back to his lair and waited for him to make himself comfortable on his throne. He summoned several of the others to come and witness what I was certain would be something bad for me.

"So, moron, run this by me one more time." His voice held that tinge of sarcasm again. "I want to be sure I understand that part about how much God cared about the Egyptians."

He was making sport of me. Satan stood up and strutted back and forth in front of his throne, waving a claw in the air for effect, stroking his ugly chin with the other, mocking deep thought.

"Let me see if I remember this correctly: all the chariots got stuck in the mud."

"Yes, sir," I barely whispered.

"And all the soldiers were drowned; even Pharaoh was drowned."

I nodded.

"Like, say, a pack of rats; it was something like that, wasn't it?" His eyes narrowed, and the sinister grin that split his misbegotten face only encouraged the others who hadn't left for Canaan yet to snicker louder at my humiliation.

"Well, then." He sat down on his throne. "Help me out here. Why don't you reconcile that unfortunate event with your insistence that God cared about the Egyptians and wanted to save them?" Everybody laughed.

One look at his sneer told me there was no way for me to win, so I said nothing.

"What? No defense? No glib comeback?"

I shook my head, avoiding looking at him directly.

"Why don't you just go on with your report? God drowned all the Egyptians, and then what happened?" One last snicker came from the onlookers.

"The Jews started singing and dancing and praising God for their salvation. That's it."

"Idiots," he spewed. The mere mention of worship and praise to God ruined his mood every time. "Have they started to move toward Canaan yet?"

"Moses was working on it when I flew back to report."

"How long before they get close to Canaan? I want their welcoming committee to be ready." He laughed, and so did everyone else except me.

"It depends. If they take the direct route, a couple of weeks, maybe a little more."

Satan turned as if to give an order to one of the waiting demons when I interrupted.

"But God is unlikely to lead them along the shortest route, sir."

"And why would that be?"

"History, sir." I hoped that answer would be sufficient, but a look in his other yellow eye told me it wasn't.

"God has rarely, if ever, led His people in a straight line to anywhere. My guess is He will lead them around in the desert for a while—maybe even years."

"Why? Doesn't He know what to do with them now that He's got them?" Several snickered.

I knew I was stepping out far beyond my actual knowledge if I ventured a guess about God's strategy, but why not? After all, I'd been watching God and humanity for eons. Besides, Satan's quotient for humiliating me had reached its peak for one day. My guess would be as good as anyone's and better than most.

"He will keep them in the desert until they're ready to fight."

"Fight against what?" Satan seemed surprised.

Here's what I wanted to say: "Oh, puh-leeze. Do you for one moment think God doesn't know what you've got planned through all of those demon-possessed people you have waiting for them on the other side? You will never outmaneuver God, and He will never let you get away with a massacre."

Here's what I said instead: "God will anticipate trouble once they leave the desert, and He wants them trained to defend themselves."

Satan leaned back on his throne as if the thought had never crossed his mind. After a while he motioned my dismissal.

"Follow them."

So, that's how it happened that I went winging it across the Red Sea to catch up with the jubilant now ex-slaves.

As I watched Moses leading the throngs across the desert sand, I wondered if he had the first idea what to do next.

CHAPTER 13

I T WASN'T LONG before they moved beyond the Red Sea toward the land of Shur. By the third day when they still hadn't found any water, the people began to complain to Moses.

"What are we supposed to drink?"

"You should have thought about water before we left Egypt."

Moses resisted the urge to scold the people for their short memories. Not even three days from God having split the sea on their behalf, here they were complaining to Moses about a lack of water. I tried to imagine what it would have been like for anyone in the demonic ranks to have complained to Satan about a lack of provision when they followed him in his rebellion.

Moses might have suspected there would be water at Marah, but he didn't count on it being so bitter as to be undrinkable. Frustrated with the people whining about how they should have stayed in Egypt, Moses cried out to God for help. God pointed out a pile of sticks, which Moses could have found for himself if he had been looking instead of expecting God to do every little thing for him.

"Throw the stick into the water, and it will become sweet," God said with no enthusiasm whatsoever.

Moses should have known to do this without being told. It was one of those bits of desert-survival training he learned while herding goats. He seemed to have a lot of trouble applying his prior life skills to his present situation. I'm not sure he ever made the connection between his training in herding goats for forty years and his present job to herd people through the same desert. The difference between the two was negligible as far as I could see.

Once the people filled their vessels with water, God told Moses He was ready to establish some laws and procedures for the rest of the trip.

"If you listen obediently to how I tell you to live in My presence, obeying My commandments and keeping all My laws, then I won't strike you with all the diseases that I inflicted on the Egyptians; I am God your healer."

If I'd been Moses, I wouldn't have let that decree pass without reminding God of a few things.

"God," I would have said. "Have You forgotten what happened with Adam and Eve when they had only one law in the entire universe to uphold? Two human beings in a garden couldn't successfully obey one simple rule. Now You're thinking about imposing multiple rules to thousands of people wandering in the desert and ready to flee back to Egypt at the first inconvenience?"

Although Moses didn't challenge God's idea, he must have been concerned about how well it could work. He sighed, roused himself, and got the people moving again. On the fifteenth day of the second month after they had left Egypt, the whole company of Israel moved on from Elim to the Wilderness of Sin, which is between Elim and Sinai. As Satan predicted, the whole company complained loudly against Moses and Aaron again, and I'm sure Moses was having chest pains.

"Why didn't God let us die in comfort in Egypt where we had lamb stew and all the bread we could eat? You've brought us out into this wilderness to starve us to death."

It was true that if God didn't intervene, the people were likely to starve because they were deep in the desert and there was no readily available food source. I could have pointed out to God in the very beginning that He would regret many times His decision to make humans from flesh and blood. To make it worse, He threw emotions into the mix, including the penchant to feel sorry for yourselves over the slightest difficulty. Human beings are simply too high maintenance to be of any real use in a pinch. Sorry to say, but none of you can be counted upon in less-than-perfect circumstances. Every few hours, you have to be fed and watered, not to mention needing sleep every single day.

For a fleeting moment, I wondered if, based upon prior history, He might not just let them starve after all. He certainly had precedent to do so. In all the centuries I had watched God and His humans, I had seen Him rescue them many times, but always in response to that "faith" requirement. You know what I'm talking about—when humans face a catastrophe fully believing God will rescue them because He loves them. Oh, yes, I've seen God swing into action more than once—often at the last possible minute—to respond to the faith of one who trusts Him in times of trouble, even when there is no visible evidence whatsoever that He intends to do anything. But would God respond to whining, complaining, and self-pity? I couldn't recall ever having known God to respond well to such behavior, especially after having proven Himself as many times as He had in their exodus from Egypt.

I don't mind telling you I was a little more than perturbed when I heard how God intended to give in to their griping.

God spoke to Moses: "I've listened to the complaints of the Israelites. Now tell them that at dawn they'll eat their fill of bread."

In the morning there was a layer of dew all over the camp. When the layer of dew lifted, there on the wilderness ground was a fine, flaky, frostlike something all over the place. The Israelites, having no idea what it was, took one look and said to one another, "*Man hu.*" ("What is it?")

So Moses told them, "It's the bread God has given you to eat, and these are God's instructions: 'Gather enough for each person—about two quarts per person—enough for everyone in your tent. Eat all of it. Don't save any of it for tomorrow. If you do, you will find it spoiled and inedible.'"

Stiff-necked people that they were, a couple of them just had to try it. They saved some of the stuff overnight, but it became full of worms and smelled all the way to the second heaven. Moses lost his temper over their action, but really, what did he think was going to happen? Especially when the rules changed for the sixth day.

"Tomorrow is a day of rest, a holy Sabbath to God. Whatever you plan to bake, bake today; and whatever you plan to boil, boil today. Then set aside the leftovers until morning," Moses instructed them.

So they set aside what was left until morning as Moses had commanded, and contrary to its prior behavior, the manna didn't smell bad and there were no worms in it. Go figure.

Moses said, "Now eat it; this is the day, a Sabbath for God. You won't find any more of it on the ground today."

True to character, on the seventh day, some of the people went out to gather anyway, but they didn't find anything. Once again, Moses's temper flared.

"How long are you going to disobey my commands and not follow the instructions God has given me for you? Don't you see that God has given you the Sabbath? On the sixth day He gives you bread for two days. So, each of you, stay in your tent. Don't try to gather on the seventh day."

Whether they were afraid of God or not I can't say, but they were definitely afraid of Moses, so the people quit working on the seventh day. The phenomenon of the manna continued for forty years.

CHAPTER 14

So they're on the way to Rephidim. What of it?" Satan seemed annoyed that I'd left my post with the Israelites to give him a location update.

"There's no water there." I paused to see if he connected with the obvious. Apparently not.

"They must have water. They're humans; they can't go three days without it."

"God will let them die of thirst? Is that your point?"

"No, no. God will lead Moses to find water somewhere, but in the meantime, Moses is tired, and the people are frustrated. They keep complaining to Moses that he should have left them in Egypt instead of leading them into the desert to die. They're in a weakened condition. If you wanted to, it's a good time for an attack."

Satan stopped polishing his claw and looked up at me for the first time. Then looking right past me, he turned to one of the other demons.

"Do we have anybody at Rephidim?"

"Um, Rephidim? Where is that exactly?" The demon stumbled over his answer, having no idea what was going on in the desert. Ever since the desert demons abandoned their posts when God showed up in the wasteland as a burning bush, Satan had never been able to quite get his tight rule back together there.

"The Amalekites are there." I interrupted the stumbling.

"You're sure?"

"Near there, anyway, and they hate the Jews. It wouldn't take much to provoke them to attack. That is, if an attack was part of your plan, Mighty One."

I didn't know what Satan had planned and neither did anyone else, maybe because he rarely made any plans. He's more of a thermometer than a thermostat. Since the Egyptian army drowned, he hadn't told any of us what his next step might be.

"Make it happen," he said, looking directly at me.

"Me?" I was suddenly queasy. "Surely, my lord is not suggesting I could provoke the Amalekite army to action? Someone else would be much better."

"You said it wouldn't take much to provoke them. Well, you're not much, so go do it."

The whole room burst out in guffaws. I didn't know what to do, so I tried to join in the laughter with them as if it were all some great big joke. As soon as I opened my mouth, everyone else became suddenly silent. I couldn't guffaw, but I was able to muster up a pretty convincing chuckle.

"You had me going there for a moment, sir."

"Get him out of here," Satan ordered one of the guard demons.

The burly demon picked me up by my wing and tail, carried me to the rim, and tossed me out over the expanse between the second heaven and the earth. I tumbled over several times through space before I could right myself and flap my way back to the desert where Moses was camped. I arrived just in time to hear God tell Moses how to get water.

"Go on out ahead of the people; take some of the elders with you. Take the staff you used to strike the Nile. I'm going to be present before you get there on the rock at Horeb. You are to strike the rock. Water will gush out of it, and the people will drink."

And that's just what happened. The people were pacified, and Moses was relieved to have quieted their grumblings for the time being.

"That went pretty much like I thought it would," I said to myself as I went in search of Israel's enemy as Satan had ordered me to do, although I didn't know what to do when I found them. How would I provoke King Amalek to attack Moses? Such a thing was way above my pay grade. As it turned out, I needn't have worried. I should have known Satan wasn't really going to trust me with an act of war. By the time I got near Rephidim, one of the other demons had already arrived and goaded the king to lay siege against Israel.

I don't know whether Moses heard the horses' hooves, or whether he saw the cloud of dust rising up over the hill, or whether it was his years of training in the desert, but somehow he knew something wasn't right. He jumped to his feet, and with one hand over his eyes to shield them from the sun, he stared straight ahead toward the hill. Then he ordered a couple of the men to go up to see what was going on. They ran up the embankment, and when they reached the top, they turned and waved their arms to signal trouble was coming.

Moses sighed and then called out for a young man named Joshua.

"Who is he?" I wondered. I couldn't recall having heard him mentioned before.

Joshua came running to Moses's side with three other young men whose names I didn't know either.

"You called for me, sir," Joshua said as he bowed his head to Moses as a sign of respect. I might not have noticed his reverent tone of voice had it not been for the pervasive tone of gripe and grumble that came from so many of the other people when things weren't going just right.

"Joshua," Moses said to him in a subdued voice. "Take some of the men with you—pick the most reliable—go up to the top of the hill. See what is coming, and be prepared to fight."

"Right away, sir." He turned to signal to his three comrades.

"Wait," Moses interrupted his departure. "It may be Amalek. If it's him, there will be a battle. You must take the front line with your men. I'll come and stand on top of the hill where I can see the whole field, and I'll signal you from there."

Joshua lowered his head again and raised it quickly to show he understood his orders and ran off toward the camp with the others following close behind. I wondered why I hadn't noticed him before. If Moses was sending him out to lead the battle, he must be important. Note to self: watch Joshua.

"Tomorrow I will take my stand on top of the hill holding God's staff," Moses said to Aaron, who had come looking for him to see what was going on. "You and Hur must go up with me."

Joshua, who seemed to have a natural sense of military maneuvers, did as Moses had instructed him in order to fight Amalek. The next morning Moses, Aaron, and Hur went to the top of the hill. He didn't show it, but Moses had to be a nervous wreck. This was the first time for the poorly organized Hebrew fighters to go up against an enemy of any kind, much less one skilled in battle like the Amalekites. Three months ago they were slaves; now they were soldiers. You can imagine how chaotic it was in spite of Joshua's precise orders to the untrained Hebrew army. In fact, the Amalekites should have been able to roll those chariot wheels right over the Hebrews, and at first, it looked like that might be the story, but then something strange happened.

Moses stood at the top of the hill, watching his troops take a beating from the Amalekite army. In a gesture of desperation, Moses raised his arms up over his head—personally, I think he was trying to get God to pay attention to the slaughter about to happen—and Israel seemed to rally. Moses lowered his arms, and the Amalekites advanced; he raised his arms, and Israel took ground. Aaron and Hur exchanged a look. This was looking like a trend.

It turned out that whenever Moses raised his hands, Israel would start winning, but whenever he lowered his hands, Amalek would start winning. It wasn't long before Moses's arms got tired. Aaron and Hur, who had definitely figured out what was going on, hurried and got a stone and set it under Moses. He sat down on it, and Aaron and Hur held up his arms, one on each side, and there they remained steady until the sun went down. By the next day, Joshua had defeated the entire Amalekite army.

I hadn't counted on that. I knew I should get right back to the second heaven to let Satan know what had happened, but I just couldn't make myself go. Instead, I flew down to the empty battlefield—empty except for the dead Amalekite soldiers—and sat down on a rock, trying to figure out where things went wrong. Not that it mattered. It was still going to be my fault. After all, I was the one who told Satan it would be an easy victory for King Amalek, one of Satan's best resources to persecute the Jews. The king might even be dead now. Oh, no, I hoped not. That would surely be my fault too.

By the time morning came, I was still sitting on my rock. No one had come to look for me, so maybe Satan had other things on his mind and had temporarily forgotten about Amalek. I decided to make one more pass through Moses's camp to see if I could find some tidbit of information I could carry back to my evil master that would lessen his ire at the failure of my idea.

By the time I got there, Jethro, Moses's father-in-law; Zipporah, Moses's wife; and Moses's two sons had arrived.

Moses went out to welcome his father-in-law, bowing to him and kissing him. Then they went into the tent, and Moses told his father-in-law the story of all that God had done to Pharaoh and Egypt in helping Israel, all the trouble they had experienced on the journey, and how God had delivered them.

Jethro was impressed. He said, "Blessed be God who has delivered you from the power of Egypt and Pharaoh and the oppression of Egypt. Now I know that your God is greater than all gods because He's done this to all those who treated Israel arrogantly."

They stood up, hugged each other, and stepped outside the tent to see more than one hundred of the people arguing among themselves as they lined up for an audience with Moses.

"What is this?" Jethro asked.

Moses sighed. "It's like this every day. From morning till night they bring their grievances before me and demand I judge between them."

"No wonder it's taking you so long to get across the desert. This can't go on; they'll wear you out, and at this rate, you'll die an old man before you reach your destination."

"Don't I know it? But what else can I do? They won't move on until I rule on their petty grievances."

"You said it yourself. Their grievances are petty. Here's what you have to do. Are there any elders here you can trust?"

"Yes. Thirty, forty, maybe more."

"Concentrate on training the elders, and then let them divide the people into groups. Let each of the elders be responsible for settling the minor issues, bringing only the big deals to you."

So, for the next few days, Moses sat about selecting and training the elders who then trained captains under themselves, and before I knew it, what had been pure chaos settled into the beginnings of organization. Satan was not going to like this. One of the telltale signs that God was in something was when the chaotic morphed into order. That had been the first signal to us long ago when the rampant waters of Lucifer's flood began to settle and clear from the middle of the sea outward as Ruah Ha Kadosh hovered over the murky seas that covered the earth.

I flew back to the second heaven to deliver my report but changed my mind and went to my perch instead of to Satan's den. If he wanted me, he could send for me. No need for me to rush over to answer questions he wasn't yet asking.

CHAPTER 15

SEVERAL WEEKS HAD passed uneventfully, so one morning I decided to sleep in. I was standing on my head practicing yoga. I picked it up during one of the rare times when I wasn't glued to the Hebrews. I was on surveillance duty around the rest of the world when I encountered a strange group of people on the other side of the earth who were practicing a different sort of religious ritual. I'd never heard anyone mention the god of yoga, nor had Satan ever said anything about a rogue demon being on the loose somewhere. It didn't seem to be the "same old, same old" of a demon pretending to be a god charade I'd seen a million other times. These particular people never claimed yoga was a god, rather that the practice itself put them in touch with a higher power, so I thought I'd give it a try. After all, if there was a mediator in the hierarchy between Satan and God, I wanted to know who it was. Maybe he/it could help me bring my case to the heavenly court. I was chanting about the unfairness of fate when God's voice rolled through the expanse between the heavens and the earth with such force that I lost my balance and tumbled right onto a hard stone below.

"Speak to the house of Jacob; tell the people of Israel," He thundered. It was so loud and so clear that for a brief moment I wondered if He might be speaking to me directly—but only for a moment. He was calling to Moses.

"This is what I want you to tell the people of Israel: 'You have seen what I did to Egypt and how I carried you on eagles' wings and brought you to Me. If you will listen obediently to what I say and keep My covenant, out of all peoples you'll be My special treasure. The whole earth is Mine to choose from, but you're special, a kingdom of priests, a holy nation.'"

I blinked hard to clear the yoga mantras from my brain as I walked over to the rim of the second heaven to take a good look at the Israelites. Granted, I hadn't been watching as carefully as I should have for a few weeks now, but I'd been terribly depressed about my lot in life and found it hard to leave my perch. I wondered if the people had undergone some remarkable change in a few short weeks to make them special and holy, because they weren't anything close to that last time I looked. I peered intently at the camp, but I didn't see any change. They were still the same unruly people as before my sabbatical. I wondered if God might be talking about some other group. No way around it; it was time for me to return to Earth and check the status of the ex-slaves. I got there just as Moses was about to address the people.

Moses called the elders of Israel together and told them all that God had commanded him to say. The people were unanimous in their response.

"Everything God says we will do."

"Oh, right. Sure you will," I said under my breath. "Don't stake your reputation on them," I wanted to call out to Moses.

Moses, ever the optimist, it seemed, took the people's unedited answer straight back to God.

Then God said, "Get ready. I'm about to come to you in a thick cloud so that the people can listen in and trust you completely when I speak with you."

Again Moses reported the people's affirmation to follow God, which, as far as I was concerned, was no more convincing the second time around.

God continued, "Go to the people. Take two days to get these people ready to meet the holy God, because on the third day I will come down on Mount Sinai and make My presence known to all the people. Post boundaries for the people all around, telling them not to climb the mountain or even touch its edge. Whoever touches the mountain dies a certain death. A long blast from the horn will signal that it's safe to climb the mountain."

For the first time in weeks I was excited. If God were actually coming down on Mount Sinai to meet with the people, maybe I could wedge my way into the crowd and at last get my audience with Him. Even if He didn't speak to me directly, perhaps if I could blend in with the throng of people, then whatever blessing He released over them might fall to me as well. After all, my exile had certainly come about from standing among a crowd in the wrong place; perhaps my redemption could come in the same way. I couldn't wait for three days to pass.

On the third day at daybreak there were loud claps of thunder, flashes of lightning, a thick cloud covering the mountain, and an ear-piercing trumpet blast. Everyone in the camp shuddered in fear, including me. Moses called the people to attention and lined them up to lead them out of the camp to meet with God.

I lined up with them, more nervous than any of them, I can tell you. We all stood at attention at the base of the mountain.

Mount Sinai was all smoke because God had come down on it as fire. Smoke poured from it like smoke from a furnace. The whole mountain shuddered in huge spasms. The trumpet blasts grew louder and louder. Moses spoke, and God answered in thunder. God descended to the peak of Mount Sinai and called Moses to come up where He was. I wondered if I should chance getting closer so I wouldn't miss anything. It was then I heard God give Moses a warning.

"Go down and warn the people not to break through the barricades to get a look at Me lest many of them die. And the priests also—warn them to prepare themselves for the holy meeting lest I break out against them."

That's when I decided against trying to get closer.

Moses said to God, "But the people can't climb Mount Sinai. You've already warned us well, telling us to post boundaries around the mountain."

"Right, I did, but I've noticed that I sometimes have to tell you more than once. Go down and bring Aaron back up with you. But make sure the priests and the people don't break through and come up to Me lest My glory break out against them."

Moses hurried back down the mountain to get Aaron, who was hiding at the back of the line, scared as could be and in no rush to go up the mountain to meet with God face-to-face. See, that's just how it is with you humans. You run around boldly declaring your search for God and how God has told you this, that, or whatever, but when God finally shows up in your neighborhood, you try to crawl under the rug until He leaves.

Moses took Aaron by the shaking hand and began leading him up the mountain to where God was waiting. I so wanted to go along, but to be honest, I was as afraid as any human. I had rationalized that if God happened to spot me in a crowd of people He intended to bless, He might just let it pass that I was there so as not to inadvertently injure one of His pet people, but in a threesome? He could take me out with just a look. Better not chance making my situation worse than it was.

I don't know how long they were up there, but when Moses and Aaron came back down the mountain, Moses's face was full of light, and Aaron's was drained of color. I've noticed that is how God seems to affect you humans—with sheer exhilaration and awe or sheer terror. Moses is the one who spoke to the people.

"The Lord your God says to you, 'I am your God, who brought you out of the land of Egypt, out of a life of slavery. Have no other gods before Me. Do not use My name in an irreverent way. Observe the Sabbath day to keep it holy. Honor your father and mother so that you'll live a long time in the land that your God is giving you. No murder. No adultery. No stealing. No lies about your neighbor. No lusting after your neighbor's house or wife or servant or maid or ox or donkey. Don't set your heart on anything that is your neighbor's.'"

If you can, try to picture it: throngs of people experiencing the thunder and lightning, the trumpet blast, and the smoking mountain, totally afraid—terrified is more like it. They pulled back and stood at a distance to rethink their bravado.

Realizing the power they were about to encounter, the Israelites developed a new humility and pleaded with Moses.

"You speak to us and we'll listen, but don't have God speak to us or we'll die."

"Don't be afraid." Moses tried to reassure them. "God has only come to test you and instill a deep and reverent awe within you so that you won't sin."

Nice try, but the people were so traumatized by the glory of God that they refused to come any closer and so kept their distance while Moses turned and approached the thick cloud where God was. I suppose God must have realized He had let too much of Himself rest upon a people who in no way were prepared for who He is. That must be why He went along with their request to speak to them through Moses.

"Give this message to the people of Israel: 'You've experienced firsthand how I spoke with you from heaven. Don't make gods of silver and gods of gold and then set them alongside Me. Make Me an earthen altar to sacrifice your offerings. Everywhere I cause My name to be honored in your worship, I'll be there Myself and will bless you.'"

If I'd been God, knowing the earth people as long as He had, I would have quit right there with the rules. Moses should have interrupted and reminded God how Adam and Eve had done with only one rule to obey; it had been a disaster. Now here He was not only giving them no less than ten absolute rules, but He was also about to pour out dozens of other regulations that no human I had ever seen could possibly keep up with. Moses could barely write fast enough to get them all down. From selling slaves to property rights to oxen in ditches to seducing virgins—He covered the gamut of every possible misdeed a human might think to do.

This seemed totally out of character for God, as I'd known Him before the fall from heaven. He never was much of a thou-shalt-not kind of ruler. I had to think awhile before I could figure out why He was going into so much detail with the Hebrews.

The people had been slaves for four hundred years. They'd never before had an option to make a decision on their own and therefore had no experience in even the most trivial of matters. God took up His valuable time to think of every possible reper-cussion for any misdeed the average person might get himself into and gave Moses a way to avoid it. When I thought about it, I remembered that was the only reason God ever laid down laws to start with: to keep the people out of trouble, even the rules about worshiping other gods. It's not because God is jealous the way humans understand jealousy but because He knows that worship to anything other than Himself is covert worship to Satan, and once the prince of darkness gets his hands on a human, well, let's just say there *will* be blood before he lets one go.

By the time He got to the ordinance about not boiling a kid goat in its mother's milk (as if anybody would think that was a good idea) I found myself losing interest. I knew Satan wouldn't care a thing about health and diet issues, and it looked like the law giving was going on for a good while longer, so

I decided to go back to my perch and resume my meditation about the meaning of life.

I must have succeeded in meditating my way right into a trance because the next thing I knew, one of the other demons was at my perch, shaking me by the hoof and yelling something about Satan wanting to see me. I must tell you, I was a little groggy, and I had some trouble remembering why I was standing on my head on my perch. How long had I been there? I couldn't be sure—days maybe. I just didn't remember. From the tone in the demon's voice, I knew to hotfoot it over to Satan's lair without further delay.

"Where have you been?" Satan had been standing near his portal through which he could view the earth when he whirled around to face me.

"At...at my post, sir," I stammered.

"I told you to watch Moses."

"I was watching him, sir. I was right there the whole time, well, most of the time." I knew not to lie. "God began giving him a plethora of rules I knew you wouldn't want to be bothered with, so I didn't...bother you, I mean. I assure you I didn't miss anything important." I decided not to mention my meditation.

"Then where is he?"

I looked around the room to see if any of the other demons might give me a little help. Not even a side wink. I could never count on them for any support. I thought it best to clarify the question.

"Do you mean Moses, sir?"

"Of course I mean Moses, idiot. Where is he?"

I began to sweat. *Was Moses missing? How long had I been in a trance?*

"You don't know, do you?"

"I'm sure he's right there in the camp, sir. That's where I left him—well, more like on the mountain actually—but he was right there taking down all those nitpicky rules God was dictating. I wasn't gone but a minute. He couldn't have gone anywhere else. And...I mean, really, even if he wanted to, where could he go?"

"Find him." Satan's eyes narrowed as he glared at me.

I kept my head down as I backed slowly out of the room. As soon as I was safely beyond Satan's sight, I began flapping my way back down to the earth.

That was it; no more yoga.

CHAPTER 16

SATAN WAS RIGHT. I made the rounds of the whole camp, but Moses was nowhere to be found. The people were agitated and angry as if they thought Moses had simply run off somewhere and wasn't coming back. I knew that couldn't be the case, but where was he? The last time I'd seen him he was up on the mountain with God, but that had been weeks ago. He wouldn't still be up there.

The loud voices coming from Aaron's tent caught my attention, so I flew over to see what was going on. A large contingent of mixed people was arguing with Aaron over what to do about the missing Moses. Did I mention mixed people before? I can't remember, what with so many of them to keep up with.

When the slaves followed Moses out of Egypt, a whole group of other people went along with them. They were the Egyptians who believed in the power of the God of Israel as a result of living through the devastation of the plagues. Hedging their bets that the glory days of Egypt might be over, they wagered on a future's market with Moses and joined the caravan they'd heard was on the way to a land of milk and honey. These people were nothing but trouble from the first day, and I never knew why Moses didn't throw them out of the gang early on. When there was any complaining going on with the Israelites, you could just bet it was the mixed people at the bottom of it.

For example, remember when the people started complaining about how good life had been in Egypt and how they missed the food delicacies they used to eat like onions and leeks? It was the mixed people doing the complaining. Come now, you didn't really think slaves dined on such things, did you? It didn't take long for the slaves to join right in with the entitlement grousing, but they would never have thought it up on their own. Manna and quail was quite a step above the gruel they usually had.

"What do you intend to do about it?" They badgered Aaron, who sat on the floor with his head in his hands.

"What do you expect me to do? Just give him a few more days; he'll be back." Aaron rose to his feet to take a look out the tent door as if hoping Moses might stroll up at any moment."

"No, he's gone. We must have a new leader. The crowds will panic without a leader. It could be a stampede."

"Do you want the job?" Aaron shot back.

"No, don't be ridiculous. I don't want it," said several at one time.

"Well, neither do I. Neither would anyone in his right mind."

"Then make us a god."

"That's right! Make us a god to lead us out."

"Are you insane?" Aaron was incredulous. "We can't just make up a god."

"Oh, sure you can. We used to do it all the time in Egypt."

"You made gods?" Aaron couldn't believe what he was hearing.

"Well, not really, if you mean like a *real* god who could, you know, do anything."

"He means make an idol. Who cares if it's a real god? If we say it's a god, then it's a god as far as the people are concerned. They lived in Egypt their whole lives. They're used to it. They'll follow the new god because we tell them to."

"This is crazy." Aaron wiped the sweat from his brow. "Get out of my tent."

"You better think this over, Aaron. You're in real danger of a rebellion here. The crowds are turning into mobs. They think Moses isn't coming back. If panic sets in, the people will disperse like frightened animals. Then what will you do?"

"Do it, Aaron, just till Moses gets back."

Aaron looked at one then the other then out the door one more time to be sure Moses wasn't about to walk in. He threw his hands up in the air in a sign of defeat.

"OK, you win. Bring me all your gold."

"Now you're talking." They ran out of the tent and began gathering up the gold jewelry and anything else made from the gold the Israelites brought with them from Egypt.

I was stunned. Never would I have predicted this. I didn't know what to do. I didn't know what to think. Maybe I hadn't heard right. How could Aaron be agreeing to such a thing? About that time Miriam, Aaron's sister, came running through the tent door. She had been standing outside and heard it all.

"Aaron, what are you doing?"

"That's right." I agreed with her. "What do you think you're doing?"

"I'm buying time. The people won't want to give up their gold. Maybe Moses will be back before the mixed people can get it together."

"But what if he doesn't come? What if the mixed people bring the gold? You can't go through with it."

"Miriam, do you see any other way? Look at them. There are hundreds of thousands of them, and me against them by myself? How long do you think I could last?"

Oh, my. It looked like Aaron might cave. I wondered if I should take off and tell Satan right away? No, better not. He wouldn't believe me anyway; better to wait and see what happens.

"Aaron, come out here," the men shouted.

I followed Aaron outside as the men came running back with a basketful of gold. Aaron was dumbfounded, and so was I, to see how quickly the people had turned over their treasure. It was a downward spiral after that, at least as far as God's plan was concerned. The mixed people built the fire to melt the gold while Aaron watched. I began to wonder about God; something like this wouldn't escape His notice. He must have known what was going on. And where was Moses anyway? I was so caught up wondering what God and Moses would do about the fiasco in process that I didn't actually see what happened next.

All I know is they threw the gold in the fire, and *presto*, there was a golden calf. Some said Aaron made it with a chiseling tool, but honestly, Aaron didn't have the skills to make something like that. Others said the sorcerers who were hidden among the mixed people had used their magic to bring forth the calf. Whatever. There it was for all to see: a golden idol, courtesy of Aaron, the priest of God.

That was when throngs of Israelites came running up to see what was going on. The mixed people shouted to them, "These are your gods who brought you up out of Egypt."

The looks of shock and disbelief on the faces of the true Israelites made it clear they could not have possibly been party to such a scheme and it really had been instigated by the mixed people. The Israelites looked first to the calf and then to Aaron, having no idea what to do next.

Aaron saw the confusion on their faces as well. He was quicker on his feet than I had previously given him credit for.

"Help me build an altar in front of the calf," he shouted to the crowd. "Tomorrow is a feast day to our God. We'll celebrate His goodness right here in front of the calf."

The people still looked confused, but if Aaron said it was all right, they thought it must be. They set out to build the altar and to party like all of this would work out just fine, not giving another thought to where Moses was.

I watched for a little while, but I'd seen unbridled revelry before in the name of religion, so it wasn't all that interesting to me. I knew I should probably leave right then and report to Satan, but my curiosity about where God and Moses might be was supplanting my good sense. I decided to go find them.

The last time I saw them they were on the mountain, so I flew to the base where the Israelites had gathered before to hear Moses deliver God's commands. All signs of life were gone, but the ominous clouds still hovered over the top, a sign to me that God was still there, and where God was, Moses would have to be close by. I wondered if I dared go to the top of the mountain to find them. I remembered how God had warned the people not to come close or to try to touch the mountain, and normally, that would have been quite enough to send me running back to my perch in the second heaven.

But I can go up the mountain without touching anything. I can fly.

Such courage was unusual for me, but I was compelled to find Moses and God.

I heard the rumbling before I saw Moses standing on a rock and looking toward the cloud. His face glowed from the flashes of lightning rolling over him as the voice of God spoke. I hovered within a crevice in the rocks, touching nothing, and listened.

"Go! Get down there! Your people whom you brought up from the land of Egypt have fallen to pieces."

"My people, Lord? Aren't they Your people?"

"You know the ones I'm talking about, the mixed hoards you allowed to follow you out of Egypt. You let them join with you without consulting Me."

"But, Lord, I thought that would please You, having true Egyptians deny their false gods to follow You. Granted, they've whined and complained the whole way, but no real harm has been done."

"No real harm? In no time at all they've turned away from the way I commanded them and made a molten calf and worshiped it. They've sacrificed to it and said, 'These are the gods, O Israel, that brought you up from the land of Egypt!' It's a mess down there."

Moses looked sick.

"I can't stand to look at them. What a stubborn, hardheaded people! Leave Me alone now; give My anger free rein to burst into flames and incinerate them."

"Surely You would not, Lord." Moses was nervous. "You must have a people to follow You."

"I'll start again. I'll make a great nation out of you."

That might have thrilled some people, but it was the last thing Moses wanted to do. I could see it in his eyes. Can you imagine? Starting all over with kids and more kids at eighty years old? No, thank you. Moses just wanted to get this over with as soon as possible.

"Why, God, would You lose Your temper with Your people? OK, I'll take the responsibility for the mixed people, but Your own people are at risk of Your anger. You brought them out of Egypt in a tremendous demonstration of power and strength. Why let the Egyptians say, 'He had it in for them. He brought them out so He could kill them in the mountains and wipe them right off the face of the earth'? Please reconsider bringing evil against Your people! Think of Abraham, Isaac, and Israel, Your servants to whom You gave Your word, telling them, 'I will give you many children, as many as the stars in the sky, and I'll give this land to your children as their land forever.'"

God listened to Moses and decided not to do the evil He had threatened against His people—at least not right then.

If only I could have found the courage to seize the moment to fly in front of God and demand justice. It would have been the perfect opportunity. He simply could not have justified letting these people get away with their sin while refusing to reconsider my situation.

"God," I should have said. "Listen to Yourself. You know those people have committed the unforgivable. How can You let them escape Your wrath just because Moses asked You to? What about me? My only sin was poor judgment. Why can't I have another chance?"

If only I had the nerve.

The flashes of lightning ceased, and I knew God had nothing further to say on the matter. Moses, his face still shining from the glory of God spilling out over him, bent over and picked up the tablets upon which the finger of God had been writing and started down the mountain. I hadn't noticed the tablets earlier. They were beautiful, engraved front and back in a way that no human of that day would have been able to do.

In my flight up the mountain, I was so obsessed with finding Moses and God that I completely missed Joshua, who'd been waiting beside the trail halfway up the mountain. When he saw Moses coming down with the tablets, he rushed to help him. Together they made their way down the winding path toward the camp.

They heard it before they saw it. The noise of unrestrained revelry grew louder with each step taking them nearer to the camp. When Joshua heard the sound of the people shouting noisily, he took Moses by the arm as if to warn him.

"That's the sound of war in the camp!"

"Oh, that it were only that, Joshua. Listen again. Those aren't songs of victory, and those aren't songs of defeat. I hear songs of people throwing a party."

And that's just what it was. As Moses came near to the camp and saw the calf and the people dancing, his anger flared. He threw down the tablets and smashed them to pieces at the foot of the mountain.

It was as if the people had awakened from a trance. The dancing and music stopped in mid beat. They saw the wrath and fire in Moses's eyes and panicked, running to and fro as if some horrible thing were loose in the camp and pursuing them. Moses strode into the camp with Joshua close behind, pushing the people aside as the two made their way to the golden calf.

With the strength of ten men half his age, Moses took the calf and threw it into the raging bonfire the people had built. The people were stunned at how fast the calf melted, but I wasn't. I'd seen the angel of the elite guard of heaven throw holy fire into the flames to increase the heat beyond what can occur through natural means. The primary purpose of God's fire is to consume His enemies; it works every time.

Aaron ran up to Moses and hugged him, but Moses did not hug back. Aaron stepped back and lowered his head in anticipation of what he knew was coming.

"What on earth did these people do to you that you involved them in this huge sin?" Moses demanded.

"Brother, don't be angry with me. You know the mixed people and how set on evil they are. Why did we ever let them come with us?"

Moses did not respond.

"They were spreading discontent among the Israelites, telling them that you had left and weren't coming back. Then they came to me and demanded that I make a substitute god to calm the people down and lead them out of here."

Moses did not respond.

Sweating profusely, Aaron continued. "So, I tried to buy some time, just till you got back. I ordered them to gather up the gold from the Israelites and bring it to me. Who knew the people would turn it over so easily? I thought it would take days—weeks even—to get the gold together, if they could do it at all."

Aaron paused again, but still Moses did not respond.

"So, anyway, they brought the gold to me, and I threw it in the fire, and just like that, out came this calf."

Up to that point, I think Moses might have been softening a bit toward Aaron and the impossible situation he had found himself in. I should have helped Aaron with his story before he got to sounding ridiculous. He should have told Moses how his very life was at stake or he would never have done such a terrible sin. He should have emphasized the role the sorcerers played in the whole thing. He should have added a lot more drama than he did. Otherwise, how could he possibly have thought Moses would believe such a preposterous story?

Moses shook his head and turned away from Aaron and saw that the people were simply running wild. He took up a position at the entrance to the camp. When the people saw him, the frenzy stopped as they literally froze in place under the fierce look in Moses's eyes. Finally, Moses raised his staff and bellowed at the people.

"Whoever is on God's side, join me!" All the Levites stepped up and stood behind him.

I can tell you it got ugly after that. If you ask me, Moses was out of control as he and the Levites went through the camp killing people all over the place. I don't know if they were aiming for the mixed people or not, but by the time it was said and done, more than three thousand corpses lay scattered throughout the camp. I didn't recall hearing God say the first thing about a massacre, and I wondered if Moses had done this on his own without consulting God.

Time to go; Satan would want to know all about it.

CHAPTER 17

ATAN ROARED WITH delight when I told him about the golden calf.

"It didn't take them long to get over the idea of their great deliverer, now did it?" he asked in that sarcastic way I hated. The others laughed along with him as they always did. No one would dare imply by failing to laugh that Satan wasn't clever.

"Well, to be perfectly accurate," I said, "it wasn't the Israelites who came up with the idea of making another god. It was the Egyptians who went with them. They're the ones who intimidated Aaron to do it; the people just got caught up in fervor."

"Whatever." Satan dismissed my comments entirely. "Tell me more, and don't leave anything out."

"That's about it. Moses threw the calf into the fire, and it melted immediately. That's when he lost all reason and began to behave like a madman. He called the Levites together and led them on a rampage through the camp killing about three thousand people." I paused, wondering if I should add my opinion; oh, well, why not? "I don't think God told him to do that. I would have heard it."

"Are you saying Moses disobeyed God?"

"No, no, I didn't say that. I said I didn't *hear* God tell him to kill so many people. If Moses acted on his own, technically, one could not call it disobedience in the general sense."

Satan sat back on his haunches as if pondering whether or not this meant anything to him.

"Is Moses still mad?"

"I don't know, sir."

Satan turned to one of his captains and ordered him to go to the Israelites' camp.

"Stir Moses up. Whisper in Moses's ear. Tell him Aaron betrayed him. See if you can incite him to kill more people—Aaron too."

"Wait, sir," I interrupted. "I don't think that will work." As everyone gasped I realized I had made the very foolish mistake of correcting one of Satan's ideas.

"What I meant to say, sir..." I tried to dig myself out of the hole I'd dug myself into. "Moses is a lot more like God than you know, personality-wise, I mean. His anger doesn't last. He gets aroused in righteous anger and punishes the disobedient, but right after that he always returns to loving them and seeing himself as responsible for them. He doesn't carry a grudge—nothing like you at all."

Before the words rolled off my tongue, I realized I should have swallowed them.

"Are you comparing that pseudodeliverer wannabe to me?"

"No, no, absolutely not; *cunning*, that's what I meant. Moses is not as cunning as you. Simpleminded really...doesn't have the...the chutzpah...that's it. Doesn't have the chutzpah to conduct a massacre for very long."

"Chutzpah? Am I supposed to know what that means?"

"You know, the Jews say it all the time when they want to communicate, uh, virility, sort of." I stopped mid sentence. There was no way to make this better. "Never mind, sir, all

I meant is Moses will not stay mad. He'll feel bad about the people for a little while and then feel bad that he felt bad and punished them."

"Never mind what Moses feels." He began to chuckle in that evil tone I hated. "No, never mind about Moses at all. The question is, how does God feel now that His precious people have bowed down to another god?"

"Idol, sir."

"Did the people acknowledge it as a god or not?"

"They acted like they did. Some of them probably; yes, I suppose."

"Then God will abandon them or, better yet, kill them. He has to do it. He can't break His own rules. No one can save them. We've won. Get ready to descend on the earth unopposed," he shouted to the onlookers.

Cheering broke out from the demon guards like it always did when Satan announced a victory, real or not. I stood quietly by, shuffling my hoof back and forth in front of me, never looking up and hoping I would be dismissed as no longer needed. Satan was basking in the shouts of praise from the others when he looked at me from the corner of his yellow eye and stopped in mid chuckle.

"Now, what's the matter with you? If you can't celebrate my victory, get out."

"Right away, sir. I'll just be leaving, then." I began slinking toward the door before he could change his mind.

"Stop him!" Satan yelled at one of the guards who grabbed me by the tail just as I was making my getaway.

The guard held me up and dangled me like a morsel on a string as the others roared with laughter at my predicament. When he saw the look in Satan's eyes, he knew recess was over, and he slammed me down in front of his evil ruler.

"You know something; what is it?"

"I just don't want you to get your hopes up, master," I said in the gentlest voice I could find. Was that ever a poor choice of words.

Satan himself came down on top of me and kicked me like a soccer ball. I fell to the floor and rolled up in the corner. The evil prince came and stood over me with those awful eyes. This was it; I just knew it. At last he would destroy me and only because I had tried to show a little concern for his feelings.

"I do not have hopes." He snarled as he bent down close to my face with breath that could wilt a rock. "I am not one of His pathetic humans. I have hope neither in Him nor in any other living thing in the universe. I am my own god; I decide how things will be; I do not hope. Do you understand that?" He kicked me one more time for emphasis.

"Yes, yes, of course. I misspoke."

"Get him up!" he yelled at one of the guards who promptly grabbed me by my tail again. Satan stomped across the floor and sat down on his throne, motioning for the guard to deposit me in front of him.

"Talk!"

"Yes, I was just about to..."

"Spare me the groveling."

"Right. OK, it's just that there is the possibility that God will not destroy the Hebrews as you are hoping." I couldn't believe I'd said it again. I tried to recover. "Not *hoping*, of course. What I meant to say is God may not be required to destroy the people even though they fell into idol worship."

"Because?"

"Because of intercession, sir."

The boos and hisses from the other demons didn't dissuade me. I surprised myself by spinning around to face them. "Has the past been so wasted on you that you've learned nothing from it? I said *intercession*, not praying, not begging. *Intercession!* Have you forgotten what God does in response to intercession?"

Satan motioned for them to leave me alone. I turned to face him.

"Master, if Moses intercedes for the people, God will not destroy them. I'm sure of it."

"You said Moses was so angry with the people that he killed three thousand of them. Why would he intercede for the rest of them?"

"Because humans are not like us."

The room was silent as each head turned to see how Satan would react. I couldn't imagine getting into deeper trouble than I was already in, so I risked it and continued.

"God's people get mad and do terrible things, but they don't stay mad. Eventually, they get over it. Demons never get over anything. Each offense just adds to the last offense. Therefore, we have no frame of reference for understanding human guilt or their penchant to care about other humans. They repent for their madness and plead with God to reconcile what the madness has brought about, and He usually does. Moses is going to intercede for the people, and God will forgive them. I know I'm right about this." I sat down hard on the floor and curled my tail up under me so no one could grab it again.

Satan leaned back on his throne and grasped the arms with both claws. He was obviously thinking about what I said. I tried to remember whether that had ever happened before. Finally, he stood up, walked over to me, and lifted me up by one wing. He then stood me on the floor in front of him. He walked around me as if examining me to see what foreign substance I might be made of. At last, he stopped in front of my face.

"Not about idol worship." No one said a word as we waited for his next sentence. "You may be right about other things, but not worship of other gods. His jealousy consumes Him. Have you forgotten why we were thrown out of heaven? He was jealous of me."

I bit my tongue so hard I was afraid a piece of it would fall out. I dared not respond with anything close to a true depiction of what happened in the war in heaven.

"Get back down there and follow Moses; you will see I'm right." The guarding demons began chanting ad nauseam that ridiculous ditty about how Satan rules.

I kept my head down and was able to walk out of the room under my own power instead of being heaved out by one of the other demons, which was usually the case.

"I'm not wrong," I said under my breath when I was a safe distance away.

CHAPTER 18

I RETURNED TO THE Israelites' camp to find them struggling with what to do with three thousand corpses. The whole mood had changed. There was no singing, no partying, and, for once, no griping going on. The people were traumatized; that's the only way I can describe it. They had seen and applauded God's judgment against Egypt, but I suppose it never crossed their minds that He would exact devastating punishment on them as well if they disobeyed. It's hard to say who they were more terrified of, God or Moses. They were virtually immobilized because of their fear. So much so that Aaron and Hur were concerned they might not be able to get the people moving again. That's when Hur asked for a private meeting with Moses.

"Unless you do something, Moses, I don't think we can get them to go either forward or back."

"If we don't get them going soon," Aaron interjected, "our enemies will think we're lost or vulnerable in some way. It's just a matter of time until one of them tries an attack."

"How do you think it would make God look if all these people He rescued are killed here in the desert?" Hur asked. "Right now the people are walking around in a fog and in no condition to fight. They're afraid to make a move."

"I agree with Hur," Aaron said. "This could all end up looking like God called the people out of Egypt and then abandoned them to their enemies."

Moses bristled. "And whose fault is it that we're in this predicament?"

Aaron dropped his head. "It's mine. I let it happen. I'm not cut out for this line of work. Let somebody else be in charge if you're planning on taking off again."

Moses ignored the comment. "All right, gather the people, and in the morning I'll talk to them."

True to his word, the next day Moses addressed the people. "You have sinned an enormous sin! I don't know if it will help, but I'm going up to God on your behalf. I'm not making any promises, but maybe I'll be able to clear you of your sin."

Moses told Joshua to follow him at a distance as he trudged up the mountain in search of God. He wasn't hard to find. The mountain still manifested the glory of God as the fire and smoke billowed upward. Moses went to the last place he had been when God talked to him, sat down on a rock, and waited. It wasn't long before God revealed Himself and spoke to Moses.

"They are a rebellious people."

"Don't I know it?" Moses stood up and paced back and forth with his hands on his hips. "This is terrible. They have sinned an enormous sin! There's no excuse for it. It was the mixed people who made the god of gold for them, but Your people are responsible for their willingness to worship it."

"Aaron is also responsible."

"Yes, I know, and believe me, he feels horrible about it. He's admitted his fault and has asked for forgiveness."

God did not respond. Moses waited a few minutes and then tried to move the conversation along.

"And now, if You will only forgive their sin."

"I will not," God interrupted.

Moses dropped to his knees with desperation written all over his face as he tried to persuade God to forgive.

"If you cannot forgive them, then erase me as well out of the Book of Life You've written."

"I'll only erase from My book those who sin against Me."

"If You don't forgive them, then I have failed You. My sin is greater than theirs, for I have been with You."

God remained silent. Moses closed his eyes and rocked back and forth on his knees, determined to wait for God to speak. After five minutes, he couldn't stand it. He opened one eye and whispered.

"Are You thinking it over?"

"All right. For now, lead the people to where I told you. My angel is going ahead of you. On the day, though, when I settle accounts, their sins will certainly be part of the settlement."

Moses nodded eagerly as if in total agreement.

"Now go. Get on your way from here, you and the people you brought up from the land of Egypt. Head for the land that I promised to Abraham, Isaac, and Jacob. I will send an angel ahead of you to the land flowing with milk and honey, and I'll drive out the Canaanites and the rest of your enemies before you. But I Myself will not go with you. They are such a stubborn, hardheaded people; I might destroy them on the journey."

I was mesmerized. God spoke to Moses the way neighbors talk to each other over the backyard fence.

But Moses wouldn't quit. He kept right on pleading with God, just exactly as I'd told Satan he would.

"Lord, first You tell me, 'Lead this people,' and now You've changed Your mind and aren't going with us? You don't even let me know whom You're going to send with me. An angel? It's not the same. And it's not what we agreed to. You tell me, 'I know you well, and you are special to Me.' If I'm so special to You, let me in on Your plans. Don't send me where You won't go. How can I know You're still pleased with me if You make me go on without You? Don't forget; this is Your people, Your responsibility. I never wanted this job in the first place."

"Whoa there, Moses," I almost said out loud. "Take a good look at who you're talking to."

Moses didn't seem to be worried about pushing God too far. He paused for a moment and then kept right on going.

"If Your presence doesn't take the lead here, and if You won't go with us, let's call this trip off right now. How else will it be known that You're with me in this, with me and Your people?"

He paused again, waiting for God to respond. When He didn't, Moses just kept pushing. I wondered how far this might go before God had enough.

"Well, what's Your answer? Are You traveling with us or not? How else will we know that we're special among all other people on the earth?"

I began to get nervous when God didn't say anything. I was afraid He might have left. From the beads of sweat on his upper lip, I knew Moses feared the same thing. After another unnerving minute, God finally spoke.

"All right. Just as you say; this also I will do, for I know you well, and you are special to Me. I know you by name, and I will go with you."

Moses clasped his hands together and waved them at God.

"Thank You, O Lord, for You are great and mighty and faithful to Your word."

Doesn't that beat all? God agreed to forgive the grievous sin of the people because Moses interceded for them. Isn't that just what I told Satan would happen? I was right; I didn't think it was fair, but I was right.

From watching all the people on the earth, I'd learned a few things about doing deals. The first thing I learned was when you get a yes from the customer, quit talking. Pack up your kit, and get out before he can change his mind. I thought surely that would be what Moses would do. He'd gotten the best deal he was going to get, so he should have moved right along as quickly as possible. But he didn't.

"Please, God, before You send me away, let me see Your glory."

What? I couldn't believe it. *Moses, are you addled from all the stress? God isn't going to show you His glory. Who do you think you are?*

I wasn't expecting God to say anything to such an arrogant request. I would even have bet money that God wouldn't respond. I would have lost.

"I will make My goodness pass right in front of you; I'll proclaim My name right before you, but you may not see My face. No one can see Me and live. Look, here is a place right beside Me. Put yourself on this rock. When My glory passes by, I'll put you in the cleft of the rock and cover you with My hand until I've passed by. Then I'll take My hand away, and you'll see My back. But you won't see My face."

When I heard God say those words, an old aching began to rise up within me. Moses had never seen God, but I had. How many times in my exile had I longed to see Him just one more time? I had to get closer. I crept up to the rock where Moses stood and set myself down right beside him. When the shadow of God's hand passed over us, I panicked and jumped down and hid behind the rock instead.

I couldn't see it, but I could feel it as God passed by Moses. When I dared take a peek, Moses's face was radiant beyond anything I'd ever seen in a human. Without saying another word, Moses bowed low and backed away; then he turned and ran down the mountainside.

I knew I should have followed Moses back to the camp as he hurried down the mountain, but I was momentarily paralyzed with indecision. Why was I such a coward? I was right there near the place where God was. I might never get this close again. Since He seemed to be in a conciliatory mood, I wondered whether He might be willing to hear my case now that Moses's issues were settled. He might get angry and not hear me, but how could that be any worse than things were for me now? I decided to chance it, and with great trepidation, I climbed back on top of the rock and tried to squeeze myself into the cleft where Moses had stood.

I hadn't as much as wedged my hoof into the opening before the weight of His glory forced me down on the rock, and I could not move. I was frightened beyond what words can convey. But it didn't matter; I was near the presence of God. Even if He destroyed me right there and then, my lot would be so much better than living under the dictatorship of an insane ruler who thought he was a god.

After a while, I got a cramp in my midsection from the weight of all that glory and wished I could stand up.

"I wonder if God knows He's standing on top of me?" I asked myself. "Did He cause His glory to weigh down on me because He knew I was here, or did His glory descend and I just happened to be in the way?" Not that it mattered, unless I was actually going to be allowed to speak to Him, in which case my opening line would be important.

I didn't have to wonder much longer. Slowly His weight lifted from me, and I knew He was giving me a chance to escape. I was torn between going and staying. What should I do? If I tried to approach Him instead of fleeing, as I was sure He was allowing me to do, He might be angry, and my window to get away could suddenly close, and who knew what would happen to me then? I couldn't chance it. I raised myself up and flew as fast as I could.

I will never know what might have been if only I'd had the courage to stay.

CHAPTER 19

I WAS IN NO hurry to return to the second heaven only to tell Satan I'd been right again about the intercession. I needed something else to report so it wouldn't seem like I was gloating about being right. Satan doesn't respond well to gloating from anyone else, although he himself is in a constant state of gloat. I figured God was sure to speak to Moses again with better instructions about going forward. I didn't dare miss anything, so I hung around the camp and waited for God to show up again.

Moses was sitting outside the door of his tent, appreciating the cool of the evening and apparently not expecting God to drop by. He jumped abruptly when God spoke to him, almost knocking me off the bench I was sharing with him.

"Cut out two tablets of stone just like the first set, and engrave on them the words that were on the original tablets you smashed."

God often started a conversation in the middle of a paragraph, so it was not surprising that Moses had to think for a minute before knowing exactly what God was talking about. God paused a moment until Moses got that clear look in his eyes, which signaled he was now tracking and all systems were go for God to continue with the rest of the paragraph.

"Be ready in the morning to climb Mount Sinai, and get set to meet Me on top of the mountain. Not a soul is to go with you; the whole mountain must be clear of people, even animals. Not even sheep or oxen can be grazing in front of the mountain."

Moses stayed up half the night cutting two tablets of stone just like the originals. He got up early in the morning and climbed Mount Sinai as God had commanded him, carrying the two tablets with him. Just as He said, God descended in the cloud and took up His position there beside Moses and then did what I thought was an odd thing. God began to call out *His own name.* Don't ask me why. I'd never seen Him do anything quite like this before, and believe me, I'd seen some odd things.

God turned, and with His back to Moses, He passed in front of him and called out, "God, God, a God of mercy and grace, endlessly patient. So much love; so deeply true; loyal in love for a thousand generations; forgiving iniquity, rebellion, and sin. Still, He doesn't ignore sin. He holds sons and grandsons responsible for a father's sins to the third and even fourth generation."

Why was God talking about Himself in the third person? I looked around to see if there was anyone besides Moses and me to whom God might have been making these declarations. It didn't seem like He was talking to Moses, and He certainly wasn't talking to me. I didn't see anyone else, so when God started talking again, I had to deduce that Moses was His only intended audience. God soon stopped with the third-person talk and spoke to Moses as if nothing at all strange had happened.

"As of right now, I'm making a covenant with you. In full sight of your people I will work wonders that have never been created in all the earth, in any nation. Then all the people with whom you're living will see how tremendous the work will be that I'll do for you. Take careful note of all I command you today. I'm clearing your way by driving out all of your enemies."

Moses really perked up at that last part. I once heard him tell Aaron privately that he feared the day his ragtag militia of ex-slaves would have to face on its own a real army. Even though they'd been successful in that earlier skirmish, Moses worried what might happen if they ever came up against a foe whose defeat God had not predetermined.

As far as Moses was concerned, the conversation couldn't get any better than hearing how God intended to remove his enemies before him, so he stood up, anxious to get back down the mountain to tell Aaron the good news, but God was not finished.

"Moses, listen to Me."

Moses stopped his exit attempt as he realized God's tone had changed from exuberant to somber.

"Stay vigilant. Don't let down your guard lest you make covenant with the people who live in the land that you are entering and they trip you up."

"I don't understand, Lord." Moses seemed confused by this warning. "I thought You just said You were going to drive Your enemies—our enemies—out before us."

"I did, but I'm going to use you as the instrument in My hand to accomplish what I promised."

Moses's face fell as if such a thought had never crossed his mind.

"Oh, come now, Moses. How else did you think I would do it? You know I have limited Myself to working through these people of yours."

"I just thought that when You said *You* were going to do it, You meant *You* were going to do it; that's all."

"If I were going to do everything Myself, I wouldn't need you, now would I?"

"Can You be a little more specific about what You expect us to do to drive them out?"

"Sure. Tear down their altars, smash their phallic pillars, and chop down their fertility poles."

"Oh, well, nothing to it." Moses ventured a little sarcasm but quickly recovered. "This isn't going to be easy, is it? They're going to fight back, aren't they?"

God ignored his questions but continued with a stern warning as to what Moses must be uncompromising about.

"Don't allow My people to worship any of their gods. I, the Lord, am jealous for My children. Be careful that you don't make a covenant with the people who live in the land lest the Israelites be tempted by the sex-and-religion abomination of their worship. Don't join them in meals at their altars. Don't allow your sons to marry their women. Those women will take up with any convenient god or goddess and will get your sons to do the same thing."

"Is there anything else?" Moses asked.

"Don't make any more molten gods for yourselves."

"That wasn't me. Aaron allowed that to happen." Moses seemed to immediately regret implicating Aaron. "I shouldn't have blamed him; it was my watch."

Moses may have thought they were through with the important stuff, but God wasn't anywhere near done. He went right on listing the things the Israelites could or could not do. Moses might not have understood why God was suddenly issuing dozens of new rules, but I did. He was trying to cover every possible way those stiff-necked people could get themselves into trouble.

Moses must have thought it was never going to be over. At least that's what I was beginning to think. God kept him up there forty days and forty nights, and I had to stay for every minute of it. I didn't dare miss a word because you could just never know which one of God's words might shift the power balance in the whole universe. Moses didn't eat any food, and he didn't drink any water. And he wrote on the tablets the entire time, until the words of the covenant, the Ten Commandments, were inscribed in the stone.

It must have seemed like an eon to the waiting people back at the camp. I was sure Aaron was beginning to sweat. When Moses finally came down from Mount Sinai, carrying the two tablets of the testimony, with me following along right behind him, the elders raced to greet him. I wondered what it must feel like to have others miss you and be glad to see you when you returned from duty.

No one ever hurried to meet me when I returned to the second heaven to report to Satan. Nobody was ever happy I'd come back. No one cared what I had to report, or at least they pretended it wasn't important. Since the humans couldn't see me anyway, I hurried and got in front of Moses and pretended all those cheering people were coming to greet me. I tell you, I was almost misty-eyed there for a moment.

Not having a mirror handy, Moses didn't know that the skin of his face glowed because he had been speaking with God. When Aaron and all the Israelites got near enough to see Moses's radiant face, they pulled back, afraid to get closer to him. Moses called out to them to reassure them even though he didn't know what they were nervous about.

"Don't be afraid. God is for us, not against us.

"Come close and listen carefully to what He has said because He loves us."

Aaron and the leaders in the community came slowly back at Moses's reassurance that they weren't in more trouble. Moses talked with them and told them everything the Lord had commanded for them. Later that afternoon, the rest of the Israelites came up to him, and he passed on all the commands to them that God had told him on Mount Sinai.

And, of course, they promised to obey every last one of them.

Chapter 20

"Is He never going to be done with them?"

Satan stood on the rim of the second heaven, staring down at the bulging camp of the Israelites far below. He had convinced himself that God would wipe them out after the golden calf affair. He refused to believe me when I tried to tell him how God would give the people a pass even for idol worship—all because of Moses's intercession. It happened just like I predicted, but I didn't dare say anything that sounded like "I told you so."

"How can He do anything else, sir? You have the rest of the people on the earth in bondage. The Israelites, pitiful as they may be, are the only team God has. If He gives up on them, game over; He has nothing."

"I can still win. I've watched these miserable humans for centuries. God has overestimated their potential. He might get them through the desert to Canaan, but they'll never be able to stand up to our forces there. How many do we have?"

"The Amorites, Canaanites, Hittites, Perizzites, Hivites, and Jebusites, sir."

"Just as I thought; my strategy is working."

"What strategy would that be, master?"

"What are you, blind? Why do you think I haven't sent forces after them in the desert? I *want* them to get across. I don't know which I look forward to the most—seeing them slaughtered at the border or seeing them seduced by the sex priestesses in my temples." He paused as if relishing both possibilities.

"I think I'll have them go lightly on the slaughter." The smirk continued. "It gives me much more pleasure to see them defile themselves with those sex perverts than to see them dead. Whatever angers God the most, that's what I want to see. He will regret the day He took me on as an enemy."

"Uh, Your Majesty..." I struggled with whether I should tell him what God had said about all those "ites." If I didn't tell him and he found out later, it could only be much worse for me than if I just told him now and gave him time to get over it. He turned and looked at me as if daring me to contradict his plan.

"What is it?"

"Well, sir, to be perfectly honest, God mentioned those people to Moses while they were up on the mountain."

"Go on."

"He told Moses that He—God—would drive them out before him—Moses. To be exact, what He said was He intended to use Moses to drive them out, but He would be behind the whole thing."

Satan did not respond right away so I thought he might need to be reminded about the rules of engagement.

"It's like this, sir: God can do anything He wants on the earth, but He has to do it through human beings."

"Really?" The sarcasm dripped from the word. "I didn't know that."

He pushed me aside as he stomped back to his den. Since he didn't order me to follow him, I didn't. Instead, I climbed upon my perch and looked at the earth. I kept an eye on the Hebrew's activities, but it didn't seem to me there was much going on there that anyone except God would care about.

Moses was still hearing from God on a daily basis with a new set of regulations to govern the lives of the people. I suppose He wanted them to have a fully functional form of government when they reached their destination so no time would be wasted in political scuffling. It would be easier for the people to fight if they knew in advance what they were fighting for. It takes a government to overthrow a government, not a band of vigilantes. That would certainly be the case once they crossed into the enemy territory where all the governments were under the reign of Satan. That had to be God's reasoning behind all the rules.

However, it did not explain the tabernacle. God ordered Moses to gather the artisans and craftsmen from among the people to begin the construction of a tabernacle, a tent of meeting, and a box. If I thought God was meticulous on the rule giving, it was nothing compared to the detail He insisted upon for this new building project. The attention to every thread, every color, and every building material that was to be used would boggle the mind of human or demon. Fascinating as it all was, what most captured my attention was the box.

God referred to the box as the ark, not to be confused with the boat Noah built by the same name. (Don't even ask. I don't know why He didn't call it something else for simplicity's sake.) God was in every detail of how it was to be constructed, how it would be carried, and what would be in it. This is where it began to get interesting. God told Moses to put the tablets of the covenant in the ark. No particular big deal; he had to keep them somewhere. But it's what God said next that thickened the plot.

"Sculpt two winged angels out of hammered gold for either end of the lid. Make them so they're one piece with the lid. Make the angels with their wings spread, hovering and facing one another but looking down on the ark. I will meet you there at set times to speak with you from between the angel figures that are on it. I will speak the commands that I have for the Israelites from that place."

Well, I was confused. What was He doing? God speaks from heaven, from the mountains, from the pillar of fire, from just about every grand thing imaginable. But God does not stand on the lid of a box to speak. Furthermore, He would certainly never get *in* the box, which was bound to be the next illogical conclusion to which the Israelites were certain to jump given enough time.

Much as I hated to do it, I needed to talk this over with someone. This was just not like anything God was known to do. Unfortunately, the only person who knew more about God than me was Satan. I supposed I'd have to tell him about the box eventually, so it may as well be sooner than later. Reluctantly, I took myself to his throne room and waited to be admitted. It didn't occur to me that Satan might outjump the Israelites en route to a wrong conclusion, but that's just what he did.

"A box? God in a box."

"Something like that, yes, sir." It was pointless to argue about whether God was on top of the box or in the box.

"And just why do you think God might do something like that?" He pretended interested in my opinion.

"I…I hoped you might know, sir." Then the tittering began among the onlooking guards.

"Well, let's see if we can figure this out. What was Moses supposed to do with the box once God got inside?"

"Only the priests were to handle the ark—the box—and even they were not permitted to touch it. They were to carry it on their shoulders on poles that would fit into rings on the sides. Once they start moving again, the priests are to get in front of the people and carry the ark."

Satan couldn't seem to get over the hilarity of visualizing God in a box, but I was figuring the whole thing out just from talking out loud. Note to self: I don't need to consult with Satan for answers; I just need to hear myself talk.

"I think I've got it, sir. God is preparing the people for war."

"By getting in a box?" Everyone roared at Satan's retort.

"Yes, yes, that's it. Don't you see? God knows what they're like. It's plain from the golden calf debacle. The people want a god they can see, one they can carry in their hands. They were willing to follow the golden calf because they could see it, handle it, and know where it was at all times."

"That has nothing to do with war."

"But it does, or it will. God knows what you've got planned with those nations lying in wait for the Israelites to cross over. He knows the Israelites will be terrified and might run away.

177

But when they see the priests carrying the box with God in it, they'll feel invincible and be willing to go to war."

Satan's face showed he wasn't connecting the same dots as me.

"You'll see I'm right, master." I probably shouldn't have made that boast. No one was allowed to be right except for Satan. "Shall I go down for a closer look, Mighty One?"

"Go down for a closer look," Satan commanded as if I hadn't just said the same thing.

CHAPTER 21

I FOUND MOSES IN his tent with his hands over his ears. I couldn't blame him. The people were back at their national sport, whining and complaining. It was the mixed people who had stirred them up again. They hadn't counted on the journey taking so long. Their soft life back in Egypt hadn't prepared them for an extended camping trip. It was inevitable they would fall back into loud grumbling over their hard life and lead the Israelites right into misery with them. Moses had learned to ignore the mixed bunch, but when it spread to the others, the din could not be shut out. Moses wasn't the only one who heard them; God heard them also.

From experience I knew there was a point at which God would have had enough. I didn't always guess right as to where that point might be, but it was always there eventually. On this day, the Israelites hit it dead on. When He heard their unabashed ingratitude, His anger flared, and He sent fire that blazed up and burned the outer boundaries of the camp.

The people thought they were goners for sure and went running toward Moses's tent, crying out for him to help. Moses stepped out of his tent to keep them from trying to get inside.

"Don't you care that He will destroy us?" they shouted.

"He's not going to destroy you. You've given Him plenty of opportunity and reason. If He were going to destroy you, He would have already done it."

"But how do you know? Look at that fire," they clamored.

Moses sighed and tried to ignore them, but they would not be quieted.

"Help us. Talk to God on our behalf. Save us." The crowd was growing.

"I'll try." Moses sighed and went back inside his tent.

He lifted his hands toward God as if trying to grab hold of Him. "You know You're not going to destroy them. Please, can't I have a little rest?"

God didn't answer, but the fire flickered out, and the people settled down. When Moses heard the cries of discontent fading, he peeked out the door of his tent to see what had happened.

"Thank You," he whispered to God as he rolled his eyes heavenward.

Anyone who knew humans the way I do would also know the calm wouldn't last. The mixed people were soon at it again. Now they had a craving for meat.

"Why can't we have meat? We ate meat and fish in Egypt— and got it free—to say nothing of the cucumbers and melons, the leeks and onions and garlic. Nothing tastes good out here; all we get is manna, manna, manna."

"Why can't we have meat?" the Israelites cried right along with the mixed people. Never mind that most of them had never had a bite of meat in their entire lives. Meat was not on the Egyptian menu for slaves.

Moses heard the whining of all those people moving toward his tent again. God heard it too, and Moses began to get worried about what might happen next.

Moses looked up and raised his hands. "Are You here, God?"

"Yes, I'm here."

"Where do I go to resign?"

"Don't be ridiculous. You're My chosen servant."

"Can't You choose someone else for a while?"

"This is the reason I created you."

"Then why are You treating me this way? What did I ever do to You to deserve this? Did I conceive them? Was I their mother? Why do You dump the responsibility of this people on me? Where am I supposed to get meat for all these people?" He lifted the flap of his tent door as if showing God the crowds outside.

"Give us meat; we want meat." It sounded like a lunchroom brawl.

"God, I can't do this by myself," Moses complained as he closed the tent flap. "It's too much for one person with all these people. If You're not going to help me with them, do me a favor and kill me. I've seen enough; I've had enough. Let me out of here."

"Get a grip. You know you can't go anywhere. Gather seventy men from among the leaders of Israel, men whom you know to be respected and responsible. Take them to the tent of meeting. I'll meet you there, and I'll come down and speak with you. I'll take some of the Spirit that is on you and place it on them; they'll then be able to take some of the load of this people. You won't have to carry the whole thing alone. How does that sound?"

"Well, OK, that's better than nothing." Moses himself was close to whining.

"Now go tell the people to consecrate themselves and get ready for tomorrow when they're going to eat meat."

"Really?"

"Oh, yes, really. I'm as tired of their griping as you are. 'We want meat; give us meat. We had a better life in Egypt. Whine, whine, whine.'

"I've heard their whining, and I'm going to give them meat all right. Not just meat for one day or a few days or even a week. I'm going to give them meat for thirty days. They're going to eat meat until it's coming out of their nostrils. They're going to be so sick of meat that they'll throw up at the mere mention of it. And you can tell them why. It's because they have rejected Me, who is right here among them, whining to My face, 'Oh, why did we ever have to leave Egypt?'"

Apparently Moses had never seen God's emotional side. But then Moses was a bit emotional himself; otherwise, he would have been a little more careful with his tone of voice.

"I'm standing here surrounded by six hundred thousand men on foot, and You say You'll give them meat every day for a month. So, where's it coming from? Even if all the flocks and herds in the land were butchered, would that be enough? Even if all the fish in the sea were caught, would that be enough?"

"So, do you think I can't take care of you? You'll see soon enough whether what I say happens for you or not."

"No, I didn't mean it like that. I know You've never failed me."

"Then do what I tell you."

I was flabbergasted. That's all I can say about it. I know what I said earlier about God and Moses talking as if they were friends, but this was too much. Even though it might sound like a real argument was going on, it was an argument between two people who respected and trusted one another. Moses trusted God so much he could pour out his anger and frustration and feel safe doing it. God trusted Moses so much He pulled no punches in letting him know just how He felt about things. I was pretty sure God would never have been that transparent with any of the angels.

Moses went out and told the people what God had said. He called together seventy of the leaders and told them to stand around the tent. Right on cue God came down in a cloud and spoke to Moses and took some of the Spirit that was on him and put it on the seventy leaders. When the Spirit rested on them, they prophesied.

Then Moses and the leaders of Israel went back to the camp. A wind set in motion by the breath of God swept quail in from the direction of the sea. They piled up to a depth of about three feet in the camp and as far out as a day's walk in every direction. All that day and night and into the next day the people were out gathering the quail by the bushel baskets. Quail was all over the place. Huge amounts of quail; even the slowest person among them gathered at least sixty bushels.

They ate so much quail some of them got sick and died. The mixed people said God had sent a plague on them. It didn't look that way from where I was sitting. They gorged themselves like pigs and died of gluttony. That would be the official story for sure. But I knew what had really happened; after all, I watched the whole thing.

The people insisted they knew more about what they needed than God did. Spurred on by the mixed people, they harangued God and Moses endlessly about something they didn't really need, something that, in fact, was bad for them. Their digestive systems were not suitable for an orgy of meat, and they were unrestrained in eating as much and as fast as they could.

So, why did God give in and let them have something He knew would make them sick? Because He won't make people do what they are supposed to do even though their lives would be so simple if only He would. His will is perfect for them if they would accept it. But when they won't, He'll hold out for a while to give them time to think through their impetuous nature. If they won't accept His will for them, He won't force them into compliance. It's sort of like He finally says to them, "Very well; *thy* will be done."

Many people died because they got exactly what they insisted on having.

CHAPTER 22

I T TOOK DAYS to take care of all the people who were sick from food poisoning and to bury the many who died. If there was a good thing for Moses in all this, it was that at least there was positively no more griping about food. I followed Moses as he walked through the outer camp, where all the dead and dying had been moved. If he intended to call on God again, I didn't want to miss it. When I figured out he wasn't going to do anything but survey the damage and console the people when he could, I got bored and decided to go back to the main camp to see if anything was going on that Satan would want to know about.

I smelled him before I got close to him. As I said before, once you've smelled a demon, you can never mistake the odor for anything else. There was definitely a demon in the camp. Satan must have sent someone to check on me, not for my well-being, of course, but probably to see if I was on the job. I found him with Aaron and Miriam. They didn't know he was there, but he was right in the middle of their conversation. When the demon spotted me, he flew over to my side.

"Why are you here?" I asked him.

"Watch and see. Satan knew you would let things get too cozy for the leaders. He sent me to stir them up a bit."

Miriam and Aaron were deep in quiet conversation, but I couldn't hear without moving in closer. When I did, it was clear they were talking against Moses behind his back because of his Cushite wife, Zipporah.

"What did she tell you?" Aaron asked.

"She's unhappy. They haven't had marital relations in all this time because Moses insists on remaining chaste in order to hear God."

"It isn't good for Moses to ignore his wife. He's coming up now; let me talk to him."

Moses joined his brother and sister to give them a status report on the condition of the camp after the food epidemic. Sensing he had walked in on a private conversation, he asked Miriam.

"What's going on?"

Miriam lowered her head as if captivated by an ant crawling across her shoe. Then peeking up, she tilted her head toward Moses as if urging Aaron to speak.

"Let me ask you something," Aaron began. "Is it only through you and you alone that God speaks?"

"What?" Moses had no idea where this conversation was going.

"Doesn't God also speak through us? Aren't Miriam and I prophets as well as you? Or are you the only one who can hear from God?"

"Yes, you can hear God; I suppose so. What's this about?"

Miriam and Aaron exchanged looks with one another. Miriam gave him that "go ahead" nod.

"It's about your wife."

"Zipporah? What about her?"

Aaron looked to Miriam for encouragement before speaking again.

"She's unhappy. She told Miriam that you haven't been a husband to her in all this time."

Moses looked embarrassed. "She told you that?"

Miriam jumped in. "Why not? You said Aaron and I are also prophets. Yet we don't have to deny our spouses to hear the Lord. Where did you ever get such an idea?"

"Or is there another reason?" Aaron asked.

"Like another woman?" Miriam whispered.

Moses was the most humble man on the earth, and he simply didn't know how to reply to such an implied accusation.

None of them realized God was hearing every word. No one expected Him to break right into the middle of their conversation, but that's just what He did. At the same moment, the loud *whoosh* by my ear told me the demon menace had taken off at the first hint of God being in the neighborhood.

God said to the three of them, "Come out, you three, to the tent of meeting." The three went out, not saying a word. I can tell you Aaron was wishing he had minded his own business and stayed out of the women's talk.

When they got to the tent, God descended in a pillar of cloud and stood at the entrance to the tent. He called Aaron and Miriam to come closer to Him, which neither was eager to do. When they stepped out, God spoke.

"Listen carefully to what I'm telling you. Most of the time, if there is a prophet among you, I make Myself known to him in visions. I speak to him in dreams. That's the way I do it with you two. But I don't do it that way with My servant Moses. I speak to him intimately, in person, in plain talk without riddles. He knows Me personally. You have no way of knowing what I've said to him or what I require of Him in our relationship. So, why did you show no reverence or respect in chastising and accusing My servant?"

The anger of God blazed out against the two of them from the pillar, and then He left.

When the cloud moved off from the tent, Miriam had turned leprous; her skin was white and covered with lesions. Aaron took one look at her, rolled up his sleeves, checked himself out, and then pleaded with Moses.

"Please, my master, please don't allow God to come down so hard on her for this foolish and thoughtless sin."

"Am I greater than God that I can tell Him what He can do?" Moses was distraught, but he pleaded with God as Aaron had asked. "Please, God, heal her. Please heal her."

Aaron dropped to his knees, sweating rivers in fear of what might be about to happen to him.

God answered Moses: "Quarantine her outside the camp for seven days. She will get well, and then she can be readmitted to the camp."

So, Miriam was placed in quarantine outside the camp for the seven days. The people didn't march on until she was readmitted. Aaron had dodged a bullet, and he knew it.

I sat down on the bench outside Moses's tent and tried to remember if I'd ever seen God in a four-way conversation with humans before. I was certain it had never happened.

CHAPTER 23

FOR A BRIEF moment, I almost felt like I was one of them. Of course, they didn't know it, but I planted myself right there beside Moses, Aaron, Hur, and Joshua as they stood quietly at the top of the hill and gazed long and hard at the land of Canaan spread out before them in the valley below. It was a picture-perfect moment. They'd made it. They'd survived the desert, and the Promised Land lay before them for the taking.

Suddenly, the realization of what this meant hit me.

"They made it!" I yelled as if waking myself up from a dream. "What am I doing hanging around here? I must get back to tell Satan."

Think talking on a cell phone and driving a car at ninety miles per hour and you can understand how my mind was not on my flying as I careened over the rim into the second heaven at daredevil speed (pardon the pun). In my zeal to tell the news, I forgot to adjust my speed for altitude and crashed right into the stone door that blocked my path to Satan's lair. Disheveled and stunned from my sudden stop, I must have also looked desperate because the guards didn't try to stop me or bother to laugh as I rushed passed them and entered in without any protocol at all.

"Lord Satan... " I was breathless.

Satan had plenty of breath and seemed only mildly curious as to why I'd barged in the way I had.

"So, speak," he said to me as his attendant held a mirror for him to check out his appearance. He'd developed new interest in preening himself, or, better said, having one of the lower-ranking demons do it for him. I was momentarily distracted by the primping; there wasn't a makeover artist in the universe who could make him pretty. I wondered what he saw in the mirror that kept him coming back to take a look. Maybe he still imagined himself as he used to be when he was Lucifer, the light bearer of heaven.

"Don't make me repeat myself," he said with irritation. "Why are you here?"

"Right. Why am I here?" The preening caused me to lose my train of thought. When he glared at me, my recall returned.

"They made it, sir. They're on the hill above Canaan. They actually made it."

"Have they entered in yet?" Continuing to admire himself in the mirror, he showed some interest in my report but not nearly enough for this kind of news.

"No, not yet. They won't go in all at once. If I know Moses, he'll send a scouting party in first."

He took the mirror from the attendant and held it closer to his face.

"One of the boys brought me some aloe gel from the earth. I've only used it for a week, but I think it's given me a smoother look. What do you think?"

"You're lovely, sir."

"Now, what were you saying?" He gave the mirror back to the attendant.

"The Hebrews have reached Canaan."

He snapped his claws in the direction of one of the guards. "Alert the Nephilim."

"The Nephilim?" I knew my voice cracked. "Are there Nephilim in Canaan? How? They all drowned in Noah's flood."

Satan looked at me as if I were too simpleminded to live.

"Og, the Nephilim king, survived. He has a new clan, the sons of Anak." He sneered as if telling a dirty secret. "Why do you think Canaan is so wicked? Og is serving me well; you could learn a few pointers from him. I never have to send anyone down there to be sure he's doing his job." Then, pressing his claws together and cocking his head with the prissiness of mock courtesy, he continued. "But manners do require me to alert him that lunch is about to be served."

The guard laughed right on cue.

"Tell Og they're coming," he snapped at one of the messenger demons who always hung out around his throne, waiting to do his every bidding. The messenger sped away with a mere nod of acknowledgment.

"And you." He turned to me.

"I know, I know. I'll show myself out."

I looked around the camp until I found Moses, Joshua, Caleb, and Aaron huddled around a drawing in the sand where Moses had sketched a rough layout of the land. I knelt down beside them to take a look.

"Go up through the Negev and then into the hill country. Look the land over; see what it's like. Assess the people: are they strong or weak; are there few or many?"

Joshua nodded, anxious to be off, but Moses wasn't through giving instructions.

"Observe the land: is it pleasant or harsh? Describe the towns where they live: are they open camps or fortified with walls? Pay close attention to the soil. Is it fertile or barren; are there forests?"

Joshua and Caleb rose to their feet. Moses grasped Joshua's garment before he could get away.

"And try to bring back a sample of the produce that grows there—this is the season for the first ripe grapes." With that, the twelve scouts led by Joshua and Caleb headed into the land God had promised their ancestors.

At last, they were on their way without the slightest notion as to what awaited them over the next hill. Motley crew though they were, they eagerly scouted out the land from the Desert of Zin as far as Rehob toward Lebo Hamath. Their route went through the Negev Desert to the town of Hebron.

"Pay close attention in Hebron," Joshua warned. "It is said to be a city older than the cities of Egypt. There's a legend that the descendants of Anak are there.

"Who's Anak?" several asked together.

Caleb looked sharply at Joshua and said nothing with his mouth, but his eyes said it all. "Too much information, Joshua."

"Never mind." Joshua returned Caleb's look and tried to change the subject.

"Nephilim," called out the skittish one who lingered toward the back of the group. "The sons of Anak are the Nephilim."

Uneasiness spread rapidly through the men.

"Nephilim? Impossible."

"They were drowned in the great flood."

"If there are Nephilim in there, we can't go in." Eagerness was giving way to nervousness.

"Like I said," Joshua answered, "it's a legend."

"A myth," Caleb said. "Never proven; now let's get going."

When they arrived at the Valley of Eshcol they cut off a branch with a single cluster of grapes that took two men to carry it slung on a pole. They also picked some pomegranates and figs. They named the place Valley of Eshcol ("valley of grape clusters") because of the huge cluster of grapes they had cut down there. After forty days of scouting out the land, they returned home.

Moses and all the people were waiting for them. Some boys from the camp had been on watch for the scouts, and when they saw them from a distance with the luscious produce of the land, they raced back and told the people.

There were loud cheers and slaps on the backs as the twelve arrived and presented themselves before Moses and Aaron and the whole of Israel.

"Just look," Caleb exclaimed. Everyone wanted to try one of the grapes that were as large as plums. "This is just a sample of the fruit of the land."

"Now tell us what else you found there," Moses said.

"We went to the land just like you told us to do, and, oh, it does flow with milk and honey. Just look at this fruit." Joshua held a pomegranate high above his head so people in the back of the throng could see.

"Tell him the rest," said one of the twelve.

Joshua and Caleb exchanged a look with each other and then sent a piercing glare to the one who had spoken.

"Yes, you must tell them," said another. "Tell them why we can't go back."

The crowd murmured. "What? Why can't they go back?"

Joshua glared at the frightened man who belonged to the voice.

"There is one challenge," Joshua began, "but it's only a challenge."

"How naïve would we be if we didn't expect challenges?" Aaron chimed in.

"Go ahead," Moses encouraged him. "What did you find?"

"Well," Joshua continued, "the people who live there are fierce; no doubt about it. And their cities are huge and well fortified."

"That's not all. Tell them the rest." The man whose voice had earlier quaked with fright jostled his way through the crowd to get in front of Moses. Joshua reached out as if to push the man away, but Moses stayed his hand.

"Let him speak," Moses said.

"We saw descendants of the giant Anak."

Some of the people looked puzzled.

"Nephilim, get it? There are Nephilim in the land. They didn't all drown."

The people gasped in disbelief and fear.

"That's not all," the man said. "Amalekites are spread out in the Negev; Hittites, Jebusites, and Amorites hold the hill country; and the Canaanites are established on the Mediterranean Sea and along the Jordan."

Sounds of concern and fear rose up from the crowd.

Caleb interrupted. "Silence all of you." Turning to Moses, he continued. "Let's go up and take the land—now. We can do it."

The mob roared and turned on Joshua and Caleb.

"Is Caleb crazy?"

"Does he have a death wish?"

"We can't attack those people; they're way stronger than we are."

"They're not even people. They're giants."

"That's right. It would be a massacre if we tried to fight them," the other ten scouts said, one right after the other. Then they dispersed through the crowd and spread scary rumors among the people.

"We scouted out the land from one end to the other. It's a land that swallows people whole. Everybody we saw was huge."

"Didn't you hear what we said? Why, we even saw the Nephilim giants. The Anak giants come from the Nephilim, in case you've forgotten. Alongside them we felt like grasshoppers.

"And they looked down on us as if we were grasshoppers," another added.

Satan would have loved it. Instead of cheering and praising God for safely bringing them into the land they had come all this way to subdue, ten scared voices turned the hope of thousands to paranoia with cries to go back to Egypt. As if that were even an option.

Moses was angry and sent them all back to their tents with a stern warning to keep silent lest the Lord hear their grumbling, but they were so afraid that nothing could have kept them quiet. The whole community was in an uproar and wailed the whole night long. All the people of Israel grumbled against Moses and Aaron.

"Why didn't we die in Egypt? Or in this wilderness?" voice after voice lamented.

"Why has God brought us to this country to kill us?"

"Our wives and children are about to become plunder."

"Why don't we just head back to Egypt?"

"And right now!"

Soon they were all calling for the inevitable. "Let's pick a new leader; let's turn and go back to Egypt." A crowd of men headed toward Moses's tent where Moses, Aaron, Joshua, and

Caleb had gathered in an emergency session to figure out what to do.

"We can surely do it," Caleb insisted. "We can take them."

"What about it, Joshua?" Moses asked. "Can we defeat them?"

Joshua paused for a moment and looked at Caleb's face, beet red with emotion.

"Yes, yes, we can," he answered ever so haltingly. "There will be casualties, but we can take them if the Lord is on our side."

The men of the camp arrived at the door of Moses's tent, demanding they come out.

Joshua and Caleb followed Moses and Aaron outside and then ripped their clothes and addressed the assembled people of Israel.

"What is the matter with you people? Where is your courage? The land we walked through and scouted out is a very good land—very good indeed. If God is pleased with us, He will lead us into that land, a land that flows, as they say, with milk and honey."

"He will give it to us as He promised our ancestors," Caleb shouted, raising his staff high above his head.

"Just don't rebel against God!" shouted Joshua. "Don't listen to those cowards who went with us, and don't be afraid of those people we found on the land that belongs to us if only we will take it. Why, we'll have them for lunch! They have no protection because God is on our side. Don't be afraid of them!"

"We can't lose," Caleb cried out, trying to assure them.

I was beginning to feel a little patriotic myself at the fervor of Caleb and Joshua. I believed they could do it and would have joined up with them right there on the spot if I could have. Unfortunately for them, however, the cowardly scouts had done such a good job of terrifying the people that instead of rushing to join up, the whole crowd was up in arms and talking of hurling stones at all four of the men.

Whoosh! A wind kicked up, so strong it knocked over many of the people. Moses and Aaron were leaning into their staffs for balance as Caleb and Joshua shielded their eyes from the bright light invading the night. If the people thought they were afraid before, they were about to learn what real terror was. There neither was nor is anything in the universe to compare to the wrath of God when Ruah Ha Kadosh splits the atmosphere as the glory of God Almighty descends into the earth realm and all created things bow to His presence.

They were on their knees, but I was face down in the dirt as the bright glory of the Lord appeared at the tent of meeting, and every Israelite saw it. God was in the house.

The voice of God rumbled to Moses. "How long will these people treat Me with contempt? How long will they refuse to trust Me? And with all these signs I've done among them! I've had enough."

"No, wait, Lord," Moses pleaded.

"Don't talk to Me about them anymore, and don't pray for them. I will send a plague and kill them."

"No, don't say that, my Lord." Moses struggled to stand.

"Don't fret; I'll keep the promise I made to Abraham, Isaac, and Jacob. I'll give the land to you. I'll make you into a nation bigger and stronger than they ever were."

"But You can't, my Lord. The Egyptians will hear about it. They'll say You delivered this people from Egypt with a great show of strength and then abandoned them. The Egyptians will tell everyone. They've already heard that You are God, that You are on the side of this people, that You are present among them, that they see You with their own eyes in Your cloud that hovers over them and in the pillar of cloud that leads them by day and the pillar of fire at night. If You kill this entire people, all the nations that have heard what has been going on will say, 'Since God couldn't get these people into the land that He had promised to give them, He slaughtered them out in the wilderness.'"

Whether or not the people on their knees could hear God, I couldn't say, but they could certainly hear Moses, and they knew he was pleading for their very lives. They continued to be very quiet and to listen as Moses cried out to God to spare them.

"Now, please, let the power of the Master expand, enlarge itself greatly along the lines You laid out earlier when You said You were their God. Remember who You are: slow to get angry and huge in loyal love; forgiving iniquity, rebellion, and sin; still, never just whitewashing sin. But extending the fallout of parents' sins to children into the third, even the fourth, generation."

I tried to lift my face out of the dirt to shout, but I could only manage to mumble. "So that's what He was doing back there!"

I was always excited whenever I learned something new about God. "Months ago when God began talking about Himself in the third person, He was writing the intercession Moses would need today to stay His hand of wrath against the nation. Moses probably doesn't even remember where he heard the words he's saying to describe God."

I shook my head the best I could and marveled at the cleverness of God. Who would ever have thought God's words of intercession released into the atmosphere could be snagged by an intercessor later on when the stakes were really high? I wondered if God had done this before. Satan was not going to like this at all.

Moses continued, "Please forgive the wrongdoing of this people out of the extravagance of Your loyal love just as all along, from the time they left Egypt, You have been forgiving this people."

Moses put his face down into the dirt near me and waited for God to answer.

"I forgive them, honoring your words," God said. Big surprise. "But as I live and as the glory of God fills the whole earth, not a single person of those who saw My glory, saw the miraculous signs I did in Egypt and the wilderness, and who have tested Me over and over and over again, turning a deaf ear to Me, will set eyes on the land I so solemnly promised to their ancestors. No one who has treated Me with such repeated contempt will see it."

Then God added a PS: "My servant Caleb is a different story. Both he and Joshua have a different spirit; they follow

Me passionately. I'll bring them into the land that they scouted, and their children will inherit it."

The people heard it all and began dispersing, relieved they would live to see another day. They were so glad to still be alive that they didn't even care about not being allowed to enter the Promised Land. They were in no mood to argue about the terms of the deal.

Moses and Aaron stayed behind. They knew God had more to say to them.

"Since the Amalekites and Canaanites are so well established in the valleys, for right now change course and head back into the wilderness, following the route to the Red Sea."

They nodded but still did not speak. Experience had taught them that a pause in a conversation with God did not mean the conversation was over.

"I will spare them, as you have asked," God continued. "But how long is this going to go on, all this grumbling against Me by this evil-infested community? I've had My fill of complaints from these grumbling Israelites. You can tell them again they aren't going into the land. Their corpses are going to litter the wilderness—everyone twenty years and older who was counted in the census, this whole generation of grumblers and grousers. Not one of them will enter the land and make their home there, except for Caleb and Joshua.

"You can tell them that their children, the very ones they said would be taken for plunder, I'll bring in to enjoy the land they rejected. These children will live as shepherds in the wilderness for forty years, living with the fallout of the unfaithfulness of their parents until the last of that generation lies a corpse in the wilderness. They scouted out the land for forty days; their punishment will be a year for each day, a forty-year sentence to serve for their sins."

By now, both Moses and Aaron were facedown in the dirt from the weight of God's anger. They didn't dare move, and neither did I.

"I, God, have spoken. I will most certainly carry out these things against this entire evil-infested community, which has banded together against Me. In this wilderness they will come to their end. There they will die."

Smoke filled the tent, and the light of the glory lifted. But none of the three of us could get up. I'm pretty sure I passed out right away. When I awoke, Aaron and Moses were gone.

It got bad for some of the Israelites after that. Right away God confronted the ten scouts who had come back with a bad report and sent fear through the people. He released a consuming plague on them, and they died quickly. Only Joshua and Caleb escaped His wrath.

Moses didn't want to deliver God's word to the people, but with good sense, he feared God more than he feared them. So when he told the people of Israel everything God had said against them, they mourned long and hard. But early the next morning they were up like nothing had happened and started out for the high hill country.

"We're here; we're ready. Let's go up and attack the land that God promised us. We sinned, but now we're ready."

I shook my head in disgust at them.

"A little late!" I wanted to shout out. I could have told them a few things about God's mercy and grace. There's a limit to it. Humans never think about it until it's too late. Part of the problem is God's own fault. He never should have taught Abraham about intercession. When people see how many times sincere intercession will stay the hand of God's wrath, they presume it will always be that way.

"It's not always that way!" I finally did shout, though no one could hear me. "Look at me; I'm living proof that God has a limit. It wasn't even my fault. I wasn't grousing and whining like you people. You deserve God's punishment. I didn't. I was innocent. I would never have rebelled against God. It was an accident."

When Moses heard what the people were planning, he ran to stop them.

"Why are you disobeying God's command yet again? This won't work. Don't attack. God isn't with you in this. You'll be beaten badly by your enemies. The Amalekites and Canaanites are ready for you, and they'll kill you. Because you would not obediently follow God and trust Him, God is not going to be with you in this. Don't go! I can't help you this time."

But they went anyway. Recklessly and arrogantly they climbed to the high hill country. If I had been one of them and turned around to see that neither the ark of the covenant nor Moses had budged from the camp, I would have turned around and run for cover. Not them, though. They simply didn't understand the line they had crossed with God. They were in the battlefield barely half an hour when the Amalekites and the

Canaanites came out of the hills and attacked, beat them, and chased them all the way down to Hormah.

They called out to God for help, and He did just what He said He would do—nothing.

Chapter 24

"**W**HY DO YOU think this is good news?" Satan's eyes were narrow and even colder than usual as he glared at me.

The longer I was in exile with this egocentric maniac, the surer I was that I could understand humanity—and I daresay God too—better than I could understand the thought processes of this mercurial personification of everything evil. Why wouldn't I think it was good news? Moses had failed. God had failed. The Israelites who were rescued and assured they were a chosen people on the way to their Promised Land were now going to die in the desert. Even Moses wasn't going to make it across because of an insignificant (in my mind) episode when he struck the rock for water like he did the first time they hit a drought. God had clearly told him to speak to the rock the second time, not pound on it. What possible difference it made as long as the water came out was lost on me.

Satan was winning the game with God for control of the earth. He wouldn't have to deal with the Israelites for at least a generation, maybe more. There would be no challenge to the land he now ruled so effortlessly. He had every reason to celebrate; why was he so macabre? He continued to stare at me, and although I wouldn't daresay what I was thinking, I knew I'd better say something.

"I thought you would be pleased to know the ex-slaves are all going to die in the desert."

"All of them?" His tone gave him away. It was not a real question, so I needed to be careful about my answer.

"Well, uh, most of them—certainly the most important ones. The ones who had witnessed God's miracles in Egypt will not cross over. He was clear about that. Only the younger ones who were too young to know what was going on have a chance to go in sometime in the future."

"So, God is going to kill all of the first generation for angering Him?" Another trick question.

"Yes and no. Not exactly but eventually." I was beginning to get confused. "He won't kill them directly. They'll die in the desert of the usual stuff—disease, accidents, things like that."

Satan didn't respond; he just continued to stare at me.

"He'll let them wander in the desert until the first generation dies. Could be sooner, could be later," I stated with certainty.

"You have no idea how long this will take, is that right?"

I was straining now to remember the fine print of what God had said to Moses and Aaron. Suddenly I remembered.

"Now I remember. Forty years. God said they would wander in the desert for forty years—one year for each day the scouts had been gone."

Satan rose from his throne and walked over to one of the demon guards and stared at him directly in the eyes. The guard did not move or blink, but he was beginning to sweat. No one could ever be sure whom Satan was mad at or what he was mad about, so the guard was as nervous under that icy stare as I would have been. Finally, Satan turned, and his eyes locked on me again. I heard the guard exhale slowly.

"Do you think I want the slaves to die in the desert?" Another trick question; now I was sweating. My eyes darted quickly around the demonic ranks to see if anyone was going to give me a little help. Every face was expressionless. I wasn't the only one who didn't know the answer Satan was looking for.

"Don't you, sir?" I managed to get the words out.

With one claw under his chin and the other under his elbow, he rolled his eyes around the room as if searching for an answer on the ceiling.

"Why don't you tell me how it helps my cause if some of the slaves die of old age in the desert?"

Now I really forced myself to think deeply. What had caused Satan to hate the Israelites to start with? Hadn't he always tried to kill them? Yes, but why? I forced myself to remember. As the memories came rushing back, it was like being there again. Why, of course. How could I forget? It started in the garden when Satan tricked Adam and Eve. In my mind I could hear the voice of God all over again. It was that day when He cursed Satan.

"The seed of the woman shall crush your head." I wouldn't dare say it out loud, but that must be it. As long as even one of the Israelites remained alive, it didn't matter how many were dead. He hated them all but feared only one. But which one? I scrambled for words to answer him without suggesting he might be afraid of the Israelites.

"I just thought, you know, the more we eliminate, the fewer you have to worry about." I knew *worry* was the wrong word the moment it crossed my quivering lips. I tried quickly to recover.

"Not that you're worried; nothing like that. I just meant they wouldn't be crossing over into Canaan to cause any trouble."

I swear he changed colors right there in front of me. Not a different color entirely, more like a deeper shade of the color he was. Saying nothing, he turned and walked back to his throne, where he stood for a moment before turning around sharply and sitting down. He leaned toward me and motioned for me to come closer with the crooked digitlike appendage on the end of his claw.

I was so afraid I could barely move, but I forced myself to inch closer to him.

"I want you to listen to me."

"Of course, sir. I hang on your every word."

"Shut up. Just shut up and listen to me. I do not want to have this conversation again. Do you understand me?"

I nodded but dared not speak.

"Dead Jews do not help me. How long they wander in the desert or how long they live or how many there are is of no interest to me. None. Zilch. Zero. Do you understand that?"

No, I didn't, but I managed to nod that I did.

"I wanted them to cross over to Canaan; the sooner the better. I do not care about their bodies. I want their souls. I want their worship. I want them to abandon God the way a frustrated wife leaves her husband for her lover. I want God to hurt for them, long for them, pine for them as He watches them come to me in unabashed worship. I want Him to watch as I ravish them. I cannot seduce them in the desert. They must cross over into my…boudoir." He laughed wildly.

I was feeling queasy as I processed what he was saying.

"But now look what you've done," he said.

"I'VE DONE?" I screamed the words but kept them from leaving my throat by swallowing them and biting down hard on my tongue. Didn't I say if things went wrong it would be my fault? I thought things had gone right, and it was still my fault.

"If you had done your job correctly, they would be crossing over instead of turning back to the desert."

"My job is to watch and report. I don't cause anything to happen," I wanted to shout.

"What do you suppose is going to happen to them while they wander in the desert for forty years?" I knew it was rhetorical question, so I looked at the floor as if at a loss for words, which was mostly the case.

"Let me tell you what will happen. They will get stronger. God will pay more attention to detail with them. He will instruct them in every aspect of life. He will leave nothing to chance. It will give Moses time to designate a successor and to train him. When they cross over, it will be harder to seduce them."

Joshua, I thought but did not give any hint that I knew who it would be.

"Now, get out of my sight. Watch them every minute of every day for the forty years. Miss nothing, and do not come back until the time of the transfer of the mantle. You are of no value to me until that time."

My wings were limp and dragging on the floor as I trudged slowly out of the throne room. Why did I feel so dejected? Certainly Satan never had any affection for me—or anyone else—so it wasn't like I'd been suddenly spurned. Why did I care whether he thought I was of value or not? My service to him was always a matter of my existence, not my devotion. I hated him. He was the reason for all of my misery, all of my loss. He was the destroyer of my purpose. It made no sense that I felt discarded as some worthless thing. He had always treated me as worthless. What was wrong with me?

I managed to drag myself to my perch and crawl up on it, letting my limp wings dangle on either side to keep me from falling off. I didn't have the strength to hold myself erect. To have been rejected by God was more pain that I thought I could bear. But to be rejected by Satan, the sum of all that is evil, corrupt, and distorted, confirmed my worst fear.

I no longer existed.

CHAPTER 25

I T DIDN'T TAKE me long to get over myself and realize that Satan's opinion of me had nothing whatsoever to do with my value. I was glad to be exiled from his presence for the forty years the Israelites were sentenced to meander in the desert. He had been right about one thing, however. God did use the wandering as a time to have Moses give the Israelites a remedy for every eventuality of life. I watched faithfully for decades, but after a while I lost interest. Besides, once the trek was over and I would be called back in before His Awfulness to report, he wouldn't care anything about how many rules God had given them. Satan wanted to know one thing: when was the handoff coming between Moses and Joshua.

I planned to use most of the years to work on my brief to present before God and the heavenly court so I would be ready when my day came. Every year I gathered more and more evidence of the disparity between how God treated humanity versus the angels. I just knew that before an impartial court, the evidence would call for my case to be reopened. I could provide thousands of instances when humans committed grievous sin worthy of death only to have God intervene and find a way to let them off the hook. Before a heavenly court, His partiality to you people would surely work to my benefit—at least, I told myself it would.

It's amazing how fast forty years can pass by. When I realized what time it was, I knew I had to check on the earth to see how near the Israelites were to the finish line. When I saw them stopped near the border at Canaan gathering around the place where Moses was, I took off immediately. Just as I suspected, Moses was giving his farewell speech to the people.

"I command you today: Love God. Walk in His ways. Keep His commandments, regulations, and rules so that you will live blessed by Him in the land you are about to enter and possess."

"We will," the people said.

Moses didn't look convinced. "But I warn you, if you have a change of heart, refuse to listen obediently, and willfully go off to serve and worship other gods, you will most certainly die. You won't last long in the land."

"You don't have to worry about us," they assured him.

"Well, good, then." Moses was still not convinced his words were hitting home. "I call heaven and earth to witness against you today. I place before you life and death, blessing and curse. Choose life so that you and your children will live. And love God, listening obediently to Him, firmly embracing Him."

"We got it," they shouted.

"Sure you do," I added silently.

Finally, someone in the crowd realized this was not a training session but a good-bye speech.

"Wait a minute, Moses. You make it sound like you're not going in with us."

"I'm one hundred twenty years old today. I can't get around like I used to. And besides, God told me I wasn't going to cross the Jordan with you due to a misunderstanding on my part about how to get water from rocks. Anyway, God will cross the river ahead of you and destroy the nations in your path so that you may dispossess them. Joshua will lead you now."

"But Joshua is untested," another called out.

"How can you say that? Joshua's proved his mettle these forty years. He's served me faithfully, and God will be with him as He was with me."

Then Moses summoned Joshua and said to him with all Israel watching, "Be strong. Take courage. You will enter the land with this people. You will make them the proud possessors of it. God is striding ahead of you, and He won't let you down. Don't be intimidated. Don't worry."

Moses didn't look worried, but Joshua did. Promotion from within is the riskiest way up the ladder. The people watched Joshua "grow up," so to speak, and knew every mistake he ever made. Joshua, on the other hand, had watched the people and knew how likely they were to duck and run at the first sign of opposition.

Then God whispered to Moses, "You are about to die. Bring Joshua quickly to the tent of meeting so I can commission him."

"Well, that's it, then." Moses took Joshua by the arm and turned to go. "Meeting adjourned."

God was waiting for them in the tent in a pillar of cloud. In a tender voice, He said to Moses, "You're about to die and be buried with your ancestors."

Now, to my mind, this would have been the place to end the conversation. Spirit the old guy off to wherever it is you humans go when you die; let him pass in peace. Moses was ready, standing there with outstretched arms and closed eyes before the pillar of cloud. It sort of ruined the mood when God decided to keep on talking.

"You'll no sooner be in the grave than this people will be up and searching after the foreign gods of this country that they are entering. They will abandon Me and violate My covenant that I've made with them. I'll get so angry I'll walk off and leave them on their own and won't so much as look back at them. Then many calamities and disasters will devastate them because they are defenseless."

"What?" Moses asked as he dropped his arms and opened his eyes.

"What?" I echoed. Really, why was God dropping all this on Moses on his retirement day?

"Don't think I don't know what they are already scheming, and they're not even in the land yet."

"I thought we were here to commission Joshua," Moses replied.

"Right, we are."

Moses summoned Joshua to come and kneel down as God spoke His blessing over him.

"Be strong. Take courage. You will lead the people of Israel into the land I promised to give them. And I'll be right there with you."

Moses closed his eyes again and stretched out his arms in obvious expectation of taking off, but no go. No chariot swinging low, no angels singing, no heaven opening up...nothing. He opened one eye to see if God was still there. He was.

"Was there something else You wanted, Lord?" Moses opened the other eye.

"I've got a few more things to say to the children of Israel."

"Can't Joshua say it?"

"No, I want you to tell them so they'll know I'm serious."

Moses sighed, looked around for something to write with, and then plopped himself down on a pillow on the floor.

"OK, go."

God began to dictate an entire new set of warnings and admonishments and told Moses to take them to the priests to put in the ark. When Moses entered the tent where the priests were, they were startled, to say the least.

"You're back?"

"I haven't left yet. I know what rebels these people are and how stubborn and willful they can be. Even today, while I'm still alive and present with them, they're thinking rebellious thoughts against God. How much worse is it going to be when I've died?"

"Does that mean you're not leaving?" the chief priest asked.

"Don't be ridiculous; gather the leaders of the tribes and the officials here. I have something I need to say directly to them with heaven and earth as witnesses, and then I'm out of here."

So, the priests hurried out and did as Moses had commanded them. It was a little difficult to get the people to assemble again. You know how it is when a crowd disperses, but when they heard Moses had something else to say to them, they hurried up. As soon as they were gathered, Moses began speaking.

"I know that after I die you're going to make a mess of things, abandoning the way I commanded, inviting all kinds of evil consequences in the days ahead. You're determined to do evil in defiance of God, deliberately provoking His anger by what you will do."

"How can you say that?"

"It would never cross our minds to do such a thing."

"Never mind," Moses interrupted. "Pay attention; I'm going to teach you this little song."

"What?" they asked in unison.

Odd as it may sound, that is just what Moses did. All those words he was writing down as God dictated were a song the people were to learn before Moses could die. Why, you may ask. The only explanation I can offer is that your race seems to be able to remember anything you can sing. How many times have you seen a grown person singing the "ABCs" because it's the only way he can remember that *j* comes before *k*.

When Moses had finished teaching the words of the song to the people of Israel, he said, "Take to heart all these words to which I give witness today, and urgently command your children to put them into practice. This is no small matter for you; it's your life. In keeping this word you'll have a good and happy future in this land that you're crossing the Jordan to possess."

Moses rolled up the scroll and handed it to the priests, and then he turned to walk back toward the tent of meeting. I followed close behind because I knew God would be there, and I wanted to hear whether He planned a surprise ending in which He would forgive Moses's one and only sin and let him enter the Promised Land. After all, He had forgiven people for a whole lot more than what Moses did. I loved a happy ending and just knew this was going to be one. Besides, if God changed His mind about Moses's punishment, it would be more ammunition for my legal brief. Everything was hushed as God spoke from the cloud.

"Climb the Abarim Range to Mount Nebo in the land of Moab, overlooking Jericho, and view the land of Canaan that I'm giving the people of Israel to have and to hold. Die on the mountain, and join your people. This is because you broke faith with Me in the company of the people of Israel at the waters of Meribah Kadesh in the Desert of Zin. You didn't honor My holy presence in the company of the people."

"I know, sovereign Lord," Moses replied.

"You'll look at the land spread out before you, but you won't enter it."

The pillar of cloud disappeared, and all by himself, Moses, the deliverer of Israel, walked away.

I was so dejected I could have cried. If God wouldn't commute Moses's sentence after all his years of service with those rebellious people because of one little foul-up, I knew I didn't have a chance.

Chapter 26

All the way back to Satan's lair, I found myself thinking about Abraham and Moses and how God had used them as both prophet and intercessor. Each of them carried so much spiritual authority that it could be said that they held both the office of prophet and the office of intercessor. In succeeding generations, things would change, and it would be rare to see one human with both offices. Prophets would be able to intercede, and intercessors would be able to prophesy now and then, but the fullness of both gifts would not normally be resident in one person. Knowing humans as I do, I find it amazing that the two groups insist on working together. The way I see it, when it's done right, the work of each cancels out the work of the other; must be horribly frustrating.

Here's what I mean: Suppose God decides to bring about a calamity to punish His disobedient people. But before He does, He tells a prophet all about the coming disaster with instructions for the prophet to proclaim it for everyone to hear. The prophet obeys and goes about warning, "Thus sayeth the Lord," to everyone.

The intercessors hear the warning, and they start repenting and praying and interceding for God's mercy to avert the disaster. God responds to the intercessors and stays His hand of judgment, and the calamity does not come about.

Who looks foolish here? The prophet. What he clearly heard God say *would* happen does *not* happen because of the intercessors; so even though he may be a *good* prophet, he will always appear to be *wrong* when it comes to judgment. It must be the worst job in town. You'd think a prophet would stay a mile away from an intercessor when he gets a word from the Lord. I know I would; believe me, I know what it's like to be thought wrong all the time. But that's not the case with these odd humans. They seek each other out even though a good intercessor will always make a good prophet look bad because right away when calamity is averted, all you humans start calling him a false prophet. It amazes me how God continues to find people willing to accept such a dead-end assignment.

As I got nearer to Satan's abode, I found myself getting nervous. After all, it had been forty years since I was allowed inside the doors of his throne room. I wondered if I should stop by my perch and spruce up a bit. What was I thinking? I have hooves, claws, and scales. No amount of sprucing was going to help that. Instead, I decided to practice my opening line.

"Lord Satan, it's good to be back. I've missed you." No, too sentimental.

"Your Majesty, I've returned victorious." Too unbelievable; I might be asked to prove it.

I was still practicing when the guards opened the heavy doors to let me pass. As I got nearer to his throne, where he perched like a vulture, I realized my tongue had tied itself in a knot. "Oh, no." I was only a few steps away. "Maybe I can swallow it," I thought in desperation. I tried—I really did—but it would not go down, and it would not untie.

"So, you're back," Satan said.

I nodded and tried to smile but did not open my mouth.

Satan leaned in toward me. "What's the matter with you? Cat got your tongue?"

"No, thir." I struggled to make a sentence, "Ith wight heah in my mout. Thee?" I opened wide to show him. He jerked back as if I'd assaulted him with bad breath.

"Is he speaking in tongues?" Satan asked one of the guards.

"It's possible, sir. We've had reports that when he's on the earth, he spends a lot of time with intercessors."

"No, no." I mumbled as Satan glared at me the way he would a common traitor. "Nofing like at." I shook my head as hard as I could and with all my might thrust my tongue out as far as it would go. It sprung undone with a snap.

"Nothing like that." I panted. "How are you, sir? I've missed you." One of the guards snickered. Satan turned a deep red, and I could have just died right there; I was so mortified.

"What's so funny?" Satan snarled at the guard who immediately tried to swallow his tongue. His natural color was coming back as the evil prince turned his attention back to me.

"This had better be about Moses."

"Well, yes, it is…sort of. Actually, Moses is probably dead by now, but—"

"Dead? Are you sure?"

"Pretty sure. I heard God tell him he would soon die, so, yes, probably."

"Where is the body?"

"I don't know, sir. God said something about his ancestors, but I wasn't really concentrating on that part."

"Fool," he yelled. He jumped from his throne, pushed me aside, and sped past the guards and out the door, headed for the rim of the second heaven. There, he stopped short and looked keenly across the hills and valleys near the land of Canaan.

"There it is. I see where He buried him." With that he was off like a rocket, headed toward the earth.

I couldn't remember the last time Satan himself had gone down to the earth. Some of the others came over to see what was causing all the commotion.

"What's happening? Where's he going?"

"What did you say to him to make him take off like that?"

"Whatever it was, say it again."

Everybody but me burst into laughter. Since none of us had a clue what had caused Satan's reaction, we remained glued in place, watching to see what would happen when he got there.

Like a lightning bolt, he flew spot-on to a place near Beth Peor, and then he came to a stop in front of a cave so hidden it was doubtful any human would have ever found it. He looked frightening—much more so than usual. He was always horrible, but now he appeared to be enraged and much larger and more powerful. Taking long, deliberate steps and clenching his claws, he marched toward the opening of the cave.

He paused and looked both ways then lunged toward the entrance. In the split of a second, a blinding light appeared before him, causing him to stumble backward as he tried to shield his eyes.

A gasp escaped from those of us who stood watching.

"Who is it?"

"It's Michael."

"Michael?" I blurted, pushing my way to the front. "It can't be Michael."

But it was. Michael, the archangel and captain of the angelic guard, blocked Satan's path into the cave where Moses's body lay buried by the hand of God. Michael's flaming sword flashed like fire as he wielded the magnificent weapon, causing Satan to stumble a few more steps back.

"Are you back for another match?" Michael chided him.

"Hand him over."

"The Lord rebuke you." Michael did not flinch from position.

"Give me the law breaker."

"Law breaker?" I said. "Moses was the law *giver*, not a law *breaker*. Why is he calling him that?"

No one answered me, but several shook their heads. Nobody knew what was going on. I tried to think. When had Moses broken any laws? Yes, there was that one thing with striking the rock, but one would have to stretch to call that law breaking. And even if that were the case, what did Satan want with a dead body, even if it was Moses?

Satan tried once more to lunge past.

"The Lord rebuke you," Michael shouted as he thrust his sword within centimeters of Satan's contorted face.

Satan pulled back in fear.

"Flee!" Michael spoke the word in a quiet voice but with such authority that Satan whimpered as he slunk back farther. Several of us also felt the power behind Michael's word and moved back a safe distance from the rim. Not knowing whether anything else might happen and not wanting to miss it if it did, we continued watching until we saw the chastened archdemon leave the earth realm.

Completely confused by what we'd seen, we were still standing there when Satan came storming back.

"What are you gawking at?" he growled. He pushed past us and headed back to his throne room.

We tried to follow him, but when we got close to the doors, at Satan's command, the guards slammed them shut and refused entry to any of us. Under normal circumstances, demons—gossips that they are—would have been a titter with speculation, but not this time. None of us had any idea what had happened or why Satan had done such a bizarre thing. Why had he tried to steal the body of Moses? Why was Michael there to defend it so fiercely? Why had God buried Moses Himself and not allowed the people to do it? We had no answers.

Till this day, we still don't.

CHAPTER 27

I WASN'T SURE WHAT I was supposed to do next, so I retired to my perch, knowing Satan would send for me when he wanted to hear my report. It wasn't long before his messenger showed up. I followed him back to the lair where Satan waited.

"Do they have a new leader?" Satan asked in a matter-of-fact tone.

Let me point out how this is an example of one of the rare ways in which God and Satan have similar speech patterns. Both of them are prone to start a conversation in the middle, assuming the other person knows what's being talked about. Fortunately, I did.

"Yes. His name is Joshua."

"Why don't I know about him?"

"I'm sure I mentioned him, sir." I wasn't sure at all, but I didn't blink and stuck to my story. "He followed Moses around for several years helping him out. Sort of like his assistant. Nothing really special about him that I've noticed."

"Keep careful tabs on him; I want no surprises." Satan motioned for two other demons to come closer to where he sat. "Moron here," he said, pointing to me, "will move out with the Israelites as they cross the Jordan. He'll keep me posted. As for you, be sure the king is ready for them. I want them stopped at Jericho, but do not allow them to be killed. I have other plans." He rubbed his claws together and licked his lips. The others laughed as though they had an inside joke and I wasn't part of it.

Satan stopped chuckling and looked sideways at me. "Why are you still here?"

I bowed quickly and backed my way out of the room. *Just once,* I thought, *I'd like to be treated with a little respect.* Was that too much to ask?

I flew toward Earth and arrived just in time to hear God speaking to Joshua, who lay prostrate on the ground before Him. God had spoken to Moses face-to-face, but let's be honest, for all he would later accomplish, Joshua never quite reached the level of intimacy with God that Moses had. Whether that was God's preference or his, I can't say, but Joshua seemed more comfortable with his head in the sand than to chance a glance at the face of God.

"Moses, my servant, is dead," God said. "Lead these people, and get ready to cross the Jordan River into the land I am about to give to them. I will give you every place where you set your foot, as I promised Moses. Your territory will extend from the desert to Lebanon, and from the great river, the Euphrates—all the Hittite country—to the Mediterranean Sea in the west. No one will be able to stand against you. As I was with Moses, so I will be with you; I will never leave you nor forsake you. Be strong and very courageous. Now stand to your feet before Me."

Joshua rose to his feet but kept his head bowed as God spoke again.

"Be careful to obey all the law My servant Moses gave you; do not turn from it to the right or to the left and you will be successful wherever you go. Keep this book of the Law always on your lips; meditate on it day and night, so that you may be careful to do everything written in it. Then you will be prosperous and successful."

"I will do as my God has said."

Then Joshua went back to the camp and called the leaders together. "Go through the camp, and tell the people to pack their bags. In three days we will cross the Jordan River to enter and take the land God is giving us."

The leaders cheered and pledged their allegiance to Joshua.

"Call the Reubenites, the Gadites, and the half tribe of Manasseh together. I want to talk to them apart from the others."

The men saluted Joshua and ran back to do as he directed them. It wasn't long before the three groups were gathered and anxious to hear Joshua's instructions.

"Remember what Moses, the servant of God, commanded you. Your wives, your children, and your livestock can stay here east of the Jordan, but the rest of you are soldiers, so you must cross the river in battle formation, leading your brothers, helping them until God gives them a place of rest just as He has done for you. They also will take possession of the land that God is giving them. Then you will be free to return to your possession, across the Jordan to the east. Am I clear?"

"Everything you commanded us, we'll do. Wherever you send us, we'll go."

"As we obeyed Moses in all his commands, so we'll also obey you."

I could tell by the look in Joshua's eyes that he wasn't sure whether this was good news or not since he'd been right there as a first-person witness to the rebellion of the people against almost everything Moses told them to do. They never obeyed the first time.

"OK. Well, good, then," Joshua said.

"We just pray that God will be with you as He was with Moses," someone called out.

"You can count on us," said another. "Anyone who questions what you say and refuses to obey whatever you command him will be put to death."

"Let's hope it doesn't come to that," Joshua said.

Joshua went back to his tent, where two men whom he had summoned from Shittim, Jehoa and Simon, were waiting for him. He motioned for them to sit down, and then he shared his plan with them.

"You know the land we are going into is occupied."

"Why should it matter if the Lord has promised it to us?" Jehoa asked.

"It does matter. He's promised it, but make no mistake, we'll have to fight for it. We need intelligence as to what's awaiting us when we get there."

"Command us, and we will serve you." They both nodded in agreement.

"Here's what I want you to do: Go secretly over to Jericho and spy out the land. How many men does the king have? What kinds of weapons are there? Tell no one where you're going."

"You sound like you're expecting trouble," Simon said.

"I'm expecting nothing but trouble. We don't want to walk into a trap."

Jehoa and Simon exchanged a quizzical look. Joshua was not a man exuding confidence and certain victory.

Simon ventured a question. "What is it, Joshua? What are you worried about?"

"Who said I was worried? We've got the word of the Lord on this, don't we?"

Jehoa and Simon knew by his eyes that Joshua was not asking a question he wanted answered. I myself was curious as to what was going on in Joshua's head. Could he be having doubts? Finally, he spoke.

"I wish Moses were here. That's all."

"Moses is dead," Jehoa quipped, obviously not thinking.

"So I've heard," Joshua shot back.

"What I mean to say is you're wearing Moses's mantle now. No one questions that."

"But I'm not Moses. I don't hear from God the same way Moses heard. What if I'm wrong? What if I'm hearing nothing but my own ambition?"

Uh-oh, I thought to myself. *This is not going to be good news for Satan.* Joshua was not a duplicate of Moses for sure. He didn't presume to know more than Moses or to be a new and improved version of Moses. This was almost unknown behavior in young successors who nearly always thought they knew more than their aged predecessors. Joshua was bringing a new element to the human equation, at least as far as mighty-men-macho-leader types go. Joshua was examining his conscience and questioning the purity of his motives. I tried to remember if any of the leaders of the Jews had ever done anything like that before; none that I could remember. Moses had been humble all right, but he never once questioned whether or not he had heard correctly from God.

Simon put his hand on Joshua's shoulder. "Be strong and very courageous. God is with you, and so are we."

"We'll leave when it gets dark so as not to draw attention," Jehoa added.

"Right, good idea." Joshua stood, shook off his moment of self-doubt, and extended his hand to each of the men as they slipped quietly out of his tent.

I wondered if I should stay with Joshua or go with the spies. "Better to go with the spies," I reasoned. "Joshua won't do anything until they come back."

It was dark when we—the spies and I—left for Jericho. It was still dark when we got near the city.

"We need a place to hide out; we could be here several days," said Jehoa.

"I may know of such a place," Simon answered.

"How could you know of a place? You've never been here before."

"I know, but I've heard of a place from some of the travelers we encountered in the desert. I've heard stories about a woman named Rahab."

"And so?"

"She owns a food market. At least that's what some people think." He lowered his voice as if not wanting anyone to hear what he said; not that there was anyone else around.

"It's only a food market during the day. At nightfall, it's a different story. Upstairs she has a brothel."

"A brothel? We're out here on a dangerous mission and your first suggestion is to find a brothel?"

"Well, look, I'm just telling you what I've heard. We have to have someplace to spend the night. I think we should try to find her."

Not having a better idea, both men agreed and set out in search of Rahab's house. I was getting kind of excited about it myself. I'd never seen a brothel. Oh, to be sure, I'd seen plenty of the temple prostitutes wherever Satan had set up idols to himself. But just a working-girl harlot? Never.

It was pitch dark on the road that night, but those two spies found the way to Rahab's house as if they'd had a map. Simon had been right about a market. Of course, it was closed up due to the hour, but right there in front were the bins where the figs and pomegranates were kept during the day and an oven where bread was baked. The boys went around to the back of the house and knocked on the door.

A young girl opened the door just wide enough to extend a candle to illuminate the faces of the men. When she didn't recognize them, she was immediately suspicious.

"What do you want?"

"We have business with Rahab."

"What kind of business?"

"Tell her we're here. She's expecting us."

"Wait here, then." The girl looked doubtful as she closed the door.

"She's expecting us?" Jehoa looked incredulous. "Is that the best you could come up with? Since she's obviously *not* expecting us, she probably won't come down."

"I didn't hear you offer any clever answer."

"Well, I might have if you hadn't jumped right in."

The disagreement ended when the door opened again and a woman early into middle age stepped out with a lantern and closed the door behind her. As I said, I'd never seen a harlot, so I didn't know what to expect, but I guess I didn't expect her. To start with, she was substantial. I don't mean that she was large, more medium sized I suppose, but her demeanor was, well, substantial. She was not timid, and she certainly was not the least bit, uh, flirty. That's it. Not flirty in the least. She looked intently into the face of each man before speaking.

"I know who you are."

"You do?"

"You do?" I said before I caught myself.

"Yes, I do. You must come with me quickly, and do just as I say. They're already looking for you." She ushered the men through the door and then stepped in front of them to lead the way. Neither of them expected such a reception, but they had no doubt they were to do just as she instructed them.

"Follow me up to the roof. Hurry."

"Come and help me, Rhoda." She nodded to the young girl who had first met them at the door. The girl dropped the basket she was carrying and scurried up to the roof behind the spies.

"Now, quickly, both of you lie down near the wall."

They hesitated only a moment before doing as she told them.

"We're going to cover you up with these bundles of flax. Do not move and do not talk until I come back for you."

Just then a warning voice from below called out to her.

"Rahab, the king's men are here. They're asking for you. Come down quickly."

"I'm coming."

Spreading the last bundle of flax over the spies, with urgency in her voice, she whispered loudly, "Not a word. Not a move."

The two soldiers were waiting inside the house when she came down. Smoothing her apron out before her and adjusting her head scarf, she bowed slightly before speaking to them.

"What do the king's men want with a widow?"

"Widow? Is that what you are now?" The captain laughed.

"Why, of course you're a widow. That explains the long line of men who visit this house," said the junior of the two.

"I'm a poor grocer. What do you want with me?"

Rahab did not twitch or display any nervousness at all as she lied through her missing teeth. I would have been a wreck seeing the swords those soldiers carried and knowing the ruthless reputation of the king of Jericho to anyone who betrayed him. But not her; not a stumble of any kind.

235

"Bring out the men who came to you to stay the night in your house. They're spies; they plan to lead an insurgency."

"Spies? Is that what they were? Yes, two men did come to me earlier. They looked suspicious, and since I didn't know where they'd come from, I sent them away. Why do you seek them?"

"It's none of your concern. Where did they go?"

"I don't know. When the gate was about to be shut, they left. But I have no idea where they went."

"You're sure they said nothing to indicate where they were going?"

"Wait, now I remember. They talked about getting to the river. They must have taken off down the Jordan road. If you hurry, you can still catch them!"

Without so much as a thank-you, the soldiers set chase down the Jordan road toward the fords. As soon as they were gone, Rahab closed and locked the door.

Gathering her skirts about her, she climbed back on the roof, where the spies lay motionless and quiet.

"They're gone. You can come out now."

Jehoa and Simon shook the flax off and stood up.

"We're grateful," Simon said.

"You don't know us," Jehoa interrupted. "Why did you help us?"

"I know who you are and that God has given you this land. We're all afraid. Everyone in the country is terrified of you."

Jehoa and Simon looked at each other, unsure of what to say in response.

"We've heard how God dried up the waters of the Red Sea before you when you left Egypt and what He did to the two Amorite kings east of the Jordan whom you put under a holy curse and destroyed."

She paused to gauge their reaction, which was hard because they were too dumbstruck to react.

"We heard it, and our hearts sank. Fear consumed us all because of you and your God. They say He is the God of the heavens above and God of the earth below. Is that so?"

"It is so," Jehoa said.

"Then swear to me by your God that because I showed you mercy you will show my family mercy; my father and mother, my brothers and sisters—everyone connected with my family. Promise me you will save our souls from death!"

"We'll protect you with our lives because you have risked your life to save us!" said Simon. "But don't tell anyone our business. When God turns this land over to us, we'll do right by you in loyal mercy."

"The soldiers will be back," Jehoa cautioned. "How can we get out of here?"

"I'll show you." She called for Rhoda to come and help her. Together they lowered the men through a window with a rope; as I said, Rahab was a substantial woman.

"Run for the hills so they won't find you. Hide out for three days, and give your pursuers time to return. Then get on your way."

Jehoa called back to her, "In order to keep this oath you made us swear, here is what you must do. Hang this red rope out the window through which you let us down, and gather your entire family with you in your house—father, mother, brothers, and sisters. When the fighting starts, anyone who goes out the doors of your house into the street might be killed."

"If that happens," Simon added, "it's his own fault—we aren't responsible. But for everyone within the house we take full responsibility. If anyone lays a hand on one of them, it's our fault."

"But if you tell anyone of our business here, the oath you made us swear is canceled—we're no longer responsible," Jehoa added.

"If that's what you say, that's the way it is," she answered and sent them off. They left, and she hung the red rope out the window.

With me right behind them, the spies headed for the hills and stayed there for three days until the king's men had returned to Jericho. The pursuers looked high and low but did not find them.

Jehoa and Simon returned to their camp to find Joshua waiting in anticipation for their report. They were out of breath from running the last mile in excitement to tell him what they'd found.

"You won't believe it." Simon bent over and rested on his knees to catch his breath.

"They are terrified of us!" Jehoa blurted out.

"Terrified?" Joshua asked.

"It's true," Simon interrupted. "Every word of it. They know who we are. They know where we've been, and they are convinced we are coming to take the land away from them."

"That wouldn't make them terrified unless they thought we could do it." Joshua seemed skeptical. "Why would they assume a people who has wandered in the desert for forty years could just walk in and take out a fortified city? Jericho is walled up. No one goes in or out without the permission of the king."

"They know God has promised it to us."

"How do you know all of this?"

"The harlot told us," Jehoa blurted.

"You were with a harlot?" Joshua's eyes widened.

"No, not like that," Simon interrupted. "She's not a real harlot."

"Not a real harlot?"

"No, she's sort of a grocer." Simon struggled for words to describe Rahab. "She's more like a part-time harlot, just to make ends meet, I'm sure."

"And, so, was she pretending to be a harlot or pretending to be a grocer when you went to her house?"

"I don't know. We weren't there more than thirty minutes, but I can tell you she saved our lives."

"That's right," Jehoa said. "The king of Jericho sent soldiers looking for us. We don't know how he knew about us or how he would have known that we sought refuge in the harlot's—Rahab's—house."

"A grocer harlot?" Joshua tried, but he couldn't get a visual. "Never mind; go on with the story."

"Rahab hid us on the roof and covered us up with bundles of flax. The king's soldiers came looking for us, but she told them we'd been there and gone."

Joshua's face was more perplexed than jubilant at such a development.

"I don't understand. Why?"

"It's like we told you. The news of us has gone before us, and the people fear us."

"It's more like they fear God," Jehoa corrected. "Rahab said the people near and far know that God is with us and has promised us the land."

Joshua put his hands on his hips and walked back and forth as if having received some important new revelation. I walked back and forth with him. I was also thinking how the scales might tip in Israel's favor if the people were already afraid before they got there.

"That settles it." Joshua clapped his hands together in newfound resolve. "Tomorrow we go out."

The three men slapped shoulders, gave each other a manly hug, and then each headed back to this own tent, leaving me to pace by myself.

CHAPTER 28

B Y MORNING JOSHUA's confidence in God and in himself had returned. He energized the people and got them moving toward the Jordan River where they set up camp. His renewed zest for life caused me to wonder about what had changed in his spirit and why. Just the day before, Joshua doubted his motives, the people, and his ability to hear from God, although he clearly had. I myself heard the promises God spoke to him. I clearly heard God say the words, "Be bold and very courageous." Yet, Joshua was feeling anything but that. Why? He had affirmation from the highest authority there was on the matter.

Depressed and unsure of himself, he shared his feelings with Jehoa and Simon, underlings in the power structure for sure. Then Simon said to Joshua, "Be bold and very courageous," the exact words God said (which, to be honest, hadn't produced all that much confidence in Joshua), and look what happened. Overnight, Joshua recovered and was squarely back in control of the situation. Why would a human's words mimicking God's words cause such a reversal in attitude, especially when there was no new information contained in them? It was just a repeat of what God had said. Do you see my perplexity? Why weren't God's words alone good enough to keep Joshua cheered up?

I feared I was about to figure out something else about God's strategy for humanity that Satan was not going to like the least little bit. God's words in the mouth of a human can carry the same authority, cause, and effect as if God Himself were speaking. Say, for example, God speaks a prophetic word into the spirit of a person. The person may know what he heard, and he may even believe it was God, but after a while when nothing seems to be happening, doubt creeps in. He begins to say things like, "I don't know if it was God or me." I've heard you people do it thousands of times. Not being 100 percent supernatural like we are, you simply don't trust your ability to operate in the supernatural and hear God without doubting yourself. If you only knew how supernatural you really are, but I digress. To compensate for this flaw in your makeup, God causes another human to audibly speak His exact same words to the same person; it's as if God is bearing witness to Himself.

I struggled for a way to describe such a dynamic. *Encouragement.* There's no other word for it. A human speaking the words of God to another human gives him courage. I don't say I understand how such a thing *can* work, but there is no doubt that it *does* work every time.

Oh my, but this was not good news for Satan.

Encouragement combined with intercession could be a one-two punch for any scheme a demon might have. If the chosen person had one human interceding for him and another speaking God's encouragement, who knew where it could end? Joshua would prove to be a textbook case for what was possible.

After they'd been by the Jordan for three days, God said to Joshua, "This very day I will begin to make you great in the eyes of all Israel. They'll see for themselves that I'm with you in the same way that I was with Moses. Now, command the priests who are carrying the ark of the covenant to go to the edge of the Jordan's waters and stand there on the river bank."

Joshua called the leaders together and told them what to do. "Get ready to go through the camp. Tell the people that when they see the ark of the covenant, carried by the Levitical priests, to start moving. Follow it. Make sure they keep a proper distance between themselves and the ark, but don't lose sight of it, because they've never been on this road before, and we don't want any wrong turns."

Then Joshua called out a rallying cry to the people: "Sanctify yourselves. Tomorrow God will work miracles and wonders among you."

Next, Joshua turned to the priests. "Take up the ark, and step out before the people." So they took it up and paraded before the people.

Joshua turned to the people. "Look at what's before you: the ark of the covenant. God Himself will cross the Jordan as you watch."

Turning back to the priests, Joshua instructed them. "Now take the ark and step into the water. When your feet touch the Jordan's water, the flow of water will be stopped and the water coming from upstream will pile up in a heap."

That's when the honeymoon ended between Joshua and the priests. The priests carrying the ark froze, stared in disbelief at Joshua, and wouldn't take another step. They exchanged fearful looks between themselves. Then, turning his back to the people, the chief priest motioned for Joshua to come to his side. He whispered so none of the people could hear him rebuke Joshua.

"Have you lost your mind? Are you mad? Look at that river. It is far above flood stage. You can't be seriously telling us to just march into the river like there's no problem."

"We can't be sure where the bottom is," came the voice from one of the other priests.

"We could drop the ark. We could drown," another chimed in.

"How about you send a good swimmer out there first, and let's see how he does before you imperil the entire Levitical priesthood?"

"Have you no faith?" Joshua whispered back.

"I have faith, but I have eyes also, and so do the other priests."

Joshua looked at the frightened faces of the priests and could see they were in agreement and in deep fear.

"Are you refusing to obey your God?"

"No, no, it's not that, but just look at that river!"

Joshua didn't respond. The priest was visibly uncomfortable in challenging Joshua, but no one with a sense of self-preservation would have dared walk into the river. Those swirling waters even made me dizzy. Looking to the other priests, then to the people, then to Joshua, the chief priest asked what no one had dared to ask before.

"Joshua, how sure are you that you've heard from God?"

This was the first real test of Joshua's leadership apart from Moses. What if the priests wouldn't obey? If they showed no confidence in Joshua, the people would scatter like frightened sheep. Oh, I could see clearly what was really at stake here, and I wondered if God had a backup plan if the priests faltered. This particular scenario hadn't ever happened before.

In other crisis moments of obedience, God spoke to His anointed, and the anointed spoke to the people who obeyed or didn't and were rewarded or judged pretty much on the spot. But this was different. Between Joshua, the anointed, and the people was a whole new layer of management: the priests. Moses and Aaron, as well as Joshua, had spent a lot of time convincing the people to respect the priesthood. The people saw Joshua as the leader but saw the priests as their religious authority, who presumably also heard from God. What would Joshua do if the priests flatly refused to step into the water? He wouldn't dare send the people into the river unless the ark went before them as God had instructed. The rest of history would depend on that moment and what the priests did.

Right then I knew why I could never be a leader. I couldn't stand the stress. I would never have the nerve to tell people to do something with real consequences for fear that they might not do it—like what was happening right there with Joshua and the priests. If they didn't obey me, I would have no idea what to do next. I was suddenly glad that my entire role in life was to watch and report and nothing more.

Joshua stepped closer to the chief priest, nose to nose and toes to toes. He did not blink, he did not raise his voice, and he did not plead.

"Step into the water, and see the salvation of the Lord."

The priest did blink—several times, in fact—but said nothing. Signaling the other priests, he turned, and with each in position and wide eyes locked straight ahead, they stepped into the whirling waters of the Jordan. When they did, the waters began to heap up just as God had said they would.

I'm telling you, this would have never happened had it not been for the encourager. If God hadn't put His words into the mouth of Simon, I'm convinced Joshua would never have had the courage to stand up to the priests.

Those priests carrying the ark stood firmly planted on dry ground in the middle of the Jordan while all Israel crossed before them. Finally, the whole nation was across the Jordan, and not one foot was wet.

God spoke to Joshua again. "Select twelve men from the people, a man from each tribe, and tell them to take twelve stones from the center of the river where the priests are standing. Carry them across with you, and set them down in the place where you camp tonight."

Joshua called out the twelve men and said, "Cross to the middle of the Jordan, and take your place in front of the ark. Each of you heft a stone to your shoulder, one for each of the tribes of the people of Israel, so you'll have something later to mark the occasion. When your children ask you, 'What are these stones to you?' you'll say, 'The flow of the Jordan was stopped in front of the ark of the covenant as it crossed the Jordan. These stones are a permanent memorial for the people of Israel.'"

The people did exactly as Joshua commanded. They took twelve stones from the middle of the Jordan, carried them across to the camp, and set them down.

The priests carrying the ark, trembling the whole time, continued standing in the middle of the Jordan until everything God had instructed Joshua to tell the people to do was done. The people crossed quickly; no one dawdled, but it seemed like forever to the priests, who thought the crossing was never going to be complete. When every last one of the Israelites stepped out of the river, the ark of the covenant and the priests crossed over as the river closed in behind them. You have never seen a group of holy men hightailing it like those priests were as they ran out of the river.

The Reubenites, Gadites, and the half tribe of Manasseh lined up in battle formation as Joshua had told them to do. All told, about forty thousand armed soldiers crossed over before God to the plains of Jericho, ready for battle.

Just as He said He would do, God made Joshua great that day in the sight of all Israel. For the first time, they were in awe of him just as they had been in awe of Moses. This was a risky move on God's part, if you ask me. He should never allow humans to get to the "awe" state. Why would God think humans could stand up under adoration any better than Lucifer had when all the other angels were in awe of his beauty and majesty? If I'd been God, I would have gone with letting the people feel gratitude and be done with it. There was way too much danger in allowing awe.

Joshua stretched out his arms over the people and proclaimed to them, "God dried up the Jordan's waters for you until you had crossed, just as He did at the Red Sea. This is so that everybody on Earth will recognize how strong God's rescuing hand is to save you."

When all the Amorite kings west of the Jordan and the Canaanite kings along the seacoast heard how God had stopped the Jordan River before Israel until they had crossed over, their hearts sank, and just thinking about it made the courage drain from them.

Figuring Joshua would ride the momentum of the moment, I expected him to go after Jericho right away, and he probably would have except that God had another idea.

God said to Joshua, "Make stone knives, and circumcise the people of Israel a second time."

Can you imagine how that news went over? I still had nightmares from the time Abraham had to circumcise all the males and I had to watch. Certainly Joshua had seen circumcisions before leaving Egypt, but it had always involved a baby eight days old—not too much blood or kicking and screaming. But when it came to circumcising grown men by the hundreds, there's no way he could have imagined how bad it was going to get.

This was a good time for me to leave. I needed to report in to Satan, and if Joshua went through with it, the men would be laid up for three days at least. I could get to the second heaven and back before the siege against Jericho began.

By the time Joshua raised his new flint knife into the air and began explaining what he was going to do with it, I was airborne and headed for home.

CHAPTER 29

SATAN LAUGHED WHEN I told him about the circumcisions.

"Why does He keep making them do that ridiculous self-mutilation?" he asked, meaning God, of course.

"I know. It sounds more like something *you* would've come up with." That's what I wanted to say. What I did say was less inflammatory.

"I really don't know, sir. As far as I can recall, He's never said why."

"Will wonders never cease? There's *something* you don't know about God? You who are always so quick to lecture me on the what and why of God?" He raised his claws and grasped his head, feigning amazement. "At last, to find something about Him you don't know."

I did know one thing: I'd better not offer a response to such a loaded remark. If I'd had the nerve, I would have pointed out to Satan that, as a matter of fact, most of the time I was exactly right in predicting or explaining what either God or humans were apt to do. But as for the circumcision business, I have to admit I'd never quite figured that one out.

Ignoring his jab at me, I went on to tell Satan about Rahab and then about the priests carrying the ark and the Jordan River heaping up so the people could cross, but he just yawned and looked bored.

"I care nothing about harlots and priests. As for the river, is God still relying on that old trick, splitting waters in half? He should know anything after the Red Sea is passé. It's a shame He hasn't moved on by now and developed a new act."

"Well, the truth is, sir, most of the people who were alive at the time when the Red Sea split are pretty much dead now. The new generation has heard the story from their parents. Not having been there, they're pretty impressed with making the waters of a river rise up and stand at attention."

He yawned again. "So, basically, you have nothing new to report, and you're only here because you didn't want to watch the circumcisions. Is that about it?"

Why couldn't I get over the need to impress him? I loathed him. I thought I was over caring what he thought about me. Why was I here again trying to get his approval? It was impossible. Why didn't I just leave right then?

"Not exactly. I thought you might want to know that God has released another weapon into the arsenal of humanity for spiritual warfare." I turned slightly as if intending to leave. "But if you're not interested, I'll just be going."

"What do you mean?"

I swallowed hard and tried to sound foreboding. "He has released the spiritual gift of... encouragement."

Satan stared hard at me for several seconds before slapping his knee and roaring into laughter. The guards also began their obligatory snickering of agreement whenever Satan saw anything funny.

"Encouragement?" He could barely get it out for his laughing. "God has released people to say sweet things to each other?" Snort, chuckle, and snicker. "You're such an idiot."

Don't answer, don't answer, don't answer, my brain kept saying as my mouth opened and my tongue escaped.

"I'm not the idiot; you're the..." My brain forged ahead and caused my jaw to clamp down on my tongue before it could seal my absolute doom.

"I'm what?"

"You're..." My brain froze. I couldn't think of a single thing. "You're wise to see what's behind God's cunning." My brain unfroze just in time.

"I am? Of course I am. I've always known His motives."

"God can't get anything by you, sir. That's why you see right away that encouragement may seem innocent enough but is really a cover for a powerful delegation of God's power."

"Of course I see that. Nothing gets by me. He should know that by now."

"Right, so that's why you see right through what God is doing by releasing His words into the mouths of one human to speak to another human, thereby empowering him as if God Himself had spoken."

"What else do I see?"

"You can see that when you send a demon to torment and accuse a human to make him feel inadequate and rejected, God no longer has to send an angel to countermand the demonic lie. All God has to do is speak to another human who will take His word to the dejected person, and just like that—" I snapped my claws—"the person is no longer dejected. His spiritual energy is renewed, and he's able to withstand whatever the demon has released against him." I paused to see if Satan was still listening. He was, so I continued.

"Fortunately, the humans haven't yet learned how to use this new weapon. They don't even know it is a weapon. But it's just a matter of time until the intercessors will see what's going on and call the encouragers to the front lines of the battle. A human who can speak the words of God to another human can thoroughly undo any demonic word curse released to the person. It's much more efficient and conserves God's angelic resources."

Satan sat silently thinking over what I said for at least a minute before brushing it off.

"I don't get it. For human number one to carry God's word to human two would have to mean number one cared about number two to start with. Otherwise, why bother?"

Now it was my turn to look perplexed.

"You don't get it, do you, moron? Humans don't care anything about each other. They only care about themselves, or maybe their blood kin, but nothing more than that. A human isn't going to stick himself in the middle of a spiritual war between a demon and another human."

"They will do it, sir."

"Maybe those weird ones, the intercessors; they might do it. But normal humans won't.

"They will, sir."

"Why do you insist on such nonsense?"

"Because they…they love each other; whether they are related or not. They care about people they don't personally know. When they see other humans in terrible situations, they have strong feelings of compassion for them and want to help."

"Only if they are going to get something out of it."

"Regardless of whether they're going to get something out of it. You can't understand this characteristic of humans because you care about no one but yourself."

Now, you may think, knowing his temper as you do by now, that this would be the point where he would do something terrible to me for my impertinence. But you'd be wrong. Satan can't *feel* things like a human, but you humans can't *think* things like demons, although you like to tell yourself you can and that's how you outwit us. Nonsense. You interpret what I said to Satan about not caring about anyone but himself as an insult. He interpreted it as a matter of fact. Not caring about anyone except one's own self makes perfect sense to him. Caring about other beings—unless you need them—in the demonic realm is silly sentimentality.

Satan stood up, signaling the end of his interest in what I had to say.

"Go down to Jericho. Watch the battle, and then come back and report when the king has backed Israel into a corner."

I flew back toward the earth, knowing full well that Satan hadn't believed a single thing I said about the encouragers. He hadn't believed me about intercession either when it first appeared in Abraham. He would learn that the encouragers would have as much or more to do with Israel's perseverance than the intercessors and the prophets put together. Gift by spiritual gift and office by spiritual office—it was so clear to me what God was doing, what He told Satan He would do oh so long ago when the earth was restored and Adam and Eve were created. He told Satan He would redeem the earth through men and women. Satan laughed. Fool that he is, he is still laughing.

"Mark my words," I spoke into the atmosphere as I flew, "God will laugh last."

CHAPTER 30

C URIOUS TO SEE what was going on in Jericho before heading back to the Israelite's campsite, I flew over the city wall for a look but decided to take a pass when I saw the entire town was tightly shut up and locked down—no one going in; no one coming out. Fearing I'd already tarried too long trying to explain encouragement to Satan, I hurried on to find Joshua. I barely got there in time to hear God speak to him.

"I've already given Jericho to you, along with its king and its troops. Here's what you are to do: March around the city with all your soldiers. Circle the city once. Repeat this for six days. Have seven priests carry seven ram's horn trumpets in front of the ark."

"When do You want us to lay siege to the city?"

"Don't raise a sword. You won't have to do a thing."

"But You must want us to do something. You're not thinking they'll just surrender to us?"

"Just do what I tell you. On the seventh day, march around the city seven times with the priests blowing away on the trumpets. Then tell them to sound a long blast on the ram's horns. When they hear that, all the people are to shout at the top of their lungs. The city wall will collapse all at once."

"Uh-huh. Just like that? The wall will simply fall down?"

"Just like that. After that, Israel can enter right in and take the city."

I suppose if God were thinking surprise attack, this strategy was the one to go with. Whatever the king of Jericho was expecting, a parade around the city for seven days probably wasn't it.

Joshua called the priests and the people and told them what God had said. I thought they might at least have a few questions, but not so. When Joshua spoke the orders, the people moved out without so much as a raised eyebrow. After the heaping up of a river in midair, Joshua's stock was pretty high, even with the priests. He could have told them to run around the wall swinging a dead chicken over their heads, and they would have done it. No one questioned the oddness of his battle plan the least little bit.

Seven of the priests with their seven ram's horn trumpets set out before God, the ark, and the Israelites and then blew the trumpets for all they were worth.

Joshua hushed the people. "Don't shout until I tell you. In fact, don't even speak—not so much as a whisper."

Then he gave the signal and sent the whole contingency on its way around the city. It circled once, came back to camp, and stayed for the night. Joshua was up early the next morning, and the whole process began again. They did this for six days.

I couldn't stand it. I had to know what the king of Jericho was thinking when he saw the parade marching around his town. I found my way to his quarters in time to hear a debriefing from one of his captains.

"What are they doing?" The king stood on his balcony where he could see the whole thing.

"Marching around the city with a wooden box and blowing horns," the bearded officer said.

"I can see that. *Why* are they doing it?"

"No idea, sir."

The king returned to his throne, leaned his chin on one hand, and tapped the arm of his chair with the other. After a few moments, he perked up, signaling that he had figured it out.

"Perhaps we've been worried about them for no reason. They may have been fierce at one time, but obviously, by now they've gone mad. Wandering in the desert for forty years could do that to a person."

"That's as good an explanation as any, Your Majesty."

"So, what do you think they'll do next?"

"Don't know, sir. Hard to predict what crazy people will do."

When it became clear that strategy was not the long suit of either the king or the officer, I tired of their uninspired conversation and went back to Joshua's tent. The next day would be the seventh, and I was excited to see if the walls of Jericho would fall down like God had said.

Right on cue, the people got up early and marched around the city the same way as before, but this day they circled the city seven times. On the seventh time around, the priests blew the trumpets and Joshua got before the people.

"Now, pay close attention to my instructions. When I tell you to shout, do it, and the walls will come tumbling down. So, watch yourselves; don't get close until it's all on the ground."

Maybe the king was right; they were all crazy. Otherwise, surely someone would have pointed out the odds against such a thing happening.

Joshua paused and raised his hands to settle the excited people down and to let them know that what he was about to say was important.

"The city and everything in it is under a holy curse and is to be offered up to God. That means nobody keeps any of the gold or silver. Everyone is to be killed except for Rahab the harlot. She is to live—she and everyone in her house with her—because she hid the agents we sent."

The excited chitchatting stopped cold in mid chat. Lots of confused looks were exchanged among the people, but not a word was uttered.

Right there was a perfect example of how I could have helped God anticipate and avoid a problem with Joshua if He had only restored my standing. My entire existence had been reduced to watching you humans. I knew all the personality types. If only I had His ear, I could have urged God to hold up a minute and think about what He had made Joshua to be: a commander/soldier type. Joshua was constructed to take orders, give orders, lead wars, and that was pretty much it. He was not a thinker, feeler, metrosexual kind of guy. Joshua had no sensitivity skills to speak of and therefore could not process what the emotional impact was going to be on the men when they heard they were going into battle where there was to be no payoff…at all. Joshua assumed the men would just suck it up and obey like he would have done, ergo his willingness to obey God's seemingly ridiculous battle plan for taking Jericho without raising an argument.

"Have Joshua take one of the priests along with him," I would have told God. "Let the priest explain the theological implications, inspire them to greater good, bigger payoff later on for blind obedience—things like that. Soften it up some. It's bound to work better than Joshua's my-way-or-the-highway attitude."

"What do you mean everything else is under a holy curse?" shouted someone from the back of the crowd.

Was I right? I could have written the script.

The excitement of the crowd was noticeably subdued as they waited for Joshua's answer.

"I meant what I said; take nothing from the city. It's under a holy curse."

The teaspoon of sugar concept was completely unknown in Joshua's world.

"Wait just a minute," another of the men called out. "We do get the booty, don't we?"

"No, and watch yourselves. Be careful that you don't covet anything in the city or take something that's cursed. If you do, you endanger the whole camp and make trouble for everyone. All silver and gold, all vessels of bronze and iron are holy to God and going into His treasury."

Well, I can just tell you this was a deal killer for some of the men. Joshua's stock took a noticeable dip, especially with the man named Achan. When Joshua turned his back, Achan gathered a couple of the other men, spoke in low tones not to be overheard, and complained about Joshua's orders.

"Do you see what's going on here?" Achan looked over his shoulder to be sure Joshua was out of earshot. "I've seen this happen before with people who think God speaks to them personally. Before you know it they become fanatics."

"His orders don't make sense. Why does he think God needs the gold and silver more than we do?" the fat one asked.

"Right," replied the third man. "What's He going to do with it? If God wanted gold and silver, He could just make Himself some more of it."

"The way I see it," Achan said, "there's no point in attacking the city if there's no payoff. We may as well leave it alone and spend our time on something worth more."

"Oh, sure. So, which one of you is going to tell Joshua we've changed our minds about Jericho?"

"Not me."

"Never mind," Achan said. "I've got a plan. Just wait for my signal."

Just at that moment the priests blew the trumpets.

When the people heard the blast of the trumpets, they gave a thunderclap shout. The wall fell down exactly as God said it would, and the people rushed straight into the city and took it. They put everything in the city under the holy curse and then set about killing man and woman, young and old, ox and sheep and donkey.

Joshua called Jehoa and Simon to his side. "Enter the house of the harlot and rescue the woman and everyone connected with her, just as you promised her."

When I heard Joshua's orders about Rahab, I lost all interest in seeing more of the wall falling down. I had to go with Jehoa and Simon. If Joshua followed through with the promise to give shelter to a harlot, I just knew it had to be good for my case. I'd have to look it up to be sure, but I was all but certain that in those thousands of laws God dictated to Moses while they wandered in the desert, there had to be one about stoning the harlot. I'd have paid more attention if I had known it was ever going to come up.

The men made their way through the fighting to Rahab's house, finding her inside huddled together with her whole frightened family. When the men burst through the door, Rahab ran to Simon and Jehoa and bowed to them.

"You came to save us!"

"We gave you our promise."

The men got the whole family out and rushed them to safety, giving them a place outside the camp of Israel for sanctuary.

Well, there it was; sanctuary for the harlot and her kin. God was all too willing to let Joshua make an exception for a habitual sinner. Rahab wasn't a fallen woman who had fallen only once. She fell several times a week. She couldn't plead the only-once-when-I-was-young-and-foolish-thought-he'd-marry-me-never-did-it-again defense. If God let her off the hook, how could He refuse to consider my case?

Meanwhile, Joshua's army burned down the city and everything in it, except for the gold, silver, bronze, and iron vessels—they put all that aside to be placed into God's treasury. Joshua didn't see Achan stuff some of the gold and silver into a grain bag and then hide it beneath some rocks behind one of the burning houses, but God did.

Knowing you humans as I do, I can see you're bothered that the attack on Jericho was so brutal. How could God, who describes Himself as abounding in mercy and love, call for the killing of every person in the city, giving them no chance to escape or repent or at least be taken prisoner? You can never understand why God released such destruction on the people He created, until you know what the people He created had become. Satan owned their souls, and you should be terrified when I tell you how he got them.

It began when the archangels whom God set over the nations of the earth were enticed by Satan to go down to the daughters of men. The fallen angels raped and pillaged humankind and brought forth the dreaded Nephilim race on the earth. God destroyed the Nephilim—most of them, anyway—and every living thing in the polluted gene pool of the earth when He unleashed Noah's flood. I believe if God had thought about it for five minutes longer, He would have anticipated what could happen if He let the guilty angels remain alive, and He would have destroyed them right there and been done with it, no doubt saving Himself and humanity centuries of grief. Instead, He barred them from the third heaven, just as He did with Satan and the rest of us. They weren't thrown out of heaven as we were; they just weren't allowed back in. That left them with no place to go. It wasn't long until the whole host of them appeared before Satan's throne.

The rest of the rank-and-file demons, including me, hid in the shadows when the archangels kneeled before the one they had once served and known as Lucifer. Even on their knees they were huge, almost as big as Satan himself. We didn't know why they were there, but if there was going to be a fight over territory, well, I for one wanted to be out of the line of fire. Satan's sense of revenge at seeing them bow before him was unrestrained.

"How delightful to see you." He mocked them with false hospitality. "I'm so glad you dropped in." His eyes narrowed as his falsetto voice changed to an angry snarl.

"Now, get out."

"Lucifer, master," the one named Molech began. "We have no place else to go."

Satan swelled up with pride like a helium balloon to hear Molech address him as master.

"And what is that to me? Do you think I've forgotten how you traitors refused to stand with me? How you did nothing when He cast me out? Now you turn to me for sanctuary? You disgust me."

Molech's jaw tightened, but he said nothing more as he lowered his head. I was so relieved. Maybe they would leave without any trouble.

That might have happened if the demons hiding in the shadows with me, the ones who never knew when to shut up, hadn't begun to chatter among themselves so loudly anyone could have heard them.

"Yeah, who do they think they are?"

"Think they can just barge right in? Serves them right. Let them know what it's like to be banished."

"You tell them how it is, master." They egged Satan on.

I started looking for the exit.

Satan rose to his feet and turned his back on the kneeling angels. They kept their heads bowed but began exchanging side glances between themselves. I scrunched down to see what might be transpiring in the unspoken language of their eyes. When I saw the narrow baleful slits that Molech's eyes had become, I broke out in a rash right there on the spot. I spun around and tried my best to hush the heckling demons but to no avail. Was I really the only one who could see what was about to happen and how the archangels were beginning to stand up, some already tapping the handles of their swords?

I raced around to his front side to see if there was any trace of expression on Satan's face that would indicate he had a grasp on what could happen if he rejected these monstrous angels. As I feared, there was none. Never in his life had Satan been able to weigh risk and consequence. I rushed to his side and whispered to him.

"Master?"

Never startle Satan. He jumped and just about knocked me over.

"Idiot! Never do that again."

"Master, what will you do with them?" I nodded toward the angels who were beginning to whisper among themselves—not a good sign.

He looked at them as if wondering whether or not he could beat them in a fight. His fallen face said it all: not a chance. They were not rank and file like the rest of us who were forced to serve him. Seeing the wisdom in not testing their power, he dismissed them with a wave of his hand.

"Let them fend for themselves. They can't stay here, not after the way they betrayed me."

"Master, I know you've thought through the possible repercussions of sending them away."

"Of course, I have." He continued to stare at the wall before glancing my way. "But which specific repercussions do you mean?"

Brain, don't fail me now! The archangels were all standing up by now. I had only minutes to convince Satan of what he was about to unleash.

"Master, if they are not with you, they will be against you. Look at them."

He turned his head slightly until he could see the troop of them as they formed a huddle, contemplating their next move.

"If you act right now, you can avoid a rebellion. They're willing to serve you. They're disoriented and haven't tested their strength now that God has rejected them. You must move while they fear you, while they still think you're more powerful than they are."

"I am more powerful."

"Of course you are," I lied. "But just think what you can accomplish with an elite force like them; makes the rest of us look weak by comparison."

I don't know if I got through to him or if he finally noticed how really big they were, but just in time he swung about and walked toward them with outstretched arms.

"I'm nothing if I'm not magnanimous."

"What did he say he is?" whispered one of my lesser brethren.

Magnanimous wasn't a word usually found in the working vocabulary of a demon.

"I'm willing to let bygones be bygones." Satan sauntered to his throne and sat down, motioning for them to kneel again in front of him. "I've decided to overlook your offense and allow you to serve me."

I held my breath as the archangels looked at him, looked at each other, and looked confused, and then, on Molech's signal, one by one they kneeled down. I momentarily lost consciousness from holding my breath so long.

When I came to, the archangels were in counsel with Satan, who was laying out the plans to establish a new hierarchy of evil just below himself. He appointed Baal and Ashtera, the most powerful of the troop, as "gods" over the other demons.

"I will allow you to rule the entire land of Canaan," he promised.

Then Satan gave them instructions as to how they were to lure the people into bizarre and exotic worship of themselves, which would be nothing more than worship of Satan by another name. The first pyramid scheme, if you will. The idea of worship from the humans they once brutalized in their lust was irresistible to the fallen princes.

"Feeble humanity will become your harlots." Satan laughed and dispatched them to the earth.

In some ways I blame God for what happened next. He has to take the responsibility for the manufacturer's default in how you people are made. In your hierarchy of needs, though you won't find it on your man-made charts, is your need to connect with the supernatural through worship. God intended it to be a means for intimate and exclusive relationship with Him. It turned out to be a good idea gone bad because He didn't install the proper safeguards. God failed to eliminate the seductive alternatives that were sure to come about by Satan's lesser gods. He meant well, but He just didn't think it through. If He were going to allow for the possibility that you fleshly creatures might choose to worship someone other than Him, then He should have cut you some slack on His intransigent command that you worship only Him or face His total and utter rejection of you. I'm not absolving you of your own stupidity by any means, but I mean, fair is fair.

"What do you think about them now, God?" Satan yelled from the rim of the second heaven where he watched the archangels seduce the people. He roared in satisfaction at perfect demonic possession occurring in the people, intoxicated with supernatural sensuality, slipping deeper and deeper into an inevitable and inescapable abyss.

The lesser demons celebrated with Satan as they lusted after the travesty taking place on the earth, but I couldn't bear to watch. I slipped away to my perch and curled up with my tail tucked safely beneath me—my version of a fetal position. I didn't want to think about the people at all. Why should I care that they were sentencing themselves to hell? Humanity certainly cared nothing about me. I did find myself feeling sorry for God, though.

"Don't worry about them, God," I cried out to Him. "It's not all Your fault. They did it to themselves. Sure, You should have reined in that free will debacle long ago, but You meant well."

I put my claws over my ears and tried to hum to drown out the sound as the converging carnival and orgy from the earth became louder and unavoidable. The men and even the women of Canaan reveled and cavorted in the ecstasy of the carnal prostitution of themselves with their gods until their minds became reprobate and they were neither desirous of nor able to repent of their choices. Satan laid out the welcome mat, but they themselves had willingly walked into an addiction from which there was no escape.

When Satan realized I wasn't watching the show with the others, he came looking for me. It was a first and a shock to me since he always acted as if he didn't know or care whether I was around or not. I hoped he hadn't heard me talking to God.

"What's *your* problem?" he demanded

"Me? Oh, nothing at all, sir. I don't have a problem."

"Good. Just remember this was all your idea."

My idea? How could such degradation be my idea? I wasn't capable of such a thing. I said nothing, but my jaw must have dropped to my knees as Satan laughed at my dismay.

"You were the one with the idea to set the archangels up as gods and let them ravish the people."

"But I...but I...but I," were all the words I could put together. He couldn't possibly have interpreted anything I said to be an endorsement of such mayhem.

"Don't take it so hard. Sure, it was your idea, but it was God's fault. Egomaniac that He is, He's the one who put the desire in them to worship."

Satan blew on his manicure and polished his nails on his cape as if he had nothing to do with the chaos. "Of course, He never once thought they'd be unfaithful to Him." Then he raised his eyes and looked straight at me and jeered.

"Too bad for God that they found me to be a more exciting lover." He laughed until his laughing turned into howls that curled my feathers. Satisfied that he had undone me completely, he went back to his ringside seat at the rim.

I knew it wasn't my fault the people had fallen into such deadly desire, but I have to admit that I found myself thinking about what Satan said about it being God's fault. I wanted to ask God, "What were You thinking?

"God, why did You make them yearn for the exhilaration of worship? Neither the angels nor mankind can handle the intimacy and power of worship. And why does it attract You as nothing else does? It's almost as if You can't resist them when they worship. When You saw Lucifer risk his place in paradise for worship, didn't that tell You something? What did You think was going to happen with mere flesh and blood?"

God didn't answer me—big surprise—but I kept thinking about it for a long time until I figured out what God must have intended. He planned for worship to emanate from people and bridge humanity to Himself. He knew once people tasted true worship, they would no longer merely love Him—they would fall *in* love with Him. I know because that's how it was with us, the angels.

If you've ever experienced true worship, then you know a love affair with God consumes every part of your life. It's even more delightful for you humans than it ever was for us angels. Ruah Ha Kadosh enters into your body, and it becomes His temple where He abides, and you become as one with God. Nothing like that ever happened with us.

God manifests His love for you, and you experience Him as holy, pure, beautiful, and powerful as He brings you into communion with Himself as in a marriage where you are the cherished bride of a loving groom. It's the perfect love for which you were intended, for which we were intended. Yet, for all the things this union with God is like, there is one thing it is not. It is not erotic. But worship of a demon god is. Satan's gods could never have lured humans into worship by love because they don't have love, so they lured them by lust.

For most of you, the desire for sensual ritual, which is prohibited to you, never rises to consciousness because God eagerly makes Himself available to you and you are satisfied with His love for you and yours for Him and you don't place yourselves in situations where a forbidden desire can become aroused. Now, to be perfectly fair to the people of Canaan, it does seem to me that God is more accessible to you non-Jews now than He used to be.

Nevertheless, what God intended for all people was a holy longing for intimacy with Himself. For some, enticed by the seduction of the demon gods, that holy longing became warped and distorted into a perverse yearning for strange flesh, an erotic experience with the supernatural. In order to fill their escalating craving for more of the thrill, the people themselves became hunters of other human souls.

That's what the people of Jericho and Canaan were like—locked into a frenzy of unspeakable worship of their gods and ravenous to bring others into it with them. The only way God could protect Israel was to destroy the predators of human souls by the hands of His worshipers.

And that's why Achan's thievery was so odious and why God's punishment would be so severe. It was as if Achan had kept an engagement ring from the dark powers who ruled in Jericho. In his greed, Achan had taken the bait of Satan and put Israel within the devil's grasp, but through the obedience of His servant Joshua, God would snatch them right out of his hand.

The worship of the demon gods made the people one with the demon, a marriage made in hell with no retreat, no repentance, and no escape for the humans who succumbed to the seduction. Eternal, irreversible damnation, and it would remain so for many more centuries until…but no, wait. I'm getting ahead of myself; that comes later in the story.

CHAPTER 31

J OSHUA WAS BLISSFULLY unaware of the breach in his camp when he sent spies to the land of Ai. They returned and guaranteed him the city would be a piece of cake.

"You don't need to send a lot of soldiers," they assured him. "Two or three thousand men are enough to defeat Ai. There's no need to wear out the whole army when there aren't that many people there."

Joshua was feeling so confident after Jericho that he didn't bother to check in with God to get His take on the situation and, instead, relied solely on what the spies told him. He ordered three thousand men to go up and take care of business at Ai. But the army had no more than reached the edge of the city when the men of Ai attacked them and killed thirty-six of them as Israel turned and fled. Ai chased them from the city gate as far as the quarries, killing them all at the descent. When news of the slaughter reached Israel, the heart of the people sank, and all their spirit and confidence were knocked right out of them.

I could have told Joshua from personal experience how it was a big mistake to rely on somebody else's judgment and take God's approval for granted. He ripped his clothes and fell on his face before the ark of the covenant. He and the leaders threw dirt on their heads, as if that would help matters, and lay prostrate until evening.

Then Joshua cried out, "O God, why did You insist on bringing this people across the Jordan? To make us victims of the Amorites? To wipe us out? Why didn't we just settle down on the east side of the Jordan? O God, what can I say to Your people after Israel has been run off by its enemies?"

"I'm sure you'll think of something. Since you didn't think it important to ask Me before you rushed off to war, you figure it out," God answered. "And by the way, brush the dirt out of your hair. You're a mess, and I'm not impressed."

"Sorry, Lord." Joshua stood to his feet and shook out his hair with his hands. "I know I jumped ahead of You. Please tell me what to do. When the Canaanites and all the others living here learn of this, they'll gang up on us and make short work of us—and worse, Your reputation is at risk."

"My reputation?"

"Won't they say You brought us here but were unable to protect us?"

"Don't grovel, and don't patronize Me. Israel has sinned. They've broken the rules by taking the forbidden plunder from Jericho and then covering up their sin. The people of Israel can no longer look their enemies in the eye—they themselves are plunder."

"But, Lord, who did such a thing? I didn't know of such a sin. Neither did my men."

"Did you examine your men after Jericho? Did you make sure the forbidden things were untouched by them?"

"Not exactly. But I told them not to do it before we invaded the city."

"You were careless, Joshua. The stakes are too high, and I can't afford for you to be careless. I can't continue with you if you don't rid yourselves of the cursed things and start paying attention."

"O Lord, is there nothing we can do to repent of this awful sin?"

Joshua was obviously distraught and worried that he'd become lax in his leadership and let the people go too far with their freedom; maybe God would crush them all. Even though they were in real trouble, I could have saved him from his anguish. Joshua simply didn't know God the way I did. Oh, He was angry—no doubt about that—and He would bring severe punishment to the guilty parties. But there was no possibility God would refuse to go forward with Joshua. It just wasn't going to happen."

"Even money says He'll find a way to spare them." I wagered with myself. As usual, I was right.

"Here's what you must do. Tell the people to get ready for tomorrow by purifying themselves," God said. "Then tell them there are cursed things in the camp and they won't be able to face their enemies until you have gotten rid of the illegal booty."

"We will obey Your every word, O sovereign God."

"All right, then. Tomorrow morning call up the tribes whose names I will give you. They will pass by in front of you clan by clan, then family by family, and then man by man until the culprit is revealed. The person found with the cursed things will be burned, along with everything he has."

Joshua hardly slept that night and early the next morning called all the people to assemble tribe by tribe until the tribe of Judah was singled out. Then he called up the clans and singled out the Zerahites. He called up the Zerahite families and singled out Zimri. Then he called up the family members one by one and singled out Achan.

Before the sifting of the tribes was done, Achan knew he was busted. Sweat poured from his forehead when Joshua stood face-to-face with him.

"Make your confession to God. Tell me what you did. Don't keep back anything from me." There was no emotion in Joshua's eyes as he stared right through Achan.

Seeing no fire escape, Achan answered, "It's true. I sinned against God. In the plunder I spotted a beautiful Shinar robe, two hundred shekels of silver, and a fifty-shekel bar of gold, and I coveted and took them. They are buried in my tent."

Joshua's soldiers ran to the tent, and there they were, buried in the tent with the silver at the bottom. They gathered all the treasure and brought it to Joshua, and in front of all the people, Joshua spread out the contraband before God. Then Achan was led outside the camp, where he was stoned. The soldiers set fire to his body along with the robe and all the silver and gold while the stunned people watched in disbelief. It would be a long time before anything like that happened again.

After it was over, God sent Joshua back to Ai where he and his men thoroughly routed the city. After Jericho, Ai was the beginning of the wars Joshua would lead until the entire land of Canaan fell to Israel just as God had said would happen. All in all, I counted thirty-one kings who fell before Israel's sword.

Year after year, nation by nation, God gave Joshua success in everything he did because he was faithful and never sinned again against God's covenant with him. That's not to say he never made a mistake. All humans make mistakes, even the chosen and anointed—like the time Joshua made a treaty with the Gibeonites without asking God about it. It was nothing but trouble for Israel, but he learned from his error and never got ahead of God again.

As I watched the kings tumble one after another, I knew I couldn't postpone it any longer and had to report to Satan how Joshua was winning and taking away the land where Satan had enjoyed unfettered rule. I stood before him and tried to give the report in as matter-of-fact way as I knew how. At first, Satan simply sat on his throne and seemed unresponsive to the news that Israel was winning.

"So, that's it, sir; in spite of how it looked there for a few decades, Israel has finally won." I bowed my head and stepped back as I finished my report.

"Won?" Satan seemed startled at the word. I wondered if he had listened to me at all.

"Well, yes, they have the land God promised them. They've won."

"They've won nothing but land, and I care nothing about the land."

"You don't care about the land? What is it you care about, then?"

"I want their souls."

"But, sir," I said out of reflex without weighing my words as I had long ago learned to do with Satan. I'd been deployed to the earth for such a long stint that I was out of practice, so the words tumbled right out uncensored by my experience or good sense.

"I don't think you can have them."

Satan leapt from his throne and rose to his full huge stature, body writhing and smoke rising up all around him as he glared at me. By now I was on my knees, trembling so hard my wings caught the air movement I was generating and I began to levitate right there in place. Fearing Satan would view this as a challenge, I forced my wings down and rolled up in a ball in front of him.

"I can't have them?" He growled at me.

"No, no, that's not at all what I meant to say. I just meant you can't have them *now*. Of course, you'll get them eventually."

He didn't respond, but his eyes told me to keep talking.

"When Joshua dies, sir, it's just a matter of time. There's no successor to Joshua like there was with Moses. No one's waiting in the wings to take over."

Satan ordered one of the guards, "Kill Joshua." The guard jumped to attention, but I interrupted before he could leave the room.

"No, wait, sir. I know you don't want to kill Joshua." There I froze for a moment. He would expect me to tell him *why* he didn't want to kill him. I dared not say the truth: Joshua was golden with God, and neither his minions nor Satan himself could lay a glove on him. I bought a little time by struggling to stand up.

"Let them win a few wars, live in peace for a few years, things like that," I said as I tried to snap my wings back into alignment. "You know what will happen. They'll grow complacent as they always have. They won't be thinking they need a new leader after Joshua. They'll be wide open when Joshua dies."

Seeming to have no better idea of his own, Satan begrudgingly accepted what I said. I went to my perch, happy to be back to the closest thing I had as home and settled in to watch the earth. Since Satan wasn't interested in the land issue and didn't seem bothered about the conquered people either, there was no reason for me to wear myself out commuting from the earth to heaven with updates nobody cared to hear.

Waiting around for Joshua to die might take decades and wasn't much of a mental challenge, so I decided to find a hobby to pass the time. That's how I got into transcendental meditation. Yoga hadn't worked out all that well for me, but it was mostly the physical challenge with my wings and hooves. When you're trying to do a headstand and your wings keep falling down in your face, it ruins the experience.

But TM was different. I found my "ooohhmmm" right away. It wasn't long until I could chant my way right into communion with the free-floating Vedas of the universe. Little did I know the Vedas were part of a telecommunication system between Satan and the lesser gods. Wouldn't you know they tattled on me right off? Satan sent one of his henchmen to tell me to hang up and pay attention to the earth.

The army of Israel moved out, taking possession of all God had promised them. There were so many battles; after a while they began to run together in my mind. As each section of land was conquered, Joshua parceled out the property rights to the tribes by families. I tried to keep track of who got what, but after a while it became mind-numbingly tedious. I quit when I remembered Satan wouldn't care a thing about who got a deed to what.

What I did find interesting was the day God came up with the idea of sanctuary cities and told Joshua to build them.

"Why?" Joshua wanted to know.

"So that if a person accidentally kills another person, he will have a safe place to go for justice."

Joshua looked perplexed, as if he were not sure this was a good use of time, but being the good soldier he was, he built the cities without argument.

"Ask God how to tell an accidental killing from an intentional one since everyone in the area is sporting a weapon and is at war," I urged Joshua from my perch but to no avail.

I thought this might be useful information for me later on—you know, when I get my day in court. It could be helpful if I could point out a time when God insisted on different treatment for those who intentionally erred versus those who were victims of circumstances.

Finally, after many long battles, God was satisfied and gave Israel rest from war and safety from all its enemies. Then it really got boring.

I waited and watched for many more years until I saw the sign I was looking for. All of Israel was coming together at the place where Joshua lived. It must be time for Joshua to die. I took off and flew quickly to his tent.

All the chiefs, judges, and officers filled the tent and spilled over to the outside to hear the words of Joshua.

"I'm an old man, and I've lived a long time. You've seen everything that God has done to these nations because of you. He did it because He's your God and you are chosen and set apart to worship only Him."

Joshua took a deep, laboring breath, and so did the people gathered around him.

"Now, stay strong and steady. Obediently do everything written in the book of the revelation of Moses. Don't get mixed up with the nations that are still around."

"We won't mix in," they shouted.

"Don't so much as speak the names of their gods or swear by them."

"You can count on us."

"And by all means, don't worship or pray to them. Hold tight to your God, just as you've done up to now."

The crowd murmured their promise to be faithful.

"Now, hear me. Vigilantly guard your souls and love your God."

I shuddered as Joshua said those words. Did Joshua know their souls were what Satan had been waiting for all this time, or was that just a lucky guess?

"If you wander off and intermarry or take up with these remaining nations still among you, know for certain that God will not get rid of them when they become a curse for you—as they surely will—until you're the ones who will be driven out of this good land God has given you."

"We would never do such a thing," several of the priests said in unison.

"How could we disobey our God who has brought us here?"

Through his aged eyes, Joshua looked to and fro among the people gathered around him. He took his final breath and spoke the warning one more time.

"If you leave the path of the covenant of your God that He commanded and go off and serve and worship other gods, His righteous anger will blaze out against you. He will leave you to the ravages of the gods you choose. He will not save you. There'll be nothing left of you and no sign that you've ever been in this good land He gave you."

"There is no God but the God of Israel." The crowd cheered.

Joshua looked into the faces of the people gathered around him and then closed his eyes for the last time.

I closed mine as well, but for a different reason. I felt a cold chill down my spine, and I knew Satan was watching every move from the rim of the second heaven. Someone must have told him I was gone, and he put two and two together and figured out it must be time for Joshua to die. He didn't wait for my report. After all, hanging out until Joshua died was all that held him back, and it was obvious he wanted to see the action firsthand.

I wondered if I should try to warn God of what was coming. He hadn't been around that much since Israel was at peace with her enemies. He might be giving Israel far more credit for the ability to self-govern than was warranted. He must have known that last admonition from Joshua to the people about not worshiping other gods was going to be the exact place where Satan would go after them.

If I could alert Him to something He'd overlooked, He might be grateful. I decided to give it a try. I slipped away from Joshua's tent and found a big rock in the desert. I knelt down behind it and hoped Satan wouldn't be able to see me.

"Pssst, God," I whispered as loud as I dared. "This is, well, never mind who this is. I thought I'd better warn You of what's about to happen down here. I know how You sometimes have a tendency to forgive and forget, at least where the humans are concerned. But Satan never forgets anything, not even the slightest offense. He's been waiting for this chance. Your Jews don't have a leader right now. You might want to appoint some judges or a king maybe, someone with an official position who can tell them what to do. Satan's about to go after them through his demigods. I've seen this happen before—whole nations succumb in a day to Baal or Ashtera."

If God heard me, He ignored me.

I was flapping my way back to the second heaven when I felt the atmosphere tremble. Soon I was in position to see brigade after brigade as Satan unleashed his soul-starved hordes back into the earth realm to go after the people of God.

The seduction of Israel was about to begin.

Chapter 32

S AMANTHA WAS SILENTLY rehearsing her opening line when the voice on the phone abruptly ended the elevator music that had been playing while she was on hold.

"Jonathan Marks here," the voice said without emotion.

"Dr. Marks, this is Dr. Samantha Yale from the University of Jerusalem. Thank you for taking my call."

Samantha had wrestled with her conscience for several days before deciding to contact the highly regarded paleontologist, New Testament scholar, and expert on religious relics and objects of antiquity.

"I'm happy to speak with you, Dr. Yale. How can I help you?"

Rehearsing her opening line was proving to be of little help as she found herself searching for the right words to begin the conversation.

"Dr. Yale?"

"Yes, I'm here. Sorry." She took a deep breath. "Dr. Marks, out of respect for your time, let me come right to the point. I've come into possession of some very ancient scrolls that appear to have been written in cuneiform."

That's good, Sam. Spill the whole thing in fifteen seconds. Don't give him any time to warm up to the idea.

"I see. Well, now, that would be interesting and very unlikely since, as you know, cuneiform predates papyrus by at least a thousand years."

"Yes, I'm aware of that."

"Then, how can I help you, Dr. Yale?"

"I've been retained to translate the writing, which I've done. However, at some point, the authenticity of the scrolls themselves as genuine relics will need corroboration. I was hopeful you might be interested in taking a look at them."

Jonathan hesitated.

Don't bring up the Torah codes; don't bring up the Torah codes. She squinted and crossed her fingers.

"This wouldn't have anything to do with the Torah codes, would it?"

She opened her squinted eyes and rolled them at the ceiling. *One little request—is that too much to ask?*

"No, Dr. Marks. This is an unrelated matter."

"You said you have physical possession of the scrolls now?"

"Yes, that's right." She decided to say nothing more until he moved the conversation forward.

It's your ball, Dr. Marks. Are you going to play?

"When would you like for me to examine them?"

"Yes!" she whispered as she raised her arms in a victory pose, making sure he didn't hear her excitement.

"I'm not certain. The scrolls are privately owned. I need permission from the owner, and to be perfectly candid, I'm not sure he will agree."

"Then, why are you contacting me?"

"The owner is an eccentric who, in my opinion, may border on paranoia. If the scrolls are authentic, they are historically priceless. Should he agree to let me seek peer-level confirmation, I would need to move quickly before he could change his mind or disappear altogether. That's why I chose to speak with you first."

"How long before you can know whether he will agree or not?"

"I wish I could tell you."

Now there's a real confidence builder, Sam. Go for broke; try to explain Wonk Eman.

"This is going to sound odd, I know, but I have no way of contacting the owner. I have to wait until he gets in touch with me."

"So, you have no idea what sort of time frame we're talking about?"

"No. It could be days or weeks, but if I should be successful in getting the owner's permission to have you examine the scrolls, would you be willing to take a look at them?"

"Yes, Dr. Yale. I'll help any way I can."

The relief in her voice was audible. "Thank you so much, Dr. Marks. I'll be in touch when I have more to share. Until then, ciao."

Samantha hung up the phone and let out a long sigh. There was nothing else for her to do except wait until the elusive Wonk Eman reappeared. "I have a feeling I won't be waiting long." She leaned back in her leather chair, closed her eyes, and thought about the last words of the scroll. *The seduction of Israel was about to begin.*

Samantha answered the phone on the first ring.

"Dr. Yale?"

"Wonk?" she blurted before she could stop herself. It had been a month since her conversation with Jonathan Marks. Where had he been all this time?

"How did you know it was me?"

"Let's say I'm psychic." She waited for him to laugh, but he didn't. "Never mind. I was expecting to hear from you soon—sooner actually. That's all."

"Have you translated the scrolls?"

I'm fine. Thanks for asking, and you?

"Yes, I have." Best to overlook his lack of telephone etiquette.

Long pause.

"Do you believe what you read?"

"Believe? I'm not sure I know what you're asking."

"Do you believe things happened that way? Like it says in the scrolls."

Choose your words carefully, Sam. Remember he's a flight risk.

"Wonk, do you know the difference between a myth and something historically authentic?"

"Are you accusing me of lying, Dr. Yale?"

"You? Why, of course not. We're not talking about you. I mean the story in the scrolls—that's all."

"It's a diary."

"Yes, I remember you said that before." She paused and then decided to press on. "Anyway, a myth is something that may or may not be true but can't be proven. The scrolls contain a myth—albeit a captivating one—but it would be careless to assume the story describes actual events."

Silence.

"I expected more from you, Dr. Yale."

"I'm sorry, Wonk. I don't want to minimize what you've got because it is quite extraordinary—no doubt about that."

"Do you want to see more?"

"More scrolls? How many more are there?"

"Do you want to see more?"

"Yes, yes, of course I do."

Deep breath, reassuring voice, ready, go.

"In fact, Wonk, I wonder if you would allow a colleague of mine to examine the scrolls...to confirm my translation."

"No."

"But I assure you he would be discreet."

"No."

"Wonk, Dr. Marks is at the top of his field. If he verifies the age of the scrolls, it could easily..."

"Especially not Dr. Marks."

"How do you know Jonathan Marks?" She tried for nonchalance.

"You gave me your word, Dr. Yale."

"And I intend to abide by it. I was only thinking of your benefit...to bring additional credibility to the value of what you have."

No response. Maybe he was thinking it over.

The ticking grandfather clock in her office told her he had been silent for a full minute, far outside her ten-second rule.

"Wonk?"

"If you don't keep your word—if you don't finish the translation—I've risked everything to bring it to you." He picked up the sentence as if there hadn't been an interminably long silence.

"I told you I would keep my word."

"You don't know how important they are. They must not be destroyed before the translation is complete."

"Destroyed? Wonk, listen to me. The scrolls are safe with me. Forget what I said about Dr. Marks. Send the additional scrolls to me as soon as you can."

"Yes, all right. I have to trust you. You must be there to personally receive them."

"I'll wait for them just like before."

She knew this was a good time to end the conversation, while they had agreement and he had calmed down, but her curiosity as a Torah scholar won out over safety.

"Wonk, just one more thing. It's about Og, the Nephilim king. I researched him, and it turns out you were right that he may have survived Noah's flood, but his death is later chronicled in the Old Testament."

More silence.

"I only bring it up because you were so disturbed that he had somehow remained alive. I thought it would make you feel safer to know he's no threat to you. He died thousands of years ago."

"Demonic beings do not die. Only the human part of him died."

"I see." If she went further she knew she risked agitating him again. "I just wanted you to know I'd looked into it."

"Thank you, Dr. Yale. I know this all seems strange to you; you'd understand if I could tell you everything, but I can't. You just don't know me; you don't know who I am. That's all I can say. Good-bye, Dr. Yale."

Samantha carefully placed the black phone in its cradle, leaned back in her chair, and breathed a sigh of relief that things were on track. Glancing back to the phone, she smiled as she spoke to the disconnected caller.

"Actually, Wonk, you just don't know who I am."

FREE NEWSLETTERS
TO HELP EMPOWER YOUR LIFE

Why subscribe today?

☐ **DELIVERED DIRECTLY TO YOU.** All you have to do is open your inbox and read.

☐ **EXCLUSIVE CONTENT.** We cover the news overlooked by the mainstream press.

☐ **STAY CURRENT.** Find the latest court rulings, revivals, and cultural trends.

☐ **UPDATE OTHERS.** Easy to forward to friends and family with the click of your mouse.

CHOOSE THE E-NEWSLETTER THAT INTERESTS YOU MOST:

- Christian news
- Daily devotionals
- Spiritual empowerment
- And much, much more

SIGN UP AT: **http://freenewsletters.charismamag.com**

8178